out of the mouths

OF BABES

out of the mouths

OF BABES

Dennis Hamley

SCHOLASTIC
PRESS

Scholastic Children's Books,
Commonwealth House, 1-19 New Oxford Street,
London WC1A 1NU, UK
a division of Scholastic Ltd
London ~ New York ~ Toronto ~ Sydney ~ Auckland

First published in the UK by Scholastic Ltd, 1997

Copyright © Dennis Hamley, 1997

ISBN 0 590 54303 2

Typeset by DP Photosetting, Aylesbury, Bucks.
Printed by Cox and Wyman Ltd, Reading, Berks.

10 9 8 7 6 5 4 3 2 1

For Mary,
with love

Prologue

It was a hot, clear night. Headlights of cars shone briefly and were gone. In the large, grandiose even, house whose lighted windows blazed in the dark, a dinner party was ending. Towards the town, other houses stood – large but not as impressive as this one. Inside them, some people slept. Others ended parties. Yet others, heavy-lidded or buoyed up with too much coffee, read, watched videos or listened to all-night radio.

Here, at the far end of spacious grounds, cherry trees had already lost their blossom and the air was heavy with the scents of honeysuckle and roses. A little wooden building sat quiet in the dark and a small figure sat equally quiet, watching it. It was as if they argued silently together in the night, reasoning with each other, daring each other.

At last the wait was over. One of the two was doomed. Perhaps, by this decision, both were.

The watcher had come prepared. A can of paraffin was opened, rags soaked in it. The watcher moved silently to the door of the little building. In the still warmth, the smell of dry wood suddenly took over the night's other scents.

The door was not locked. The watcher opened it, stood in the entrance and lit matches, methodically, put them to the soaked rags and threw them inside with jerky convulsive movements. After a while there were no more rags.

The watcher stood in the doorway until forced away by

heat and fumes. Now the top of the brick wall marking the bottom boundary of the garden was the vantage point for watching satisfying orange flames eating away at the compact silhouette and the collapse of roof and beams. At first, the watcher ignored the sudden opening of windows in the nearby house, the emergence of people in evening dress, the cries of alarm. It was worth the risk waiting for the fire engine to arrive, so pleasantly and inevitably too late to save the little structure. But the real target had not been there. More fires must be lit another time.

At last the watcher slipped off the wall to the ground and, half-empty can in hand, disappeared before anyone decided to look further afield for a culprit.

Part One

Three Childhoods

Chapter One

When Julian Claverhouse was born, his parents put a notice in *The Daily Telegraph*:

Claverhouse To Georgina and William, a son, safely delivered at St John's Nursing Home, Beaconsfield, September 15th.

For Julian's father, the new arrival caused little change in routine. Having held his son, kissed his wife and left flowers, he departed the heavy atmosphere, full of women's pain, of the private hospital. He passed without greeting younger, more fertile men waiting to be fathers. His only concession to change was to park the Bentley at the station, travel first class into Marylebone and take a taxi to the City, instead of driving down the new M40 and across London.

There was much to do now the sex of his offspring was known. God knows he had waited long enough to perfect his plans! There were insurance policies to take out for school fees, telephone calls to make, old promises to call in, family connections over generations to re-activate. There must be no surprises in the first twenty years of his son's life. Prep school, public school and Oxford must follow in due order as they always had for male Claverhouses. Rocks in swirling currents. The seventies were halfway through. This cataclysmic century was three-quarters over but some things still could be – had to be – depended on.

Grizelda Grissom's mother Wendy would not have wanted the same things for her daughter as William Claverhouse for his son. Even as the puling infant was first placed in her arms, she resolved that she would *never* go away to boarding school. Her husband Larry, who had been at the birth throughout and cut the cord himself, put his arm round her shoulders. As she felt his presence near she knew they were now a family, an indissoluble trio, and felt a surge of expansive, expectant happiness. Larry would go far, she would go with him and their daughter would want for nothing. Grizelda would flourish as the green bay tree under the great arch of their love.

When Gary Lugg was born, no newspaper printed a notice. Social Services and health visitors were alerted, a home help organized. Gary's mother Chrissy would go back to a council maisonette on a big estate. No man would be waiting for her. As soon as he was able, Gary Lugg would have to shift for himself.

Julian Claverhouse's christening filled the church as colourfully as his parents' wedding had eight years before. His name was down for the schools his father favoured – and some others too, just in case (though the prospect was unthinkable) Julian's intellect turned out not to be of a level to justify the first choices.

William Claverhouse had made sure that his old Oxford tutor was one of Julian's godfathers. It was not coincidence that the other was an up-and-coming young MP whom Mr

Edward Heath was said to be considering for future high office.

Grizelda Grissom was not christened. Wendy and Larry had first met at art college, were veterans of Glastonbury and Knebworth festivals and would have been at Woodstock if they had had the money and had known about it in time. They did not consider christening their offspring – at least, not in church.

Christening Gary was not on his mother's agenda. Chrissy was too busy coping with social workers, the DHSS, the damp and cold maisonette, the gas, the electric and finding clothes in Oxfam.

Besides, who would have been Gary's godparents? Chrissy Lugg didn't even know where to find his real father, let alone two prospective godfathers.

When Julian's christening was over, he was brought back to Mockbeggar House, a substantial Edwardian pile designed by an architectural pupil of the great Sir Edwin Lutyens. The house had belonged to Julian's great-grandfather on his mother's side and had been given to Georgina by his widow, her grandmother, when she married. The house stood well back from the road in several acres of grounds, shaded by trees and approached by a long gravel drive. Anyone passing would get only the merest glimpse of its well-proportioned windows, its red-tiled roof. The house had been completely refurbished by William Claverhouse; it was ironic that the extensive nursery and playroom had not found a use for eight years. Julian knew nothing of this, nor about the striped marquee set up on the close-mown lawn, the immaculately suited and expensively frocked and summer-hatted guests who drank champagne and ate canapes in his honour.

The warm September sun was low before the live-in nanny bore him away to the nursery to be fed with his prepared formula and put into his cot on which the hanging mobiles, toys, dolls and teddies gazed benevolently down.

The party in the north London flat was a celebration. Grizelda was much admired before she was left to sleep in the Habitat crib. The guests stayed very responsible: the music was muted, only a little pot was smoked and it was understood that Wendy Grissom would leave her hostess duties every few hours to feed her daughter. But what mingled cheers, sighs and cries of "Believe it, man. This is real!" there were when she appeared again, her baby at her breast, and sat proudly on the cane chair under the old Che Guevara poster.

Nobody came to see Gary Lugg except his grandparents. They looked at him, then at his mother. Then his grandmother said, "Now see what a mess you've got yourself into! Well, we can't afford to help you."

His grandfather said, "You find that man of yours. He should be here facing up to his responsibilities."

Chrissy's hand instinctively flew to where the skin had once been bruised and cut and vowed again that never more would that man come near her.

"We've got no room for you at home," said Gary's grandmother. "Not since Terry and his wife came to live with us. And she's expecting. We can't have two babies in the house."

"That's all right, Mum," said Chrissy.

Nothing would make me go back there, she thought. So even if you did want me, you'd be wasting your breath.

"Anyway, we've brought him something," said Gary's grandfather.

Chrissy took the little baby-paper wrapped package. Inside was a cheap plastic rattle. For a moment she had a childhood memory of her mother knitting and making clothes, turning the handle of the Singer sewing machine so that it purred oilily for hours. She wondered where all that had gone.

Life in Mockbeggar House returned to serenity. William Claverhouse always tried to move with the democratic times, which told him he could not maintain the domestic staff Georgina's grandfather had in mind when the house was first built. Apart from the live-in nanny and a succession of au pair girls who came with fractured English and left with a specialized vocabulary concerning sheets and kitchenware, nobody shared the seven bedrooms and three reception rooms, study and library, spacious nursery and newly-equipped playroom, the expensively converted laundry and utility rooms.

There was not even a resident cook for the glistening kitchen. William Claverhouse knew who to hire for dinner parties, while from day to day Georgina prepared light snacks, Wanda Gates – the live-in nanny from Ilford – cooked solid English meals and the successive au pair girls proudly and sometimes inedibly reproduced their own national specialities. Two dependable ex-servicemen looked after the garden with great care but only a little money to supplement their pensions. Georgina was always there to supervise the flower borders and shrubberies. There was, of course, a daily cleaner, Mrs Duffy. The most willing au pair could never cope with such a house on her own.

But both William and Georgina sighed for their grandparents' days, before excessive wage demands and the employer's contribution to National Insurance.

Wendy often told Larry that by taking a job in an advertising agency he had sold out to the forces of capitalism and she was ashamed of him.

"They're all creative people where I work," said Larry defensively. "We've always moved among creative people and this is just an extension. Anyway, remember Timmy Green – Isle of Wight, 1970?"

Wendy did, amid the tents and mud and amplified but still only dimly heard and seen rock music.

"Well, he's my new boss."

In a month, Larry received a salary cheque which seemed to Wendy almost obscene. But not for long.

Larry put his arm round Wendy's cheesecloth-draped waist and looked down on the sleeping Grizelda.

"Think of what this will mean for *her*, my love," he said.

Chrissy Lugg ended up quite lucky. Nobody could deny that at first Gary was a quiet baby. Even so, during the day the maisonette became a prison, with a few hours of remission for good behaviour when she strapped Gary into the lopsided pushchair with its odd wheels that she had bought at least sixth-hand, and wheeled him to the Wavy Line grocer on the estate. Here she bought provisions and heroically fought down the familiar tickle in her throat when she saw the rows of shiny, colourful cigarette packs.

Only here and occasionally at the clinic was there any conversation. "Isn't he getting big?" "She gets on my wick, crying all night." "I could strangle her sometimes." "I told Kevin, either help me a bit or get out. So he went. I wish I'd kept my mouth shut now."

And then back to where the damp-flecked walls pressed in on her and life was a weary round of mixing powdered baby milk, putting teats and bottles in the Milton sterilizer, washing out terry-towelling nappies and wishing, wishing there was a man in the house still. Then recanting: what good had the last one been? Then wishing again. But who would take on a three-month-old baby?

So why was Chrissy Lugg lucky?

The old couple downstairs, Mr and Mrs Pike, had never complained even when Gary's cries threatened to crack the thin walls. They were sympathetic in a way which she found quite different from how other people seemed to be.

"You poor girl," Mrs Pike said one day as Chrissy hung some newly-washed but still stubbornly grey nappies out in the tiny yard. "You need a break sometimes. Would you like us to keep an eye on him now and again while you go out?"

Wouldn't she? That very night she was sitting in the Angel, a cheerless pub on the edge of the estate, smoking a blissful Park Drive and sipping a small lemonade shandy, looking round like a tourist in a wonderful new holiday attraction.

That was the night Kieran Brady came into her life.

Mrs Duffy was complaining – not for herself, she hastened to add, but on behalf of poor Ingrid, who cried privately and for two pins would go home to Sweden, following the path to Heathrow already taken that year by Chantal, Annelise and Inez.

There was just too much work for two women. They needed help – especially with hoovering those long, wide staircases and keeping those expensive carpets clean, and particularly after all those people came for big dinner parties. They needed a second and larger automatic washing machine in the utility room if all the bedclothes – especially Master Julian's cot linen, not to mention his nappies (Georgina would have none of these new-fangled disposable things) were to be kept perfect and fresh.

Georgina agreed about the washing machine but she demurred at the extra cleaner. Privately she regretted that she hadn't known when she interviewed the six applicants that Mrs Duffy's husband was a local official of the Transport and General Workers' Union. Mrs Duffy was a wonderful worker, but something of that terrible Socialist cancer seemed to be spreading into Mockbeggar House.

Three weeks after the extra washing machine was delivered, Mrs Duffy renewed the second half of her demand. The case was logical and incontrovertibly put – the influence, Georgina suspected, of the husband.

Georgina said she would think about it.

Wendy Grissom felt she was committing treason towards her sex. While Larry was away at the agency in Camden earning lots of (she now had to admit) lovely money, she should carry on with her painting, consolidate her reputation, make sure she was not forgotten.

But this chuckling, gurgling little creature took up every delighted moment of her life. Wendy's only gesture towards creativity was occasionally picking up a sketch pad and dashing off quick pencil drawings of Grizelda asleep, Grizelda smiling, Grizelda reaching for the dancing coloured mobiles swinging over her cot and pram. Grizelda gripping rattles, examining fluffy toys, rolling round her playpen, attempting to crawl...

All the time, the undercurrent in her mind of "I should be doing serious work" was drowned by laughter at one thought: calling her daughter Grizelda had been a challenge to the gods. And it had worked. Grizelda was no grizzler. She was sunny and radiant from the first.

When the weather allowed, Wendy loved to walk across the common to the High Road where she often met other mothers with pushchairs for long and laughter-filled coffee mornings. And she smothered at birth the fear that she was letting down the whole of womankind. Being maternal took up all her life – so sod Fiona, Germaine and the rest whose books and articles were telling her that it shouldn't!

Kieran Brady worked on a building site. Kieran Brady was earning good money. Though cement dust was lodged permanently under his fingernails, Kieran Brady was young, strong, with a fund of jokes, an easy Irish charm and the power of making women look at him and not easily forget his shiny black hair and blue eyes.

Suddenly, Chrissy Lugg felt carefree. She had something stronger than a shandy. She was young, attractive, wasting herself.

Kieran wanted to meet her again. Mr and Mrs Pike wouldn't mind looking after Gary again, would they? No, they wouldn't. They loved it. And he was such a *good* little boy, wasn't he? As long as the call didn't come *too* often.

Within a week, Kieran had moved in with Chrissy.

Mrs Pike was tight-lipped.

"I didn't think you were that sort of girl," she said.

"It's all right," said Chrissy. "We're getting married."

Mrs Pike was mollified. Now she only felt for Chrissy's welfare.

"Will he be all right with Gary? You know what they say about other men's children?"

"Of *course*, Mrs Pike. Kieran *loves* Gary."

"So he should. And I hope he always does."

William Claverhouse had what he saw as the correct attitude to his son. Women surrounded the baby all day, ministering to his physical needs, bringing him carefully to the next stage. Then William's detailed plans for him would come into operation. Sometimes, after he was home from the City and Wanda had put Julian down for the night, Georgina and he would stand in the nursery looking down on the baby's quietly breathing form and William would expand on them yet again.

"Of course, he'll follow my path through school. There's a good kindergarten and pre-prep not five miles way; I've already had a word there. Then my own old prep and public schools. Then Oxford. Frobisher, I think. My college, of course." Georgina listened attentively and with some awe. Nobody had suggested that her own boarding school education should be topped off by university. "Frobisher's got the right tone. The trouble is, things are changing. There were separate entrance exams for the colleges in my day, with scholarships and exhibitions to keep up a proper pecking order. It looks as though all this Advanced-level nonsense is taking its place, letting in all those awful state school people. We've got to keep Julian's name clear above the rest – not let them lose it in the rush."

"I'm sure Dr Raeburn won't forget he's Julian's god-father, my darling," murmured Georgina.

"He'd better not," said William. "Anyway, after Oxford, what do you think? The bank? I'll smooth his way there." And so you should, thought Georgina. Being the youngest director of one of the oldest merchant banks in the City of London must carry some influence. "And then, I thought," William continued, "one step further than me. Into politics. Safe seat, Parliament, Cabinet – we could be looking at a future Prime Minister."

"I hope his other godfather knows his duty," said Georgina.

"He will," said Williams. "When the time comes."

"And what about marriage?" said Georgina.

"Goes without saying," William replied. "Julian will know who to pick. The right sort. And if he doesn't know, we will."

Julian slept on, unaware of his destiny.

Wendy and Larry were also musing on their child. Wendy sat by the Habitat crib, rocking it slightly.

"What sort of world will she grow up into?" she said. "War? Starvation? Pollution? Catastrophe and disaster?"

"A nuclear holocaust before she's twenty?" said Larry.

Sudden gloom enveloped them both.

"Should we ever have had her?" said Wendy.

"Should *anybody* bring children into this mess?" said Larry.

"Should we have more?" said Wendy.

They felt for each other's hands in the semi-darkness and knew they would.

Wendy bent down to her daughter.

"Just be yourself and be beautiful," she said. "What else can we ask?"

Nobody planned Gary's future. Sometimes Chrissy felt the baby's eyes following her. They had a quality she could not understand. Were they asking her something? *Demanding* something? Or were they accusing her? Of what? If he grew up angry, would it be with her?

Sometimes, even in those first few months, his movements and gurgles seemed more than just random. His arms made purposeful gestures; his noises had a rhythm, a shape. They were nearly words already, as if her son had brought messages from inside the womb or from wherever his spirit was even before he was conceived. Then Chrissy felt none of the pride of the parent with a precocious child. She was frightened, as if she had given birth to a little explosive package.

And when Kieran came to the flat there was a change. Overnight, as if he sensed hostility, Gary became fractious, difficult. Chrissy had an obscure and dreadful feeling, for which she had no words, that Kieran was protecting her from her son.

Anyway, Gary was no longer a contented child. He cried, was bad-tempered, slept in his own time, not Chrissy's. The only people who could calm him and for whom he would sleep at once were the Pikes. Kieran made him worse.

Kieran was not good with children and did not help Chrissy with Gary. And why should he? He works hard all day, Chrissy thought. He has to be up early for the bus – or rather, the back of the lorry which collected all the workers

16

and took them to the huge site of the half-finished shopping mall. He needed his sleep.

But sleep, with Gary there, was not always easy.

On the same night that William planned for his son and Wendy and Larry feared for their daughter, Gary was especially bad. Chrissy had given him a feed at one o'clock in the morning. She had made him bring up a prodigious belch which should have sorted him out. Then she put him back in the cot with a dry nappy on and a dummy dipped in orange juice in his mouth. He should have slept – some nights he would have. But not tonight. The thin cries sounded hour after hour.

At three o'clock, Kieran sat up in bed and hissed at Chrissy, "Shut the little sod up or I'll shut him up for you!"

Chapter Two

Four women came round for the post of heavy cleaner at Mockbeggar House, three days a week, 50p an hour. Georgina interviewed the applicants as carefully as if selecting for the Foreign Office. Mrs Cammel won the day: a woman in her forties with bony, strong hands and a sinister face. Ingrid took one look at her and sighed again for the lakes and forests of the far north.

Grizelda blossomed towards her first birthday. Larry continued to progress in the advertising agency: in the summer of 1975 he went with his old friend Timmy Green to the first of many conferences in the USA. Wendy could have gone but decided not to. She would not leave Grizelda, even with benevolent and trustworthy grandparents. Besides, she was finding time and inclination again for her own painting.

After that dreadful night, when Kieran's terrible threat rang in Chrissy's ears throughout the sleepless hours until morning and she willed Gary to silence if not sleep, there was a lull. Kieran never spoke like that again but kept aloof, as if he and the baby were not under the same roof. Gary seemed to be much quieter – not more co-operative, not less fractious but, at night, quieter. It was as if, Chrissy thought (but knew it could not be true) the eight-month-old baby

18

had heard, understood and decided to call an uneasy truce.

But it meant that for some months Chrissy walked on eggshells. She wanted no harm for her child, but she also wanted Kieran to stay and make good his promise to marry her.

Julian's first birthday was celebrated in the morning by the staff. Wanda Gates had put up a notice, HAPPY BIRTH-DAY JULIAN, ONE TODAY, which she had painted herself. She, Ingrid, Mrs Duffy and Mrs Cammel were joined by Georgina, who brought a bottle of sweet sherry (which she abominated but presumed the others would like) and the third-best glasses. They drank Julian's health, then cut the rather dry sponge cake with icing and one candle which Ingrid had made. They looked at the cards and pre-sents Julian had received, read aloud such cards as seemed suitable and pushed into his hand such presents as seemed grippable. Julian showed little interest but crawled across his playpen towards more familiar objects.

Further celebrations consisted of a large dinner party to which Wanda, Ingrid and the rest were not invited.

On the day of Grizelda's first birthday, the hallway of the block of flats was jammed with prams and pushchairs and the sitting-room floor was alive with crawling babies while their mothers sat drinking wine poured from boxes and screaming with laughter. All the mothers thought it was a marvellous way of celebrating and probably the babies did too.

On Gary's first birthday, Chrissy bought him a card from the newsagent's. She was about to write – under *Have lots of happy hours of play/Dear Birthday Boy, you're ONE today, All my love, Mummy* when she realized Kieran might look at it, so she wrote *Lots of love, Mummy* instead. Then she placed in the cot a fluffy – though rather hard – toy rabbit with floppy ears from the Oxfam shop. Gary examined it with interest, smiled at her, then gravely laid it aside.

Mr and Mrs Pike looked after Gary that evening, bringing cards of their own, while Chrissy and Kieran went out.

William Claverhouse calculated that a two-year gap between children was ideal, and soon after Julian's birthday he informed Georgina that they would now make serious efforts to add to their offspring.

Alas, to no avail. Julian's conception had taken eight years, and it looked as though any brothers or sisters would be equally elusive. Repeated and expensive tests showed no physical reasons for this: changes of routine and scene to exotic holiday locations, with Julian left at home with Wanda and Ingrid, brought no change of fortune. It seemed as though Julian would remain an only child.

Wendy knew she was pregnant again not long after Grizelda's first birthday. She and Larry hadn't planned this, but she was not very methodical about taking the Pill and they were content to go on playing an innocent form of Russian roulette. Wendy was pleased, so was Larry. They looked fondly at Grizelda and knew she would be pleased as well.

Now Gary was getting more mobile, he was proving a hazard in the tiny flat. Chrissy was forever picking him up

20

and plonking him down elsewhere to keep him out of Kieran's way. She noticed that now, when Kieran was present, Gary was very quiet – almost as if he had decided to be on his best behaviour. But he was only fifteen months old, so she knew that was impossible.

But three months later, something she knew was all too possible was causing her real worry. There was no escape. She would have to tell Kieran.

She waited until one evening after she had fed him on steak and chips (an unaccustomed luxury) and poured him a can of Guinness. Then she said, "Kieran, I think I'm..."

Kieran said, "Yes, I know. You're up the duff."

Unable to restrain joy at this equable reaction, she said, "Don't you mind?"

"Why should I? I've always wanted a sprog of my own. Now we'll get married."

Chrissy couldn't believe it. She'd been sure he would storm out of the place like Gary's father had. What a jewel she had found in Kieran!

Wanda did not like Mrs Cammel. One day, she accused the cleaner of stealing money out of her housecoat pocket. Mrs Cammel furiously denied it. Georgina made everybody empty out handbags and pockets. No unaccounted-for money was found.

"I'm not working with a thief. Either she goes or I go," said Wanda.

Georgina valued Mrs Cammel's hard and uncomplaining work. But she had come to depend on Wanda almost completely. So Mrs Cammel, angry and injured but supplied with a glowing reference saying that she had only left "for personal reasons", stalked out of Mockbeggar House for the last time. And another advertisement for a heavy cleaner, with the same hours and terms as before, appeared in the local paper.

Grizelda's brother was born just two days before her second birthday. Grizelda was walking and talking now. Two months before, she had been to the seaside and had walked in the sea with Wendy and Larry holding a hand each and lifting her up in the air over the waves. She had sat down and felt the water whoosh! over the sand and past her and then whoosh! back again to leave her high and dry. There had been lots of other children in the hotel. In Grizelda's mind now as her birthday approached was just a general impression of something magical, entirely wonderful. She knew, as well, that something else wonderful was approaching: a day that was *hers* when lots of things she wanted would come to her, like more dolls, like toys, like a *real swing* of her own. And perhaps, Mummy had said, the biggest present of all.

Then, suddenly, Mummy wasn't there. Mummy had changed: she was slow and fat and frequently asked Grizelda to pat her tummy and say hello to her new brother or sister. Grizelda did so not knowing what it all meant, then slipped away to her toys with a strange unease in her mind.

But Daddy was at home more now, and Mummy's mummy was there as well. Seeing things different and changing was partly exciting, partly threatening.

Then Mummy went away. Grizelda heard her cry out in the night, then the door open, footsteps die away and the sound of the car outside. Mummy's mummy said, "When Mummy comes home she'll have a big present for you." Well, the birthday came and Grizelda *had* the presents:

dolls, toys, books with pictures in which Mummy's mummy read to her, a swing of her own to be set up outside. And in the afternoon Mummy came home looking small again and Daddy was with her and they had the new present with them. And they showed it to Grizelda and it was tiny and red and nasty and wrinkled and made crying noises and everybody was looking at it and not at her and she had strange and sad feelings which, though she did not know it, were the first inklings of jealousy and loss.

As Gary began to walk unsteadily and the sounds he made stayed sharp and clear but were still not words Chrissy recognized, so the atmosphere in the flat became warmer, happier. For the first time in her life Chrissy felt joy. Kieran showed a new gentle side. They married a month after her announcement to him, in a register office with Mr and Mrs Pike as witnesses. Chrissy wrote to her parents, whom she had not seen since Gary was born even though they only lived ten miles away, and invited them, her brother Terry and his wife and children. They did not answer.

She asked Kieran if his parents would be there. "If the old people back in Kerry knew their good Catholic boy was in a godless register office to marry an English heathen with a bastard already, sure they'd drop dead with the shame of it," he replied.

Chrissy realized with a shock that she knew nothing about Kieran. They were two completely isolated people.

She found a nice two-piece suit in the Oxfam shop which fitted well. Kieran had a dark grey suit already which, when cleaned, would make him look very impressive. Gary was dressed up neatly and viewed the register office ceremony and the meal and drink in the pub afterwards with, mercifully, impassive inscrutability.

Kieran became an attentive husband. Chrissy liked being Mrs Brady. But things were not so rosy when Kieran was at work. Just as before, Chrissy was cooped up in a tiny space with a growing child. Even more than before she found Gary's presence disturbing. He had passed into almost complete silence now. He walked unaided and would, if she let him, be off out of the door and down the road. Besides, his inscrutability had become oppressive. He looked at her fixedly for hours. Deep down, Chrissy knew what he was staring at and thinking: the rival was coming, the supplanter, the creature that would put him a poor third in her affections.

But how *could* he know? He was only a baby. He couldn't be *that* clever.

She had bought him a battered, second-hand wooden train: a red engine and four green carriages which joined together. Gary had pushed them, pulled them, put them together in different combinations. Then he had tired of them. Chrissy had not seen him playing with them for weeks.

It was a pity she did not see them one morning a month after the wedding and a day before Gary's second birthday. For they were strung out in a line across the doorway just outside the kitchenette, right in Chrissy's way. She walked through the door, tripped, went sprawling, tried to pull herself up, felt searing pain, screamed – and, even as Gary watched expressionless, Mr and Mrs Pike came running in and she blacked out, she knew there would be no baby for Kieran after all.

Julian Claverhouse passed his second year with only Wanda

and Ingrid for regular company. Georgina had so much else to do while William's weighty concerns were all in the City. Mrs Belswain had taken Mrs Cammel's place: a sturdy and talkative lady who took on all the worst tasks with what Mrs Duffy regarded as suspicious enthusiasm.

Georgina did not worry about Julian's lack of child or male company. After all, he *should* be kept exclusive. Later there would be three mornings a week at kindergarten – that would be company enough with children who were all of good background. And a *big* second birthday was approaching when all the family and friends would be there and for the first time Julian would know he was the central attraction.

Wendy and Larry tried to ensure that Grizelda did not feel left out, but they knew full well that she resented her little brother, Barnaby. They resolved to stay attentive to her and let her anger run its course. Besides, there were lots of children that she could be taken to play with now – and there was a good playgroup nearby to which Grizelda would soon go.

Besides, the flat was too small for such an expanding family. Larry was salting money away at the moment – Wendy could not get to grips with the agency's success. So a move to a house – and a big one, in which the family could expand still further – was on the cards.

And another possibility showed itself. What about something special for Grizelda's education?

"I'm not letting my child go to any of these stuffy private schools and have her end up some toffee-nosed snob no good to anybody," cried Wendy.

"I don't mean that," said Larry. "But what about one of

these progressive schools where there's freedom and liberal values and a real artistic sense? What about an international school where she'll meet children from other countries and be a real citizen of the world and not just this tiny, spent island?"

Well, what about them? Wendy knew nothing. But this affluent, confident person her once hippy, raffish husband had grown into was very persuasive.

"Schools like that will be right for our children," he said. "I'll get the brochures."

Wendy remembered her first vow at Grizelda's birth – that she would *never*, *never* go away to boarding school. Where was that vow now? Trampled down in Larry's enthusiasm.

Mr Pike rang for the ambulance from a public callbox. With siren shrieking, the ambulance took Chrissy away. Gary was taken next door where he stayed, docile and uninterested, with Mrs Pike, while Mr Pike waited in the flat for Kieran.

Mr Pike was not prepared for Kieran's reaction to the news. He slumped into a chair and howled like a dog. Tears ran down his cheeks. Outside, rain fell from a grey sky. Even so, once quietened, Kieran rushed out to wait half an hour for a bus to the town centre, where he had another wait for a second bus to the hospital on the other side of town.

The Pikes heard no more of him until a clatter on the stairs at three in the morning. Mr Pike rushed out, taking care not to wake Gary, whose cot they had brought into their flat. He found Kieran sprawled on the landing, dead drunk, an empty bottle of Irish whiskey in his hand, the last quarter of its contents flowing down the stairway. Mr Pike left him there: there was nothing else he could do.

There were no surprises in Julian's second year of life. The little nursery society carried on as always. There were occasional trips away – with his father on a launch along the river watching long, thin boats rowed by men with flashing oars; with his mother to other houses where he sometimes met different children of his age and they circled each other with wary suspicion. But most of the time he lived surrounded by his toys, whose number grew steadily. Sometimes Wanda Gates read him rhymes and little stories; sometimes Ingrid told him tales of dark forests, laughing trolls and evil demons. These frightened him and stopped him sleeping at night because he thought they were in the house and hiding behind the curtains.

Afterwards, Wendy realized that the matter of the school was the nearest she and Larry had ever come to a real fight. She accepted that the way the contracts were coming in, Larry was going to be seriously rich and, once he was a partner in the firm, their income would be stratospheric. She agreed that not to spend it on the children's welfare would be irresponsible. She agreed with all Larry said about progressive education, liberal values and internationalism. But she would hold out to the death against her children going away to boarding school.

Fortune smiled on them. They realized the ideal place was not four miles away, in a superb Regency house in (for London) lovely grounds, with tasteful extensions and annexes. The Anglo-World Citizens School. Exactly what they wanted – costing a bomb but full of the children of foreign diplomats, American, Japanese, Arab, European businessmen, British media people. They took children into the nursery department at three and sent them out at eighteen to universities all over the world.

Perfect for Grizelda, for Barnaby, for whoever followed. What's more, it settled where they would move: a lovely four-bedroomed detached house on the edge of the Heath ten minutes' walk from the school, with a price which made Wendy catch her breath in horror. In the town fifty miles north where her parents still lived, she could have bought five houses like it and still have change for a new car.

But then she looked squarely at the circumstances. Larry was never forthcoming about the money he earned and she had not taken sufficient notice about what his work with Timmy Green was doing to them. She had not even cottoned on to the full significance of the fact that when they watched television and the advertisements came on, Larry repeatedly said "One of ours" or "That was my idea" or "Timmy and I slogged our guts out over that one". Or, more frequently recently, "That was a real team effort. We've got some bright young people coming through."

But now she knew exactly what it meant. They could buy almost anything in the world they wanted.

Chrissy was brought home by ambulance. Kieran was already at the building site, hollow-eyed and unshaven. Mrs Pike had not had time to tidy the flat after he had gone. The place was a mess of scattered sheets, dirty socks and pants all over the floor, plates congealing in the sink. Chrissy gasped; Mrs Pike smoothed the bed and made her lie down while she cleared up. She would keep Gary for a while. She had noticed with alarm how indifferent Kieran seemed to his stepson.

Kieran came home that evening as usual. But it was a significant homecoming: the first night of the new order.

There was only one flaw in the domestic society Georgina Claverhouse supervised. Mrs Belswain had started so happily doing the heavy cleaning but, as the months wore on, Georgina noticed her become quieter, even sullen. There was no complaint about her work: something was wrong.

She asked her one morning.

"Everything's fine, ma'am," was the answer.

"Is something at home bothering you? Perhaps I can help."

"No, ma'am. Couldn't be better."

"Or is something upsetting you here?"

Mrs Belswain looked away and continued grimly stripping the beds.

"Not at all, ma'am. You're all too good to me."

"I'm glad," said Georgina.

But something *is* wrong and I'm going to find it out, she thought as she made her way upstairs, where William had had a huge Hornby-Dublo train set assembled for Julian so that he could watch Wanda make *Flying Scotsman* chase the Inter-City 125 round the track.

The frighteningly large mortgage was taken on, the move was made. The cosy flat, first home for the Grissoms, was left behind. Wendy felt a lump in her throat as Larry locked the door for the last time. But the new chapter had to start. Soon Grizelda would be three and ready for her first day at the Anglo-World Citizens School.

Kieran had changed. Chrissy had changed. Only Gary was the same.

This was what most enraged Kieran. Chrissy could see it:

she waited fearfully for the first blow, the first act of violence. But that was not Kieran's style. Oh, how he resented Gary still being there, healthy, a reminder of another man, while his own baby had perished months before its time! Kieran knew the bare facts about what had caused the miscarriage. Chrissy would never tell him about the fleeting, ridiculous idea she had had as she fell over the wooden train set and caught a glimpse of Gary sitting there, watching.

Chapter Three

The time was coming for Julian to be dressed nicely so that his mother could take him in the Range Rover to kindergarten. She knew Wanda would miss her charge for the three mornings a week he would be there. Wanda's future, when Julian went full-time to school and in the absence of brothers or sisters at home, was in the balance anyway.

But Wanda was worth her weight in gold with her politeness and her efficiency and Georgina would not let her go until she had to. Why, if she and William failed to produce another child, it might be worthwhile to adopt one just to keep Wanda.

It was about that time that Wanda brought the first complaint about Mrs Belswain.

"She's uncooperative, lazy and dirty," she said.

"But Mrs Belswain's work seems excellent to me," said Georgina.

"You don't see her all the time like I do," said Wanda. "You need eyes in the back of your head to make sure she does any work at all."

Wanda was so conscientious that Georgina decided to ask William if she could be employed as chief housekeeper when her duties with Julian were finally over.

The Grissoms were settled. Grizelda was kitted out in a

miniature school uniform which made Wendy laugh and cry at the same time. Barnaby's first and Grizelda's third birthdays came and went together: there was a nominally joint party which Wendy forecast would, in future years, expand into a huge gathering. And then, as the months passed, she realized that she was pregnant again.

Any magic had gone. Kieran went to work each day, came back, ate, went out. He seldom took Chrissy. He never showed her any violence, but was remote, uncommunicative. He made love frequently, but roughly – as if it were a necessity, like going to the toilet. The Pikes he resented. Gary he plainly loathed – but mercifully silently. Chrissy had never forgotten that whispered threat of long ago: "Shut the little sod up or I'll shut him up for you!" She never lost the fear that one day Kieran might carry it out.

But now it seemed there was no fear of it. Gary did not need to be shut up. He too stayed quiet and uncommunicative. When the two were in the flat, the silence was oppressive, like a dead weight on her. Often she wanted to break it with a long, wordless scream, but she knew she never could. She was too frightened.

Of what? Of whom? She knew the answer: of *both* the men in her life.

Julian was now a regular at kindergarten. A kind lady called Mrs Jenkins bore him away, and when either Georgina or Wanda returned to collect him, he would be wearing a little white apron blotched all over, as were his hands and face, with bright poster paints.

"We have *lovely* times, don't we, Julian?" Mrs Jenkins would say.

Thus progressed Julian's first encounter with the independent school system.

Wendy and Larry were very impressed with the language
laboratories, gyms, all-weather hockey and football pitches
in the upper schools, as well as the multilingual notices and
the chattering mix of tiny children of different nationalities
and colours in the nursery department at the Anglo-World
Citizens School. This place would give all their offspring the
broad horizons they needed to face the terrible world they
were growing up in. Wendy and Larry had made up their
minds at once. There would be no difficulty with the fees.
Grizelda would enter the nursery school when she was three
and a half. With good progress, there was no reason why she
should not stay until eighteen and then have the pick of any
university she wanted.

The earlier indulgence of dressing Grizelda up in a little
school uniform was suddenly not a fanciful game. But before
nursery school, Wendy and Larry had decided, she should
spend a few months at playgroup to get used to other children.

In a strange way, Chrissy grew used to her gaol – even came
to like it. Now Gary was bigger and could walk quite long
distances she went out more, round the dismal estate and
sometimes beyond, up to the low chalky hills which fringed
the town. For these longer expeditions Gary was strapped
into his pushchair, by now far too small for him. Sometimes
he demanded to be let out and carried. He was heavy but,
oddly, Chrissy liked carrying him. She could almost believe
she was a happy mother in a happy home with a child who
did not frighten her and would not enrage her husband into
near-murder.

Now, for the first time during Gary's short life, Chrissy found her mind full of thoughts of his father. Already Gary was beginning to look like him, with a face which, though chubby now, would one day be thin and fringed with black hair. She often caught a searching look in Gary's eyes: only now did she realize that it was the look of his father – that moody, restless man she had once thought she loved. How clearly now she remembered his periods of taciturn gloom, the intervals when he spoke quickly and urgently, using words and ideas which seemed to come from nowhere, were entirely beyond her and made her parents certain he was mad. There were those sudden bursts of violence, especially when he thought he was being tied down, made a fool of. Like the night that she had told him she was pregnant. She would never forget it. He had risen suddenly, looked down on her and hit her – three, four, five times. Then he strode out of the flat, slamming the door behind him and leaving his meagre possessions behind. She never saw him or heard from him again. He disappeared completely from her life as suddenly, mysteriously and explosively as he had entered it.

When she looked at Gary she often wondered whether she had given birth to a little replica, whether he would go the same way, whether there was anything she could do to stop it. Or was her son, like his father, just an elemental force, tameable by nobody?

She had no idea. And she didn't want to think about it. She simply wanted Gary's fourth year to pass without incident. And so it did, until something happened to change everyone's routine.

Wanda had come to Georgina with further complaints four

months after Julian's third birthday. She carried a nursery pillow case.

"Look at this," she said disgustedly. "Half-washed. Mrs Belswain is a lazy slut."

Georgina was still surprised. Mrs Belswain had always seemed an excellent worker. She said so.

"Oh, I've caught her out many times," replied Wanda. "I didn't want to make a song and dance about it so as not to cause trouble. I've been covering up for her as well as I could. But it's too much now. Either she goes or I go."

That dreaded phrase again from Wanda. Georgina felt the same sinking of the heart as when faced with Mrs Cammel's supposed thievery. Wanda meant this. She must have good cause. And while it would be unfortunate to see Mrs Belswain go, to lose Wanda would be an unmitigated disaster.

So again she would have to do the deed. She found Mrs Belswain on the top landing unplugging the vacuum cleaner. To Georgina, everything looked spotless.

"Mrs Belswain, I wonder if you would drop by to see me before you go today," she said.

"Yes, ma'am," said Mrs Belswain. Georgina could not mistake the "I know what's coming" look.

When Mrs Belswain came into the study where all the wages were paid in cash each week, Georgina stumbled over the reasons for her dismissal. She would not, could not, repeat the accusations Wanda had made. She merely stammered out excuses about needing to economize, looking afresh at their domestic needs now that Julian went to the kindergarten, changes in the duties of Wanda and Mrs Duffy.

Mrs Belswain was not fooled.

"It's Wanda Gates who's done this, and the Duffy woman hasn't stopped her. Mrs Claverhouse, you mark my words: the day is coming when you'll regret you ever set eyes on Wanda Gates. She's a selfish, evil woman."

Georgina was outraged.

"Mrs Belswain, I won't have you say such things about a trusted servant, colleague and – and *friend*!"

Mrs Belswain's mouth clamped shut in a straight line.

"Mrs Belswain, nobody regrets this more than I do," Georgina continued. "I will write you an excellent reference. Meanwhile, I am giving you a month's wages in lieu of notice."

Mrs Belswain pocketed the cash and was gone, not answering Georgina's last "Goodbye, Mrs Belswain."

Georgina sighed. More advertising, more interviewing.

The playgroup was so lovely and Grizelda was so happy in it that Wendy almost regretted that the move to the Anglo-World Citizens School would take place so soon. However, at least it showed that Grizelda could mix and play constructively. This indicated a sunny path forward for her and – Wendy felt pride here – showed how well she had done her own job. Now to do as well with Barnaby.

The shopping mall on which Kieran had worked and earned such good money was finished. The men were laid off and paid off. Where would Kieran work now? The country was in one of its many recessions: construction work had slumped. No houses, no offices, no factories were being built. Kieran was on the dole.

Kieran did not like being on the dole. Not working was a terrible blow to him but there was another, more immediate difficulty. Dole plus housing benefit plus family allowance did not add up to a sum which would keep them fed or clothed, even from the Oxfam shop.

For Chrissy there was something even more pressing. She could not face having Kieran and Gary together every day in the flat. There was only one way out of this that she could think of: she would have to find a job – any job, paying any money. And a job where she could take Gary with her.

It was a tall order. Even before she mentioned taking Gary, Kieran was scornful.

"Job? You? What can *you* do?"

What indeed? If a strong, semi-skilled man with years of experience was out of work, what chance had she, without a single qualification, a single talent?

"Cleaning?" she said hopefully.

"That's about all," he replied.

William Claverhouse was not consulted over the employment of cleaning staff. He was quite content to leave it to Georgina. He knew hardly anything about the troubles with Mrs Cammel and Mrs Belswain – such people were of no account. He only cast the most cursory glance over the advertisement before it was placed in the local paper, and then only to check that there was no increase in the wages offered.

Situations vacant
Wanted as soon as possible. Cleaner for heavy duties in family home. Three days a week, excellent conditions. 50p per hour. Write c/o Box 31.

William certainly approved of the fact that applicants would not know the address until they received an answer.

The day had nearly arrived for Grizelda to enter the Anglo-World Citizens School. She knew all about it. She had told all her friends at playgroup. She told Barnaby as he chuckled back at her from his pram.

"Going to school, Barney. Going to school."

Her jealousy of him was long buried, but she enjoyed the feeling of superiority age and change gave her.

She also had a keen sense of the order of things. Only when she was sure that Barnaby had fully grasped the point did she tell her toys – dolls first, teddies second – because she knew the difference between the human and animal kingdoms.

When all these formalities were over, she was ready.

"*Heavy* duties? What are they then?" said Kieran.

"Only one way to find out," said Chrissy, laboriously writing her letter.

> *Dear Sir or Madam,*
> *I have seen your ad in local paper. I am interested in the job with much experience of same. Please advise.*
> *Yours truly,*
> *C Brady (Mrs)*

She showed Kieran the letter. He looked at it without expression. Then she took Gary with her to the Wavy Line shop and sub-post office, bought a stamp, posted her application, bought baked beans, a packet of skinless beef sausages, potatoes and milk, and came back to await events.

Wanda was taking a firm line on the new applicants.

"As I'm going to have more time with what goes on in the house now Master Julian's flying the nest, I should be with you when you interview the new people," she said to Georgina.

Georgina only wondered for a second whether Wanda was presuming beyond her position. If Wanda's job was going to change into that of a housekeeper (nothing had been said outright about that yet but Wanda must see which way the wind was blowing) then in future she would have a right to. So why not now?

A fortnight passed with only three answers: Mrs Phelps, Mrs French, Mrs Brady.

"We must see them all," said Georgina.

Wendy cried again when she saw Grizelda in her new uniform, so small that she looked like a walking schoolgirl doll. But Larry was elated.

"The start of a long process," he said. "My girl will go to the very top."

Wendy just knew that now the four-bedroomed house would echo with comparative emptiness, even though she would very soon be busy with the third in the family.

Chrissy stared in dismay at the address on the letter asking her to an interview.

"It's a bus ride away," she cried.

"What did you expect?" said Kieran.

What indeed? Nobody within walking distance was likely to want a cleaner, but bus fares would make a big hole in the £12 a week she calculated she would earn.

Should she go at all? Kieran was full of advertisements

he'd seen for building workers to earn good money in West Germany, Saudi Arabia – anywhere, it seemed, but here in Britain. Hard work for a few months, good money, then home again until the next chance came up.

So what was the point of going for this job? Especially when they surely wouldn't let her take Gary. Even if the Pikes said they would look after him all day, which they wouldn't, she couldn't let them. Those two had been showing their age lately.

But something stubbornly told her: *Go. See what it's like, at least.*

So she went.

And now Grizelda's first day at school was really here. Wendy had felt nothing when she took her to playgroup but today, when the little girl disappeared holding the teacher's hand and became lost in the crowd of identically-dressed children, she could not hold back a snuffle and a tear.

Today marked the end of something big and the start of something bigger.

Chrissy got off the bus at the end of the road where Mockbeggar House stood. As she walked between the imposing iron gates, felt the gravel under her feet and saw a house that looked like something in a film, she thought: *This is no place for me. I'm going back home.*

But she fought the urge and toiled on up the drive. She passed the huge front door and walked as directed to the servants' entrance.

Mrs Phelps and Mrs French were big, middle-aged, strong ladies who looked able to turn mattresses without raising a sweat. So why, Georgina thought, was Wanda so insistent upon the young, slight, pale, mousy-haired Mrs Brady who looked as though the first morning's work would kill her?

Strange. But she did realize by now that if the new appointment was not made with Wanda's approval, it would not last.

Then Mrs Brady came out with an extraordinary request.

"I've got a three-year-old son, Gary. Can he come with me?"

Quite unsuitable, Georgina thought, and she was about to say so when Wanda cut in with: "Oh, how lovely? He'll be company for Master Julian when he's at home, won't he, ma'am? I'm sure they'll play together *very* nicely."

Georgina shot her a furious look – but then found herself unable to contradict. Mrs Brady seemed keen on the job, Wanda liked her, so she would come under her protection, which obviously meant a lot in this house and – well, perhaps Julian *ought* to see children who were not his own sort.

So it was agreed. Chrissy had got the job. Gary would come with her.

Chrissy went home rejoicing. When she arrived, Kieran was rejoicing as well. He was off to Germany, to work on a big site in Mönchengladbach.

So on the very day that Grizelda's die seemed cast as she entered the Anglo-World Citizens School, the scene was set for the first meeting between Gary Brady, born Gary Lugg, and Julian Claverhouse, with all the consequences that would spring from it.

Chapter Four

The years passed and Julian, Grizelda and Gary reached their twelfth birthdays. For each, life had changed.

Grizelda had been nine years at the Anglo-World Citizens School. From that first day when she was three, she had loved it – loved her American, German, French, Indian, Japanese, Saudi, Taiwanese, Bajan, Nigerian and British friends. She revelled in the work: teachers told Larry and Wendy she was gifted, was a certainty for Oxford or Cambridge, or Harvard, Yale, the Sorbonne, Madrid, Vienna – any university you cared to name.

Wendy smiled on her. Grizelda would take many steps beyond her parents' humble art college background. Barnaby, then Joel and Amy, had followed Grizelda to the school. Their lives seemed so secure, self-contained – they were not aware of the burgeoning crisis under the surface.

Wendy, however, often wondered whether everything was really as it seemed. Larry was strained, pale, tight-lipped recently. He was working far too hard. All right, so everyone was in a mess as the eighties ploughed on: unemployment was horrendous and once-busy and thriving factories lay derelict. But, Wendy reasoned, what happened to industry didn't affect the course of advertising, surely? Wouldn't Larry's advertising benefit? If firms were in a mess, they would have to try harder to sell what they made.

Thus she comforted herself as Larry came home later and later at night, slept less, lost more weight, grew more silent. At last she was beginning to doubt her own logic.

"Larry, is everything all right?" she said one night, when he staggered into bed at two o'clock and slumped down with his back to her without even the most perfunctory kiss and "goodnight".

"Of course," he muttered sharply. "Don't worry. Go to sleep."

"Why won't you *tell* me things?" Wendy cried, trying to put her arms around him. He shook her off with an angry convulsion which seemed to Wendy like a shudder expressing despair. For hours they lay awake, far away from each other, eyes glistening in the darkness, sharing a silent misery, but as Larry drifted into a dozing sleep, Wendy heard him mutter, "The cheating young bastards!"

Two days later Wendy saw the item on the business page of The *Guardian*.

Crisis at Grissom Green

The struggle for control of Grissom Green, Britain's fastest growing advertising agency of the seventies which has come to a shuddering stop in the eighties, took a new turn yesterday. A boardroom revolt of directors, aided by shareholders and fuelled by discontented young staff, finally succeeded in ousting the firm's founder, Timmy Green, and his partner Larry Grissom. Undoubtedly the firm has been losing ground during the last three years: contracts have dried up and accounts have been lost to newer rivals. General consensus has it that the whizz-kids of the last decade have lost their way and only a complete change of direction can save the agency from bankruptcy or a humiliating takeover by a more stable competitor.

Wendy read the article three times more to make sure she understood it exactly. Then she found herself shaking with rage. She must be the only person in the whole world who didn't know what was happening. How *dare* Larry keep all this from her? A humiliating takeover? She was the one who was humiliated, who felt a fool. Cocooned in her lovely house, surrounded by her wonderful children, still painting whenever she got the chance – and, she was convinced, with her talent at last finding a true and individual voice – she had been allowed to drift along in the greatest fool's paradise of all.

She took a big decision. She was alone in the house. Larry always kept their financial affairs to himself and she – so *stupidly* – had never questioned that.

Right. It was time for a change. She marched into his study and up to the desk drawer which held all his documents.

Locked. Where was the key?

She searched vainly. He'd hidden it or taken it.

OK, desperate measures.

She went outside to the garage, opened the big red toolbox, brought out a hammer and chisel, came back and hammered until the lock broke, the wood splintered and the contents of the drawer lay before her: bank statements, unit trusts, letters from financial advisers, building society managers. At first she found them difficult to understand, but eventually their remorseless logic told its tale.

As a family, they were virtually bankrupt. The current account was in huge overdraft. The shares were almost worthless. The mortgage on the house had not been paid for three months.

In a daze, she wandered into the kitchen. She made herself a cup of black coffee and wondered about something stronger. No. She had to keep a clear head.

For the fifteen years since she had met Larry she had trusted him to tell her the truth and he had never let her down – until now.

But he was doing it for *you*, hiding the truth to save you, a voice inside her said.

But you and I, Larry, are the *real* partners, her own self spoke. I'm your partner far more than Timmy Arsehole Green. I'm the one you should confide in.

What should she do? Who could she turn to?

It was now midday. She didn't expect to see Larry until late at night. Should she ring him? March into the Grissom Green offices herself? But she couldn't leave the children waiting at school – she always picked them up.

Suddenly, the front door opened. Larry walked in.

Wendy rushed to meet him.

"Larry, why didn't you tell me? Why couldn't you trust me to understand? I could have helped. I know I could."

He pushed past her.

"No time," he said. "I've got a plane to catch."

"But Larry..." she started.

He turned to her, face haggard.

"Chicago. Timmy and me. Patching a deal with the Yanks. Last chance. If it works, we're quids in. If it doesn't..."

He didn't finish the sentence but rushed upstairs to pack.

Oddly, he had left the airline ticket by the telephone in the hall, right where she could see it.

Convincing me he's telling the truth, she thought.

She looked at it. EnglandAir, a small, mainly charter airline. Economy class from Gatwick.

Wendy was no stranger to air travel. With Larry and the children, she'd been all over the place. She knew full well that when Larry and Timmy flew to the USA on business, they went first class by British Airways from Heathrow, not in a clapped out DC10 with students crossing the Atlantic on the cheap.

Had he left the ticket out not just to show he was telling the truth but also to let her know how bad things were?

He rushed downstairs, snatched the ticket and hurtled past her out of the door.

"I'll ring when I get there," he called over his shoulder as he flung himself into a waiting taxi.

The afternoon wore on. Wendy picked up Grizelda, Barnaby, Joel and Amy. They all ate a silent supper, then the children did homework, watched television, went to bed.

So did Wendy. She lay there, lonely and sleepless.

At five o'clock she drifted into a shallow doze racked with dreams she forgot as soon as she woke, but which left her shaking as if by some awful revelation she wished she could remember. She got up, gave the children their breakfast, then drove them to school, hardly seeing the road in her daze.

Once home, she forced herself into making some coffee, then switched the radio on. It was 10am and an hourly news bulletin was beginning.

"Reports are coming in that a DC10 of EnglandAir, on an overnight flight to Chicago from Gatwick, crashed in the early hours of this morning attempting to land at O'Hare Airport in a snowstorm. Eyewitnesses say the plane exploded

in a ball of flame on impact with the runway. It is already confirmed there could be no survivors. It is believed that most of the two hundred and fifty passengers were British. Accident investigators are on their way to the scene and a search has started for the flight recorder. Instrument failure is thought to be the most likely cause..."

Wendy heard no more. She was numb, paralysed. She sat staring sightlessly forward for a long time, then she stirred herself to telephone the Anglo-World Citizens School. Only then did grief, dark and cavernous, take her over. When her children were brought home and rushed in to find the cause of her echoing, racking sobs, she stared at them as if she had never seen them before.

Part Two

Grizelda

Chapter One

The young man played his flute mournfully. Pitifully few coins lined the open case in front of him. Nobody cared to stop or listen.

He did not worry. There was a strange instinct deep in his mind that his flute was calling someone, over the miles, over the years, who might not be here yet but would surely arrive one day.

Grizelda Grissom stood in the wind outside the Viking Boatbuilder. Saturday morning shopping crowds swirled round her. She was not one of them.

The Viking Boatbuilder had been a sad disappointment. The landlord – if the person in charge of such a drinking shed stuck over with bits of tasteless fake "history" deserved the title given to generations of hosts of *real* hostelries – had been no help. He had hardly spoken, obviously not impressed by this young visitor from Speakeasy Television, too busy almost to give her the time of day.

Anyway, the Viking Boatbuilder was no good, stuck on the end of the ghastly bleak 1960s-built concrete shopping centre, through which gales howled as if through a wind tunnel. Sagging strippers and awful groups were all the entertainment here. Grizelda needed a pub with *atmosphere*, a meeting place for a tight-knit society.

Could there be such a thing in this horrible town?

Anyway, thankfully she was out of the Viking Boatbuilder – pretentious name for the stub-end of a jerry-built pile of breeze blocks! Where next?

The first thing was to get out of this bitter wind. She sheltered in a doorway of Littlewoods, took out her pocket book and scanned the list of addresses she had taken back in the London office. The Caravelle? Another pretentious name – and the mirror image of the Viking Boatbuilder at the other end of the shopping centre. The New House? Not exactly an enticing prospect. The Jolly Angler?

That sounded better. She paged through her *A–Z* and found the road. Yes, quite promising. No new tower-block-torn road-grid here but a little knot of narrow streets. Quite *Coronation Street*. But what an outlandish name for a pub just there! Had it served generations of fishermen before being swallowed up by the Industrial Revolution?

Yes, this must be a real pub for real people. So there would probably be real entertainers, of the sort Quentin wanted her to find and which she'd so far been so rotten at doing.

She stepped out of the doorway into the cold blast, extreme even for late September in England, and walked towards the multi-storey where the company's Vauxhall Calibra was parked.

Pray God it had not been stolen or vandalized!

Quentin's big idea had sounded a loser to Grizelda. He was boss of Speakeasy Television, a small company he had set up in the wake of changes at BBC and ITV to make programmes for the big channels. Grizelda had joined a year before, straight from university. "Researcher", she was called.

"Really, you'll be a leg-man," Quentin had said at her interview.

"Sexist," she had replied.

"You'd walk out now if I said you'd be the leg-woman," Quentin had retorted.

"I want the job." Grizelda had said that very quickly to convince herself. The exchange had nettled her slightly.

"Researcher," Quentin had answered. "I won't let anyone call you anything else."

They agreed on it and ever since had treated each other with wary respect.

So here she was, lowly in a team making mainly documentaries for BBC2 and Channel 4, only as secure as the next contract. Even that seemed still somewhere out of sight.

As a way of getting them out of the mire, Quentin's idea seemed a sure-fire loser.

"We'll do an on-spec documentary," he had said. "We'll show it to all the channels and whoever takes it, we'll tailor it to one of their slots. *Modern Times*, *Inside Story*, *Without Walls*, *True Stories* – they'll all love it."

Quentin was speaking very fast to show enthusiasm. Grizelda already knew that was a bad sign.

"Pub entertainers. The real no-hopers. The ones who won't even make it to the club circuit, who tell bad jokes and sing their hearts out and nobody listens because they're all getting tanked up. There's pathos and lots of human interest there. And there's art in it. We could sell it to the *South Bank Show* or *Omnibus*."

Now she *knew* he was desperate.

"And I can get Maurice Cracknell to front it."

Maurice Cracknell was about the biggest name in TV documentary.

"He'd never do anything on spec," said somebody.

"I happen to know he's between contracts at the moment. And he'd do it for an old friend."

Quentin pushed the idea through against everyone else's judgement. That was why Grizelda had been dispatched to this God-awful Midlands town with a list of pubs, a reservation in a too-hot hotel room and a mission to unearth the documentary's subjects.

"I'm sending you to the heartlands," Quentin had said, "where the pulse of the people still beats strong."

He really was losing his grip.

The multi-storey car park was at the far end of the shopping centre. Grizelda could not help noticing how many of the shops were boarded up or had "Closing Down" signs. It was even worse than the town forty miles south where her mother had lived since the terrible death of her father. She walked uninvolved, separate, through the milling hordes of people, anxious only to get out.

And then an unexpected sound soared over the hubbub of voices and walking feet. What was it?

Grizelda stopped to make it out.

A flute.

The unlikelihood of such a thing *here* made her want to laugh. What was this – a bazaar on the other side of the world, where a cobra would rise swaying out of its basket?

She had to see for herself.

She pushed her way to the source of the sound.

At the very middle of the shopping centre was a clock tower and a row of telephone boxes. The sound came from that direction but Grizelda saw nothing. Was the melody being played through a loudspeaker hidden in the clock? Surely not. It sounded live, not relayed.

She walked round the other side.

Then she saw him.

The awful wind had lessened and the sun was trying to shine, though the morning was still cold. Grizelda had needed her sheepskin coat. But the young flute-playing man seemed not to need any such protection. He wore a black sleeveless singlet printed with orange lightning bolts zigzagging across yellow flames, dirty jeans and old trainers. His upper arms were tattooed with more lightning bolts on the left, a face staring through flames on the right. His own face, though, was thin, sensitive. Long black hair flopped each side of it from a centre parting. His nose was long – distinguished, even, thought Grizelda – and his eyes were brown, liquid and expressive. Thin, elegant pianist's fingers touched the keys on the silver flute.

She knew the soulful melody he played. It had been popular when she was little – "Stranger on the Shore". Even now, she saw in her mind's eye the jazz musician Acker Bilk, with his little bowler hat and waistcoat, playing it on television. But he played the clarinet, didn't he?

There was a stereo cassette player behind the flautist. From it came an accompaniment of full orchestra – he was playing to a karaoke tape. Grizelda listened. There was something wrong. What was it?

The young man was playing the melody very well indeed, accurately, with phrasing and feeling. The taped orchestra was full, rich and warm. So what was wrong?

It took her a full minute to realize. The flute was a bar behind the orchestra throughout. He had started late and kept playing unwaveringly late throughout; when there was a pause and he had time to catch up he had ignored it and continued marching on late, with absolute discipline, as if he knew perfectly well what he was doing.

It all followed on in perfect harmony: the tune still fitted without making the ears protest. But why? He could obviously play well. And when "Stranger on the Shore" finished and "Greensleeves" began he started right and finished right.

It was odd, though. The effect had disturbed her.

Time to push on. The flute case open in front of him had few coins in. Shoppers weren't stopping. Grizelda felt a sudden impulse of pity for this man. Did he need her pity? Or anyone's? She shook her head angrily. How should she know? But she felt it nonetheless.

She dipped in her bag, took out three pound coins, bent over and dropped them in the case. Then she straightened and gave him an encouraging little smile. He continued playing without the smallest reaction.

Grizelda shrugged and walked on to the multi-storey. No one had vandalized the Calibra. She sat in it for a few moments studying her street map, then drove cautiously down the winding ramps and on to the Jolly Angler.

That thin face, those long fingers and the sound of the eccentric "Stranger on the Shore" would not leave her.

"No, miss. Have a bite to eat here. On the house."

The landlord of the Jolly Angler was plainly very pleased – indeed, flattered – to see her, so Grizelda was happy to accept a microwaved vegetarian lasagne for lunch.

"On TV, eh? That'll be something. You're in luck. Tonight's our big Show Night. We've got Darlene Nash.

She's a country singer. She'll be as big as Dolly Parton one day. In fact, she already is." He roared with laughter and jabbed Grizelda with his elbow. "Geddit? That's what I say when I introduce her."

Yes, Grizelda got it. She smiled instead of pursing her lips and walking out. She was at work now.

"Then there's the Rocket Ravers. A group from Wolverhampton way. They'll go a long way, mark my words. Very popular round here."

Grizelda took notes.

"And last, there's Tommy Trefoil."

"Who?"

"Tommy Trefoil. Young comic. Not been here before. An agent put me on to him. Said he was starting out, had a bit of talent, would I give him a run? Well, of course I would." He stood up straight behind the bar; his voice changed to what was meant as serious and to Grizelda sounded merely self-satisfied. "I see Show Night at the Jolly Angler as a nursery for young talent."

The landlord was big, plump-faced, with well-oiled black hair combed straight back over his head. One for the limelight himself, Grizelda thought: it was surely no accident the big Show Nights were at the Jolly Angler and not at the pub down the road. She decided to check her impression.

"You say you introduce the acts, Mr..."

"Welsted. Reg Welsted. Reg to you."

Grizelda did not invite him to use her first name.

He went on.

"I *must* be MC at my own show. I played the pubs and clubs once myself. Romantic baritone."

Yes, thought Grizelda. You've got the lungs for it.

"So I've always wanted to give the young ones a leg-up, like. I know what it is to fail."

Grizelda looked at him sharply. She'd not expected that from this large, complacent man. Suddenly, she warmed to him.

"Anyway, I'll be telling them there's someone in tonight from TV. That'll put spice in their acts."

"I'm not talent-spotting," cried Grizelda in alarm. "This is for a documentary. I'm only interviewing. We may send a crew in later but it won't be for an entertainment slot."

"Even so, it may get them known," said Reg Welsted.

Not for what they want, Grizelda thought.

She declined an invitation to stay at the pub for the afternoon during all-day opening hours, but allowed Reg to give her a look at the tiny stage, curtains, lighting and sound equipment, of which he was plainly very proud. Then she listened intently as he expanded on the idea that the club tradition of the North had never really spread here and if it wasn't for people like him local live entertainment would have died out completely.

Soon she was sitting outside in the Calibra, tapping numbers into her mobile phone. First she rang Quentin to let him know progress. Quentin seemed pleased. Then she rang Julian at their flat – but that was silly: she should have known he wouldn't be there. She heard her own voice on the answering machine, then Julian's with the second half of their instructions. After the tone, "Darling, if I haven't spoken to you already, this is to let you know I won't be home till tomorrow."

Now she did what she should have done at first. She rang his direct line at Lombury Hazards merchant bank in the City.

The voice which answered was sharp, incisive, packing purpose and efficiency way out of the ordinary into the single, barked surname.

"Claverhouse."

"Julian, it's me."

The voice changed at once – laid-back and languid.

"Hello, sweetie. How much longer is our enforced separation?"

"I'll be home when you get in tomorrow night. I'll have dinner ready."

His voice was suddenly petulant.

"Aren't you tired of the wild-goose chases your fat gay friend sends you on?"

"Julian, it's my job."

The slightest sniff on the other end of the line spoke volumes about what Julian thought of it. Grizelda pretended she didn't hear and went on.

"I really may be on to something. And you know I love you."

Petulance changed to satisfaction. "I know, darling. And I can wait."

She put the receiver back and consulted her road atlas. There was a stately home not twenty miles away: Puttrington Hall, home of the Duke of Whitchurch. She'd known his son at Oxford and there was a unique collection of porcelain there. Much better than an afternoon in the saloon bar of the Jolly Angler.

As Grizelda filed round beautiful roped-off exhibits, bumping into Teddy, who remembered her from university so she suddenly became a guest instead of a customer, the young man with the flute finally stopped playing.

Amazingly, he hadn't been moved on today. The coins in the instrument case were probably worth less than their weight suggested. Back to the squat now. There was an evening to get through – and another identity to take on.

The little arena was packed. The blue haze in the air made Grizelda certain passive smoking was taking years off her life. The Rocket Ravers had a driving beat, a dreadlocked black lead guitar and vocalist, an identical bass guitarist, a plainly demented white drummer and an indistinct figure poring over a keyboard. Grizelda knew she would interview none of them. This was just *not* their scene. They should be doing proper gigs with proper audiences.

Most of the audience listened respectfully to Darlene Nash singing "Stand by your Man". Grizelda thought she was rather good. Sadly, a tight ring of lager drinkers at the back kept up a chant of "Show us your boobs!" Nobody tried to stop them. Grizelda saw Darlene was completely unfazed by this: indeed, she showed with one look that she could eat them all for breakfast. Grizelda's angry revulsion on her behalf must be a London luxury.

"I promise that to round the evening off you'll all see more of Darlene!"

Grizelda was furious when she heard Reg Welsted's announcement as Darlene left the stage. He was playing up to the louts. Their raucous cheers showed her he wanted it that way.

Suddenly she was sorry for anyone appearing at the Jolly Angler.

"And now a young comic fast making a name for himself wherever he goes."

Grizelda felt sudden keen anticipation. Was she about to see the new Frank Skinner or Paul Merton?

"I give you – Tommy TREFOIL!"

After the great amplified shout of the surname, Grizelda expected some larger-than-life creation in a baggy, coloured clown suit to bound on to the stage. Instead, a small, shy man dressed in a dark suit with all the jacket buttons done up crept apologetically to the microphone.

The sudden drop in interest by the audience was palpable.

Tommy Trefoil gripped a straw hat in both hands and held it slackly in front of him. He spoke into the microphone.

"Hello, everybody."

Grizelda thought, *Why does he look familiar? He's not been on TV.*

"It's me."

If he wanted any response, he was unlucky.

" 'Ow are yer?"

Nobody was disposed to answer.

A young, thin face, black hair, brown eyes.

Of course! Grizelda was looking at this morning's flute-playing busker. At once she became his only attentive listener.

"I'll tell you about me brother."

Grizelda was fascinated. A comedian by evening, a flautist by day – what odd patchwork life was this?

"He's got a job in a warehouse. They store clothes there and send them all over the place."

The only sound was of people starting their own conversations.

"He works in the garage on the lorries they send them in."

No reaction.

"He's a diesel fitter."

Still nothing.

"He walks round the clothes, picking them up and saying, 'diesel fit me da, diesel fit me ma, diesel fit me gran...'"

No laughter, but a shout from a lager drinker: "Reg, get a stripper next time!"

That got the biggest laugh of the night.

Tommy Trefoil struggled on. It was sheer, toe-curling embarrassment for Grizelda; it was surely purgatory for him. Why did he expose himself to it?

She resolved that she would interview him. She could see a whole programme devoted to him alone.

Chapter Two

Next afternoon, Grizelda was back at Speakeasy Television in Quentin's office.

"Quentin, listen to me. Forget about pub entertainers: it was a duff idea anyway. There's this *one* person — we could do a whole programme on him. He's *fascinating*. He's so *bad*. But there's so much more to him than that. I think there's a really amazing story behind him. Maurice Cracknell would *love* it. It's right up his street. Half the best docs are about single odd-ball characters: the bag-lady, *Gail is Dead* – this could be as big as any."

"He's certainly the worst comic in the world from what you say," said Quentin thoughtfully. "What's that old quotation about marring a good tale in the telling of it?"

"Any tale in particular? It was all marred."

"You mentioned the diesel fitter gag. That's an old Liverpool story. All the scouse comics have told it – Askey, Ted Ray, Tarbuck... But this fellow ruined it. Our man's just a diesel fitter on Liverpool docks. The joke is, he's looting the cargoes. 'Diesel fit me ma,' et cetera – it's using your imagination a bit that makes the joke funny. It's like this fellow couldn't bear to use his. Or dare to."

"That's right," said Grizelda wonderingly. "He was exactly literal, as if he couldn't trust us to think for ourselves. So he sets his joke in a clothes warehouse where the subject is servicing lorries so everything's accounted for and it makes ordinary sense. And ruins the gag doing it."

"Exactly," said Quentin.

Grizelda remembered something.

"When I heard him on the flute yesterday morning, he was playing 'Stranger on the Shore'. He started a bar late and kept on being late all the way through, though he had plenty of time to correct himself. I don't think it was because he couldn't. He really can play."

"So what does it mean?"

Grizelda thought.

"It's as if he can't let himself go. He *wants* to express himself but he's hooked into reality, the here and now, what he can see and hear and feel. He doesn't want to be – but he's clinging on and if he lets go, if he casts himself off, he's finished."

"So he's lacking the most important quality of a good comic," said Quentin. "But as for what you said just then – that's presuming a lot, isn't it?"

"You weren't there when I talked to him," said Grizelda. "I'll play you my tape."

It had been one-thirty in the morning before Grizelda had deposited Tommy Trefoil at the end of a row of houses with boarded-up windows. Only now she knew that his name, whatever else it was, was not Tommy Trefoil. She had reams of notes and two complete tapes.

Most of what he said lay in an undigested lump in the back of her mind. A lot didn't seem to make sense. It would need sifting.

She had returned to her hotel twenty minutes later, been let in by the night porter, gone to her room and slept at once.

Next morning saw her off down the motorway back to the

flat she lived in with Julian, and a quiet hour making sense of the night before.

At twelve-thirty Julian rang on the off-chance that she was back. They decided to meet for lunch in their usual City wine bar. As she entered, she saw him waiting. His rather handsome face was slightly flushed and puffy: he had been there some time already. Not for the first time she realized that as the years went on his face would become more flushed and more puffy.

He rose and kissed her.

"Good to have you back, sweetie," he murmured.

He was not eating yet. Grizelda ordered a quiche salad for herself and to set an example in her campaign to slim him; with a slight grimace Julian ordered the same. But he had already worked two-thirds of the way through the bottle of red wine and poured her a glass before ordering another one.

He took her hand.

"Don't go away again," he said. "I don't like being on my own."

She withdrew her hand.

"Don't play little boy lost with me, Julian," she said. "You're tough as old boots. You love it without me."

"You don't have to go," said Julian stubbornly.

"For the hundredth time, Julian, it's my job."

"You don't need a job. I earn enough for ten."

True. Julian was rising high in the bank. Fewer now earned the City silly money than did a few years before, but Julian was certainly one of them.

"Julian, we're not married. I wouldn't want to be a decorative wife. I'm *certainly* not going to be a decorative girlfriend."

Grizelda often took stock of herself. She had loved her time at Oxford – for her first year she could never quite believe her good luck in getting there from the comprehensive school she had gone to after Larry's death and her removal from Anglo-World Citizens. What had her three Oxford years gained her? Good memories, a reasonable degree and a job with Quentin. But Julian was certainly her most substantial university trophy. She had met him at a party in his college at the start of her second year. He was something of a university celebrity. He moved in higher, richer circles. He knew, drank and sniffed cocaine with sons and daughters of Dukes and Cabinet Ministers. She had no idea why she'd been invited to this party. Sometimes she wondered whether she had been spotted and her invitation was a genteel form of procuring. But the expensive, gold-embossed invitation stood on the desk in her college bedsit like a challenge for so long that in the end, inevitably, she had gone. Fateful decision: fateful meeting. She had never found out who invited her. Julian strenuously denied any plot on his part. But they had met when the noise of the party was at its highest, the lights at their most kaleidoscopic, and had ended the night shell-shocked with each other. She never knew such intensity of experience was possible. All her previous fumbling encounters dissolved into risibility. She knew the future course of her life was now defined.

Well, Julian made her second year a whirl socially – but it was nearly a disaster for her work. During her final year, when he had already gone down with a surprisingly good degree and was busy getting his feet under the table in Lombury Hazards Bank, most weekends saw her with him in London, knowing full well that come the end of her Oxford career she would be moving into his flat in St John's

Wood. In the end, after a late spurt of work, she did better in her final exams than she had feared. Julian's way, though, was always clear. Public school a cut above the rest, family connections everywhere – he had moved with seamless ease into the City, big money early, one day perhaps into politics, a life of real power. It fascinated Grizelda. Her real ambition in that final year was to leave and move in with him. The job with Quentin and Speakeasy was a bonus: at the time she would happily have joined Julian as the decorative girlfriend she now so despised.

But Quentin gave her the job and she was now in the media and could one day – in a different way – be as powerful as Julian. This realization came as a jolt. Before she met Julian she had had her own ambitions. Now they returned. Besides, she had to be true to herself. However lovely it was being there, however stimulating, Oxford had a veil of escapist glamour. The real world wasn't like that, nor was Julian's life, however privileged. She had to be sure she could look after herself. She was convinced she loved Julian, wanted to be with him, but the relationship was going to need a lot more work than she had imagined. Despite having lived together for over a year, they weren't finally committed to each other. Julian could still get bored and kick her out. It was, after all, his flat. His refusal to let her help with any of the running costs was, she was sure, not pure generosity. Should she worry about this?

At the same time it was dawning on her, clearer by the day, that she could walk out herself.

Julian had returned to the subject which irked him most.

"Running round the country at the behest of that poofter" – Julian couldn't stand Quentin – "ending up in the back of beyond mixing with oiks. It *demeans* you, Griz."

"You haven't a clue, have you, darling?" Grizelda murmured.

Julian leaned right up close to her.

"Give it up," he whispered. "For my sake."

Grizelda pointedly edged a couple of centimetres away.

"Most men in your position would be pleased for me," she said.

Julian swigged the remaining wine in his glass, poured himself another, drank it in two quick swallows, pushed his empty plate away and said, "Got to go. See you this evening."

He rose, strode through the throng and outside. Grizelda was left to pick at the remains of her salad and dispose of three-quarters of a bottle of paid-for red wine on her own.

She left fifteen minutes later. With a care for economy Julian would never understand she called for a cork and slipped the bottle into her bag. Once outside she hailed a taxi and fifteen minutes later she was with Quentin, reporting on her encounter with Tommy Trefoil.

Grizelda played the tape. Quentin listened carefully. When it was finished, he was silent for a moment.

"Well," he said at last, "he's either very deep, in which case you may have got a point, or he's a complete airhead and I don't want to know."

"Which is it?" said Grizelda.

"What do I pay you for?" said Quentin. "It's your job to find out."

"Does that mean I have to—?"

"Yes, back to Necropolis-on-the-Bog, I fear. And another meeting with the obviously appalling Welsted."

"So you think I'm right?"

"I'm not saying that. But it's worth spending time proving you're wrong."

Grizelda's heart leapt. Whatever else he might be, Tommy Trefoil was no airhead. This could be a great programme. And underneath the famous names presenting it and Quentin's undoubted big billing as director would be *hers*: she'd make sure she got the credit she was due. Her career would really be on the move.

She was home before Julian. She expected him by seven o'clock and prepared a meal accordingly. Carrying on her attempts to curb his burgeoning puffiness, she selected a low-fat pâté from a health-food shop, prepared the ingredients for tagliatelle with salmon and broccoli which she could cook quickly as soon as he came in and made a fruit salad with fresh melon, pineapple and banana. She made sure Perrier water was chilling in the refrigerator and – knowing Julian would never eat a meal without alcohol – put a bottle of white Chardonnay with it. Slim him, yes; crucify him, no!

He arrived on time, genial and expansive. He had had a good afternoon, shared convivial time with colleagues afterwards and Grizelda suddenly felt deep satisfaction in seeing him. He was here in his own surroundings and she was with him. But this was *her* place as well: she was meant for it and was not going to lose it. For a moment the thought of going away again was positively repulsive. She lit the candles on the table, put on a favourite CD and relaxed in the atmosphere she had set up.

Julian enjoyed his meal. Afterwards they sat by the fire, finishing the wine and watching television. Julian talked about his arcane but evidently triumphant doings of the day; Grizelda reflected how strange it was that while money on a world scale was his great obsession he hardly seemed to acknowledge its existence in relation to their own affairs.

Then she tried to interest him in her own days away. It was hard going. She told him about the town, the Jolly Angler, Reg Welsted, Tommy Trefoil. Julian showed a quite blatant lack of concern.

"Julian," she said after a while, "this is pretty unfair. I try my best to keep an intelligent interest in all your doings, though God knows it's hard sometimes. I'm pleased for you when things go well; I sympathize when they don't. Why can't you do the same for me?"

"You know why," he said, roughness in his voice. "You shouldn't be doing this. It's not what you are *for*."

Grizelda was angry.

"Don't think I'm going to get into that decorative girl-friend argument again. That's *finished*."

"I don't mean that. Of course you should work if you want to. What century do you think I live in? But do something decent. PR, perhaps. Or in the City with me. That's no male preserve any more. Or what about a job in Conservative Central Office?" Grizelda winced. Julian continued, not noticing. "That could do me a lot of good one day. They won't always be out in the wilderness, you know. They'll come back and they'll take me with them."

"If you cared to think about it," Grizelda replied icily, "me having a job in television could help you rather better."

"Not the same," Julian said stubbornly. Grizelda had only recently become aware of this mulish streak in him.

"Why not?"

"How does it help me to have you swanning off to terrible

places which should be *nuked* off the map today?''

Julian's voice was rising. She had detested the town while she was there: now she sprang to its defence.

"Julian, however unpleasant it may be, *people* live there. *Real* people who matter.''

Oh, God! Was she going to start talking like the politician Julian wanted one day to be?

"People? What people? A scum-of-the-earth barman, a busker and a so-called comedian with the evident intelligence of a dung-beetle? Grizelda, what are you *doing*?''

"Julian, these people *count*!'' She was screaming at him. "They may not be the sort you'd invite round here but they have concerns, worries, feelings the same as anyone else's. And these feelings matter. There's millions of viewers who'll be fascinated one day by Tommy Trefoil. He's got a story to tell and there's some who'll say 'How fascinating' and others who'll say 'How terrible' and others who'll say 'There but for the grace of God go I'.''

Julian's lips pursed so much they nearly disappeared.

"They're not like us,'' he said. "They have nothing to offer. They are different in kind; another species. They live on the other side – thank God! – of a great divide. They are of no account. They mean nothing, make nothing, they *are* nothing. They're a drag on our nation. They'll be fatal for it in the end. Better for all – including themselves – if they were not there. They are...'' he struggled for a word to sum up their entire inadequacy and came out with something so anti-climactic as to make Grizelda almost laugh "...they are *OIKS*!''

It was the second time he had used that word today. His public school must have taught him there could be no greater insult.

"Be careful, Julian," Grizelda said levelly. "You and I are not of the same background. I was once an oik myself."

"But not now, my love." Julian's voice had found a note almost of eagerness. "Don't you see? You've crossed the divide. You've become one of us."

"That's not true," murmured Grizelda. Then she remembered the childhood days before Daddy's death. A thought which had often come to her but which she had never expressed to Julian needed saying. "When my father was alive and I was at the Anglo-World School, everybody said I was clever. But after we lost everything, nobody said it any more. I had to find it out again for myself. What if I hadn't? Where would I be now?"

Julian did not reply. Instead he fixed a gaze on her which was almost frightening in its intensity. Unable to stop herself, she quailed slightly. She could have no idea of the sights suddenly peopling his mind, the ghosts from long ago, the doubts they brought, the unspeakable truth they spoke but which he could never accept.

She had to break this awful silence. Quick – something to divert his mind completely.

"I dropped into Puttrington Hall yesterday. Guess who I met there?"

Julian found his voice. The ghosts had disappeared. He would make sure they never came back. He was himself and his life was not founded on sand.

"Not Teddy? Wonderful! How is the drunken old sod? What's he doing?"

It was on the tip of Grizelda's tongue to say, "Not contributing very much." Instead, she contented herself with, "He'll have his work cut out looking after the house and the estate and coping with the visitors."

Julian laughed. "Not Teddy. He'll have a team to do all the heavy work. Good at delegating, our Teddy."

Grizelda did not point out the contradiction.

They sat quietly, relieved of anger, lovingly agreeing to differ – until Julian said, "I've got some work to do before we turn in tonight. I'll go in the study."

"And I want to prepare for tomorrow," said Grizelda.

Julian rose and left. Grizelda took the tape with Tommy Trefoil's interview out of her bag, slipped it into the stereo and started listening in a further attempt to make sense of it.

Within a few seconds she was reliving that strange time immediately after Show Night at the Jolly Angler.

Chapter Three

After Tommy Trefoil's disastrous act, the Rocket Ravers had come back. They were not so energetic as before. Grizelda wondered if Reg had waved some money – but not quite enough – at them to play a few more numbers to make up for Tommy Trefoil not appearing for an encore. But as she was the only one in the audience not making frequent journeys to the loo or bars, she was probably the only one who noticed.

Then Darlene Nash returned. She was really good, Grizelda thought. When she was singing her final encore, "Tie a Yellow Ribbon Round the Old Oak Tree", she was really getting through to her audience. Even the lager louts were rapt and, despite herself, Grizelda felt tears sting the back of her eyes. Angrily she wiped them away, blamed the smoky atmosphere and remembered something Noel Coward once said about "the potent effect of cheap music".

Grizelda had waited until the very end to talk to the performers. She knew they had to stay to get paid cash in hand, though she had an uneasy suspicion that Tommy Trefoil might have gone without waiting to be thrown out by an angry Reg. In spite of what he had said about "knowing failure", Grizelda wouldn't put it past him to give the hapless jokesmith a good rollicking and no money.

She entered the cramped backstage area in time to see Reg doling out notes, thanking the performers and saying quite affably to Tommy, "You were crap, lad. I'm taking twenty-five quid off you and giving it to the Ravers. They had to do extra because of you."

Tommy had already changed. He wore the black singlet Grizelda had seen that morning as well as an old black leather jacket, loose-fitting and unzipped. Beside him was a dirty backpack, no doubt containing his props and suit and hat. Head down, he took the small roll of notes without a word; then he looked up, saw Grizelda, and the faintest flicker of recognition seemed to cross his face.

"Like I said, miss," said Reg. "You can talk to them in the public bar. I live over the pub and never go to bed before three. I'll be around all the time."

"I only want to see Tommy," said Grizelda.

The disbelief on Reg's face was almost comical. The others took the news with equanimity.

" 'S all right," said the Ravers' vocalist and lead guitarist in a broad West Midland accent. "We'll pack the van, then."

Darlene laughed.

"I knew it," she said. "All your swans are geese, Reg."

Her voice bore little trace of any accent deeper south than Milton Keynes.

Tommy Trefoil said nothing. He followed Grizelda meekly into the empty public bar. They sat between pool tables, fruit machines and dartboards. Reg looked in and said, "You can't have a drink because it's gone closing time."

"We don't want one," said Grizelda. "And I'll drive Tommy home if he wants a lift. Don't worry about him."

"I won't," said Reg and disappeared.

Grizelda was glad her recorder worked off batteries; Reg might have begrudged her the electric current.

She looked closely at Tommy Trefoil. The black hair hung lankly on each side of his face, still marked with make-up only partly washed off. But his eyes, brown, liquid, were even more impressive close to than when she had seen him busking. They had a deepness, a ... she searched for the word to describe their quality ... *significance.* Suddenly, she realized that his inept performance on the stage had at least shown one talent. He had looked small, shrinking, shy, of no account. But, both with the flute and here now in front of her, he was none of those things. Was this acting of a high order after all?

He stood in front of her.

"Sit down, please."

Without a word he did so.

"Please call me Grizelda," she said. "I just want to ask you a few questions."

No reaction. Just those intense brown eyes.

"Of course, you don't have to answer if you don't want to."

A slight blink. *This will be a complete waste of time,* Grizelda thought.

"What shall I call you? Tommy? Mr Trefoil?

At last he spoke.

"That's not my real name," he said.

"Oh." *Not surprising,* she thought. "What is your real name?"

"It might be Darren. It might be Kevin. What do people like you think people like me are usually called?"

The riddling answer and its question reduced Grizelda to silence. While she pondered on an answer, she wondered about his accent. It was regional of some sort. She thought she could hear scraps of everywhere in it – north, south, east, west. As if he had spent his life listening to them all and absorbing bits of each.

But for the moment, he was not helping. She came out with what seemed the only possible question.

"Is there any reason why you call yourself Tommy Trefoil? Apart from the alliteration, it seems an odd choice."

Silence again. Then he spoke. "There's no reason for you not to know. It's because of the three endeavours."

"The three endeavours?"

"The three tasks I took upon myself when the sun rose after I was cut adrift."

Is he mad? Or does he speak in metaphors that will explain themselves in time? Grizelda said aloud, "What tasks were they?"

"To master the arts of music, magic, comedy."

Now we're getting somewhere.

"So music is the flute," said Grizelda. "Comedy is all this – the routines, the suit, telling jokes. What about the magic?"

Tommy Trefoil produced a pack of cards from the back pocket of his jeans. He opened it, tipped the cards out, fanned them and laid them face up in front of her.

"An ordinary pack," he said.

"As far as I can see."

He closed the fan, picked up the cards and shuffled them expertly. Then he fanned the whole deck out again and held it face down towards her.

"Take one," he said.

She did.

"Look at it, memorize it, don't tell me, give it back."

It was the seven of diamonds. He slipped it face down back into the deck, shuffled the cards and put them back into the pack, which he slipped back into his pocket. He spoke as Grizelda looked at him, baffled.

"Trefoil is a three-pointed leaf. I have three endeavours. One leaf point stands for each endeavour. I call myself Trefoil."

There was little she could say to that except "How clever!" So she said nothing. Patronizing this man would, she knew, get her nowhere.

He spoke again.

"I thought I asked you to give me back the card you took."

"I did," said Grizelda.

"Then what is this?"

He leant forward and lifted the tape recorder. Underneath lay a card face down.

"Pick it up, look at it, say nothing."

She did all those things.

"It is the seven of diamonds," he said.

"Yes," she said weakly and gave the card back. Without looking at it, he replaced it in the pack.

Sitting in the spacious flat in an exclusive part of London, Grizelda realized why that little episode had bothered her. She listened to the tape again, heard the finality in his voice – "It is the seven of diamonds" – saw again how he had lifted the recorder and slipped the card back as if it were of no account after all.

But it was of *great* account. Most conjurors would have pounded their heads, asked, "*Is* it the seven of diamonds?" as if struggling to solve a near-impossible equation, and waited for the gasp of baffled wonder at the reply, "Yes, it is."

But this man turned wonder into inevitability, cut out all imagination, just as with "Stranger on the Shore", just as with the diesel fitter joke. Quentin was right: he dealt in imagination but could not use it.

Grizelda played the tape again.

"It is the seven of diamonds."

Grizelda paused the tape and sat silent. There was no sound from the study. Julian was either absorbed in mastering the details of some extraordinary financial occurrence or had gone to bed without her hearing.

She set the tape in motion again and was at once back in the Jolly Angler.

"That was wonderful," she said weakly. Then, stronger, "Why didn't you do that for the people tonight?"

"I do what I want to do when I want to do it," he said. "That is a privilege hard-earned and it is going to be kept."

Everything he says, she reflected, comes out as if carefully rehearsed.

"I agree there," she said. "We have to work for our rights. They don't just come to us."

Unless we're called Julian Claverhouse, she thought grimly.

"To some easier than others," he replied.

An opening at last.

"Did they come hard to you?" she said.

Another silence. He looked at her as if turning words over in his mind. Finally he spoke.

"First there was misery. We were oppressed, scorned, rejected. We beat our minds and our tiny fists against walls of ignorance and fear. Then came a great release, a great light, a great warmth. But it was a false dawn. We entered a darkness worse than before: forces of darkness pushed us there, serried ranks of darkness kept us there until we returned to a new light, a hurtful light because our eyes were damaged."

For a moment, Grizelda was frightened. She was alone with an evident lunatic. This was a mind full of delusions, hallucinations. Like some mad prophet.

"Is this any help to you?" A complete change of tone.

"Oh, yes," she said.

He's not mad at all. He's just putting on an act. He's having me on. She was suddenly angry with him.

"You think I'm off my trolley, don't you?" he said.

The modern idiom so soon after something like the Book of Revelations made Grizelda quite sure she was being laughed at.

"This is all an act, isn't it?" she said.

"An act? Why should it be an act?"

"I can't make sense of what you're saying."

"Why should you? Who can? Can I? Why should I?"

Grizelda said nothing. Disturbing thoughts flew round her mind. *I've no right here: this recorder shouldn't be on.*

"I did not ask for my life to be as it is," he continued. "I came out of darkness into light; what could come next? And what of the light before the darkness? Does that alter the question? What if the blinding light *really* blinds? Who would it blind? Me? You? Why should you know? Why should I? How *can* we know?"

Riddles again. But Grizelda latched on to these last words even as he spoke them. They could be a rejection of her and all she stood for, but they might also be a plea for help.

She listened to the tape yet again. Those two long speeches:

did they both say the same thing? That once he was free, then he was not and now he was free again? Was he, in different ways each time, trying to tell her his story – but when it came to the crunch he was unwilling to commit himself to it? Or – and here Grizelda hugged herself with all the triumph of the television researcher who is given the challenge to set up the best programme of all – *he did not know it himself*?

There was more on the tape. She set it going again.

Grizelda had asked a question.

"Why don't you know? You haven't lost your memory, have you?"

He looked at her with an expression near contempt.

"What use is memory?" he said.

"I don't understand—" Grizelda began. He interrupted.

"I want to go home. I've said enough."

Grizelda did not switch the tape off.

"Can we meet again?"

"You know where you found me."

That must constitute consent.

"Look," said Grizelda. "Here's my card. You can get me there in working hours. I'll put my home telephone number on the back. And my mobile phone number. Oh, and if you can't find me at either place, here's my mother's number. She doesn't live too far from here and I sometimes go there at weekends."

He put the card in the back pocket of his jeans.

"But I might want to contact you. Could you write down an address for me?"

She tore a page from her pocket book and handed it to him, together with a pen. He pushed them back to her.

"You know where you found me," he repeated.

There was no point in asking again.

She had switched the tape off and called out to Reg that they were going. He clumped down the stairs and let them out.

"Thank you very much for your help," she said. "You'll get a credit if we do make a programme."

He grunted ungraciously.

Tommy Trefoil sat in the Calibra gingerly as if it were an electric chair. He gave directions in a gruff voice. Grizelda memorized the name of the street where he asked her to stop and watched him walk along it. She counted the houses carefully, to be sure she knew which one he let himself into. The sixth along. She would return.

She took the tape out and slipped it into her bag.

She listened. The flat was silent.

She went to the bathroom, then the bedroom. Julian lay there, not asleep.

"So both our long days are finished," he murmured.

No, she could never willingly leave this place.

She slipped into the bed beside him.

Chapter Four

Julian was in a happy mood over breakfast. Last night's tetchiness seemed gone. Grizelda almost forgot that last night she had thought he was a fascist.

That evening they were going to dinner with friends. They were Julian's, but Grizelda liked them and was looking forward to the evening. No more arguments of social principle would get in the way.

Julian left, going east in his BMW. Grizelda headed north on the tube. She had a lot to talk to Quentin about.

"Here's how I see it now," she said. "Something happened when he was young. He might even have been sent away because of it. When he came out he started 'the three endeavours' – that's a good phrase he used. It could be a title."

"I don't see what you're getting at," said Quentin.

"I've been thinking about this most of the night," she replied. "He's doing three things – flute, comedian, conjuror. He doesn't seem to know quite who he is – perhaps he doesn't *want* to know. We know there's this curious thing in his jokes and his flute-playing where he won't let his imagination go, he holds back, can't seem to trust himself. Well, it was the same when he did the trick with the cards. It was *really* clever and well done. But he wouldn't let me be amazed. No suspense, no chance of a gasp of surprise. Just "It is the seven of diamonds" – end of trick. Can you see

Paul Daniels playing down the end of a trick like that?"

"Go on," said Quentin.

"And then all this talking in riddles, in metaphors. I mean, poets use metaphors to make meaning clear. He uses them to hide it."

"The two don't go together. You can't be afraid of imagination and then say everything in metaphors. Metaphors *are* imagination."

"They go together if he's deliberately keeping the truth away."

"Who from? You or himself?"

"Both, probably."

"So what have we got? A man who can't face up to what's happened to him. Look, Griz, if we made a documentary about all of those we'd fill the available air time till Doomsday."

"But can't you see, Quentin? He's more than that. You said better about him yesterday. Airhead or incredibly deep, that's what you thought. Well, I'm on the way to sorting this out. I lay awake half the night thinking about it. He's no airhead. He's very, very deep."

"You're sure?"

"Positive."

"OK." Quentin laughed. "I agree. I was only being devil's advocate. You go back and get everything you can from him."

"Not now," she cried in alarm. "We're going out tonight."

"Tomorrow. I've got other work for you today."

"Just as well. Julian would go apoplectic."

Julian was not pleased that she was out next day. At first he

84

was sulky then, all through dinner, he made general but snide remarks about crèches and maternity leave ruining British industry along with the woman-dominated Labour government and the ludicrous Social Chapter, the family as the backbone of all decent societies, women's place being pre-ordained in some great scheme of things and the forces of biology having the last word in all these arguments. Grizelda found herself countering with such spirit that their hosts cast covert looks at each other. When they got home, Julian rounded on her.

"Well, thank *you*. Sophie and Piers won't be inviting *us* again."

"Don't be childish, Julian. It must have been quite a shock for them to find they'd got a Victorian workhouse master at their table."

"As well as a frenzied, politically correct harridan."

That night, they faced away from each other, teetering on opposite edges of the bed.

Grizelda waited until the rush-hour traffic subsided before she left Speakeasy. By ten-thirty she was on the motorway north; by one o'clock she was locking the Calibra in the same multi-storey car park.

The weather was better and the sun shone benevolently on Grizelda as she made her way through smaller crowds than last time to the clock tower and telephone boxes. No flute called her there this time. Where he had played before, now a guitarist sat, playing and singing soulfully. Grizelda walked hopefully all round the clock tower. There was nobody on the other side. She returned to the guitarist and waited until his song was over. Then she spoke.

"There was a man here playing the flute the other day.

Do you know where he is now?"

The guitarist tuned his instrument without looking at her.

"Buggered off, if he's got any sense," he said.

"Do you know where?"

"Why should I?"

Grizelda dropped a pound in his upturned hat and left.

She looked round the shopping centre for more buskers' pitches. None. Frustrated, she returned to the car park and, once in the Calibra, looked carefully at her street guide for the road where she had dropped Tommy Trefoil after the interview.

The street was deserted. She drove slowly up it until she reached the sixth house, which Tommy Trefoil had entered that night. She stopped the car and got out.

The terrace house, partly boarded up, was plainly empty. She walked through an alley to the back. None of the houses appeared lived in. She tried the gate at the back of Tommy Trefoil's: it opened. Cautiously she walked through the back yard and tried the door. It opened too. She went inside.

There was a strong smell of damp, but the house must have been inhabited recently. Packing cases stood on the floor, old cushions on them, together with a couple of sagging armchairs that looked as though they had been found on a tip. She saw a couple of split mattresses.

But there were no cups, plates or cutlery in the sink where a tap dripped. The house was no longer lived in and Grizelda had an indefinable feeling that it would never see occupation again. But the desertion seemed very recent.

Baffled, Grizelda returned to the car. She picked up the phone, rang Directory Enquiries, then the Borough Council. She asked to speak to anybody who knew about licences for street entertainers. She was shunted from person to person until someone talked sense to her.

"Strictly speaking, busking isn't allowed in the shopping centre, though unless we get a complaint we tend to turn a blind eye. But we keep no record of buskers here."

"Has there been a complaint in the last few days?"

"Not to my knowledge. Try the police. Perhaps they've had a blitz and moved a few on. They do sometimes."

So she tried the police. No, no buskers had been moved on during the past week. Her informant's tone of voice suggested they had better things to do.

Then she rang the housing department. The squat had been cleared by bailiffs and police two days before.

Grizelda replaced the phone and sat back feeling annoyed. She would have to go back to the Jolly Angler and speak to the newly hostile Reg Welsted.

The pub was crowded, though any reasonable lunch hour should have been over. Obviously a lot of people took advantage of all-day opening hours. Grizelda sat at the bar and ordered a St Clements. A barmaid with more than a passing resemblance to Darlene Nash served her. Reg was at the far end of the bar serving and laughing with a group of middle-aged men. He must have heard Grizelda's voice over the hubbub: he cast a quick glance at her, then looked away.

But ten minutes later things quietened down. Reg's companions left. Grizelda stayed where she was; she wouldn't beg Reg Welsted to speak to her.

In the end he came over himself, unwillingly and mainly, she thought, out of curiosity.

"Well?" he said, ungraciously. "What do you want this time?"

"I wondered if you could tell me if Tommy Trefoil's appearing here again."

"Him?" It sounded more like a bark than a pronoun. "I wouldn't let him in here again. Useless berk!"

"Only I'm trying to find him."

"Given you the slip, has he? Tough. It's your own fault. I put good artistes in front of you and you chose the dud."

Grizelda's voice remained level with a huge effort.

"Please, I do need to know where he's gone."

"Slung his hook altogether, has he? I'm not surprised. He wouldn't dare show his face after that shambles."

Grizelda looked squarely at him.

"Mr Welsted, please help me. I'm sorry if you thought I snubbed you after all you did. I certainly never meant to. Believe me, I really appreciated it. But I do need to speak to Tommy Trefoil."

Reg looked mollified.

"Look, miss, I really can't help you."

"But you must have his details. What's his real name?"

"Tommy Trefoil's all I know him as."

"Didn't he have an Equity Card?"

Reg gave a hoot of sarcastic laughter at the thought.

"Haven't you got files on your performers?"

"Word of mouth, cash in hand. That's how I work," said Reg.

And a fortune gained in saved VAT, thought Grizelda. Still, she wouldn't shop him. Then she remembered something.

"You said an agent recommended him. Can you put me on to the agent?"

"I could, but it would do you no good."

"Why not?"

Reg leant over the bar and pushed his face close, his lips twisted with anger.

"First thing next morning I rang the agent to ask what he thought he was doing sending shit like that. He'd never heard of him. Trefoil wasn't on their books at all."

"So what are you saying?"

"I'm saying that the little sod rang me up himself. He took me for a ride and if I see him again I'll half-kill him."

"Terrible!" said Grizelda, inwardly creasing herself with laughter. The more she found out about Tommy Trefoil, the more interesting he became.

"So I can't help you. Sorry."

There's no point in laughing at Reg, thought Grizelda. I'm just as big a fool.

She thanked him and left the Jolly Angler. She sat for a moment in the Calibra, made up her mind what to do next, headed out to the motorway and, deflated and depressed, was talking to Quentin two hours later.

Quentin was sympathetic. Grizelda was pleasantly surprised that he understood and did not immediately halt the whole idea.

"We'll put the project on the back-burner," he said. "Our friend will show again. There's no point in getting our knickers in a twist. There's things I want you to do now and meanwhile we'll get back to the first idea: the pub entertainers."

Oh, not again! Anything to escape that turkey of a scheme.

"Give me a rest from it for a while, Quentin, please. I couldn't face Reg Welsted or his like just yet."

"No sooner said, love..."

* * *

None of this helped Grizelda cope with the sense of failure that grew for the rest of the day and was nearly suffocating her by the time Julian came home.

After last night's upset she hesitated to share this with him. His triumph would be odious. But there was no one else to talk to. They had finished dinner and he seemed more like the Julian she knew and could say anything to with complete trust.

She might have known his reaction, however.

"See? What did I tell you? Slippery, untrustworthy, undependable, like all his sort."

"That's not fair, Julian."

"Fair? I'm stating the simple truth."

He had made her angry.

"Look, Julian, Tommy Trefoil might not have had your advantages but he's a person of resource, ability, constant surprise, with a brain on him and a history which I mean to find out whether you like it or not."

"Some village Hampden?" jeered Julian. "Some mute inglorious Milton? Don't give me that crap!"

"And why not?" demanded Grizelda. "There are fifty million people in this country. I don't believe the only ones who have a right to exist are you and me and our friends."

"Ah, but that's where you're wrong," Julian said. "Fifty million? More than half are expendable."

Grizelda couldn't believe what she was hearing. Pale with anger, she cried, "What? Into the gas chamber with them?"

Julian's voice rose with hers. His face took on a high colour; a vein in his neck throbbed.

"I didn't say that. But now you mention it – what do they do? What do they give? Throw anything worthwhile to them and they break it, ruin it, spit on it, throw it back in your face. *They're worthless!"*

His face was contorted. Alarmed, Grizelda thought he was near a heart attack. This was *her man* she was watching: he needed help. But could *she* give it? She had a sudden, dreadful feeling that she was out of her depth. There was more to this outburst than pique at her absence or impatience with her job. What was it? An awful word crept into her mind. There was something here that was *pathological.* But who could help him except her? With an intense effort she composed herself and spoke levelly but firmly.

"Julian, you're not rational. I've heard people argue like you, but I've never heard anybody go over the top like you. They're prepared to listen to other points of view."

"There *is* no other point of view."

Grizelda stared at him. One of the things that had attracted her to him was his light, laid-back sense of humour, his way of taking nothing really seriously – except her. Fair enough, he was right-wing in his views and she was prepared to have a go at him about his opinions any time. And he was happy to take her on. Why shouldn't he believe in one of the major streams of thought which runs through this and all other democracies? But where had his lightness of touch, his balance, gone? Was it her? Was it his job and he wouldn't tell her? Did he know himself? Especially these last few days – he had changed awesomely and terribly. Did he realize? She had to ask him directly.

"Julian, why are you like this? We've never argued so savagely before; you've never screamed at me like tonight. It all seems to have started over one person you've never even met. I don't understand."

"There's nothing *to* understand. I'm right. That's all there is to it."

"No, Julian," Grizelda said musingly. "There's more. Something about this has really got to you, wormed its way under your skin."

"Rubbish!"

"Is it something personal?"

"I'm merely stating facts."

"No, you're not, Julian. There's more. I've touched you on a raw nerve and I don't know how."

Julian jumped up and seized her by both shoulders. The sudden movement shocked her into gasping silence.

"I've touched *you* on a raw nerve because you're meddling with *scum*!" he shouted right into her face. "And I won't have it!"

He pushed her back, marched into the bedroom and slammed the door behind him.

She could not, *would* not follow him. She sat staring into space. Did this unaccountable anger mark a terminal stage in their relationship? Ought she to be tracing Julian's history just as much as Tommy Trefoil's? It was plain she needed to know a lot more about this man in her life. Part of her was thinking that, looked at dispassionately, Julian's story would be just as interesting as Tommy's. "The brutalization of the upper-middle classes." It could be a whole series.

She came back to earth. Her rational mind pointed out the irony that she was treating the man she was supposed to love, and was almost committed to, as a basket case.

But how could she commit herself to someone whose unreasoning reaction to everything she was doing and saying attested to – what? Fear? Guilt?

Guilt? Julian feeling *guilty*? He didn't know the meaning of the word.

There was a lot to think about: too much all at once.

Unnoticed, her job and her private life had jarred disastrously together like the *Titanic* and its iceberg and provided her with the biggest crisis of her life – even bigger than...

She drew her knees up to her chin in the chair, shivered slightly and tried to compose herself for a lonely night.

Chapter Five

For nearly an hour, Grizelda sat without moving, almost as if she dare not for fear of breaking some fragile, precious arrangement carefully put together. There was not a thought in her head, just wordless, bottomless misery.

At last she dozed, half-thinking, recalling vividly and accurately. What she thought about brought shock and tears just as it had on the day itself eleven years before.

She had been studying German in a large, airy room with lovely windows looking out over lawns. The language lab was here, a place of wonder to Grizelda. She and her best friends, Harvinder (whose father worked at the Indian Embassy) and Chantal (whose father ran the British arm of a big French car firm) had been recording little speeches to each other in German and laughing. Fräulein Herrmann had stood over them and they could see she was pleased.

Every school day passed like this, with happy friends and smiling teachers.

Then the door had opened and Mrs Lubbock, the secretary, had come in. Fräulein Herrmann and she whispered together and looked at Grizelda. Then Fräulein Herrman said, in English, "Grizelda, will you go with Mrs Lubbock, please? Dr Raybould wants to see you."

Grizelda was halfway through a German greeting to Harvinder and Chantal. "I'll finish it when I come back," she said. Then she trotted off with Mrs Lubbock to the headmaster's large study, which she had never been in before. There were bookshelves, armchairs and a huge desk, with Dr Raybould standing gravely behind it.

She never went back to finish her greeting.

Her father was dead and they had no money any more. Mummy had to go to America with a lot of other people whose relations had been killed on the plane. Grizelda had never known her father was going to America. He usually told them all and brought back presents. Her room was full of them.

Granny looked after the children until Mummy came back, pale and crying. There was a big funeral with lots of people, and a man in a black suit had come to the front and said nice things about Daddy which made Mummy – and Grizelda – cry a lot more. Then the coffin went through the curtains with a little rumbling noise and her father was gone for ever.

They had moved to Granny's home, in a town fifty miles north of London, where her mother had grown up. Grandad was dead, like Daddy. Grizelda began to think that all males in her life were destined to disappear before she was properly grown up. Apart from a few things which none of them would let go, all the furniture in London was sold. So was the house. Grizelda asked why that would not give them a lot of money to make things all right again. Mummy said they would not be getting very much of it. They were poor now.

Mummy sighed and said, "Back where I started."

Mummy's paintings were sold as well – except for a few she really wanted to keep. When they had settled in

Granny's house, Grizelda waited for her mother to set up her easel and start painting again.

She would have to wait a long time. Her mother never did.

Her mother was pale now, thinner, and never laughed like she used to. She got a part-time job but did not want to hand over the responsibility for four children to someone getting old so the hours were short and the money hardly worth earning. Once, Grizelda heard her crying and saying to Granny, "It was all wrong, Mum. We got too much too quickly. We were never meant to live like we did. It's a judgement on us."

Granny replied, "I've never heard such rubbish! You pull yourself together, my girl. You start painting again. It will be the making of you. And it's what your father and I made sacrifices to see you do."

But Grizelda's mother never did.

It was strange that, while her parents had been so artistic, Grizelda showed little inclination for painting, sculpture, pottery or anything to do with her hands. Her leaning, it seemed, was towards languages. Barnaby seemed to carry on his parents' tradition. At the Anglo-World Citizens School, Fräulein Hermann and the other language teachers had thought the world of Grizelda. Once, after a parents' evening, Daddy had said, "I'm more pleased about your foreign languages than anything else. After all, that's why we sent you to an international school. You live in a big world, not a tiny island."

Daddy's praise had made a big impression on her. She remembered it when she started at Heathwell Comprehensive School.

* * *

Grizelda had looked forward to the first day at her new school. She wanted new friends, she wanted to write on new, fresh-smelling paper, see her words come up on the screen of one of the computers which would no doubt be ranged round every room. She wanted to laugh as she and the new Harvinder and Chantal made their delighted way through new ideas and strange language constructions.

Alas! Her first day showed her things might not be like that. The buildings of Heathwell School were echoing, full of dangerous, rushing staircases. The others in her new class looked at her with stony hostility. When she spoke, they laughed. Her voice sounded different from theirs. All the voices round her at Anglo-World had been different as well, but in different ways. She distinguished between English accents and those of other nationalities. Here, everyone's voice was English. But to her they were weird, alien. Yet they thought *hers* was the odd one.

"You talk like a toff," said Karen next to her.

Scott, on the other side of the room, heard. "She wants it knocking out of her," he shouted.

Grizelda looked across and saw resentment in the blue eyes.

And he doesn't even know me, she thought.

French came. Mrs Blaney asked Grizelda to read a sentence off the board. *Now I'll show them*, she thought.

She put on her best accent.

"Very good," said Mrs Blaney, looking at her sharply.

Grizelda sat down. She felt a sharp dig in her back.

"*Boff!*" a voice hissed behind her.

"Boff?" What was that? A nickname? It didn't sound too bad. But why. Unless it rhymed with "toff".

97

The bell rang and Mrs Blaney left the room. "Boff" suddenly didn't sound so nice chanted at her by everyone in a horrible, cumulative rhythm.

By breaktime, both "Boff" and "Toff" seemed forgotten. The glories of her name had taken over.

Until that moment, it had never occurred to Grizelda that her name was at all out of the ordinary. These new, disturbing, hostile people, though, thought it was. "Grizzle, Grizzle, make her grizzle!" the mocking cry went up at break.

Grizelda couldn't help it. She tried to fight it. She gritted her teeth, pushed her fists into her eyes – but the lump in her throat would not go away. Soon tears were coursing down her cheeks. At that very moment, Chantal and Harvinder might be examining mulberry bushes in the school gardens or getting a first look at the new children's books as they came into the huge library. Perhaps they were sparing a thought for her as well.

So her first day at Heathwell had passed with excruciating slowness and absolute torture. And now, so many years later, sitting cold in Julian's chair, she found it etched in actuality in her mind – desolation for the loss of an old, loved life; frustrated hatred of the new leering, shrieking, malevolent crew, stronger, dirtier than she was.

And what sorrow for herself! *Nobody* was as unfortunate, sad, unlucky or unhappy as she was.

The years that followed constantly modified what she had felt on that first day. Poor Grizelda, who had lost her father, but what about Jason in her class, who had never had one that he knew and was knocked around by the man who stood in his place? Poor Grizelda, who had fallen on hard times and was left with just the dregs of a fortune, when Karen, Tracy, Glenn and Carol were brought up on benefit.

Their thin faces and sallow skins were caused by under-nourishment and they did not pay for school dinners while she did. Poor Grizelda, turned out of her lovely, spacious house by the Heath and forced to live with five others in a mere three-bedroomed semi and share a room with her sister! Some of her schoolmates came from families twice the size with half the space to live in – and behind with the rent at that. And hidden in the lives of some she saw every school day was worse, much worse.

All this she found out as time passed and it brought shame for her self-pity.

The clock struck three. Grizelda was now wide awake. She stood, tiptoed to the bedroom door and opened it. From the big double bed she heard Julian's breathing. As she watched, he turned over, thrashing with one arm and muttering indecipherably.

In God's name, what was she doing with this man? Look at the last two nights. There was *no* meeting ground. He stood for *everything* she abominated. "Oik!" That word made her so angry. Even more than "scum". Why was he so savage with people he knew nothing about? What assumptions about his fellow creatures had been bred in him from birth? By what right did he aspire one day to *rule* these people?

More, what right had he to class her with him?

Julian muttered as he slept, as if he were having a bad dream. To Grizelda, his muttering was as good as plain speaking in her ears.

"What right have *you* to think you're not? Oxford, all the privilege that gives, the social life, the partying, a respect-able degree, straight into a good job in the media? What's oikish about that, Griz? What a hypocrite you are!"

99

No, he hadn't really said that. Her conscience had spoken with Julian's voice.

She hesitated, suddenly feeling affection for that sleeping form. But no, she would not slip into the bed beside him. She turned back to her chair to think again.

The worst had passed at Heathwell. She had merged into the crowd, kept her head down, her nose clean. She had ended up friends with Jason, Scott, Karen, Tracy and Glenn and the rest. She stopped wishing her parents had given her an ordinary name when they forgot the strangeness of hers and "Griz" became an affectionate abbreviation. She was *with* them. When new pupils joined, she gave them hell with all the rest.

Memories of the Anglo-World Citizens School dimmed. One night Grizelda, now fourteen, said – quite out of the blue – "Mum, why don't you start painting again? I used to love watching you. I know Barnaby would be pleased."

Wendy Grissom looked at her with acceptance, not sadness.

"Because I never will, Grizelda. That's my old life and it's vanished, with all the old ambitions."

An intriguing question occurred to Grizelda. She asked it.

"Did you have ambitions for me?"

"Your father wanted you to go to university. Your old school said you were Oxford or Cambridge material for languages when you were eleven."

Oxford and Cambridge. Dizzy names on the edge of imagination.

"But that's all gone. I couldn't afford it," Wendy continued.

Now Grizelda remembered her father. For long stretches of time in the old house she had not seen much of him, but when she did, how warm he was! How full of praise! How generous!

"I'll go there," she said. "I mean it. I want to."

Wendy sighed.

"If only you could!"

That thought had filled Grizelda's every waking hour. When she read Thomas Hardy's *Jude the Obscure* in the sixth form, she realized with a shock that she was reading about herself.

For some time she kept her ambition secret. The fact that she was clever no longer caused mockery or resentment. Anyway, she knew very well that both Jason and Karen were cleverer than she was, if only they would realize it.

With sudden shame, she remembered that the last time she had been home, Jason was working in a garage and Karen was a single parent with three children.

In year 11 she told Mrs Blaney she would like to read Modern Languages at university.

"I thought so," was the reply. "And you will. If only some of the others would see they could so easily go with you!"

And she made it. She went into the sixth form, filled in all the forms, got her provisional offers. She would make Oxford if she managed three As at A-level. Her heart sank at the task – but she got them. She was in.

When she knew, she looked back to count the cost. Friends had dropped off, one by one. There was little life left for her in this town. At the end of her school life she was in a small, tightly-knit group, all university-bound, knowing that plenty of their classmates, as talented if not more so, had dropped off on the way. She'd been to hardly a single disco or rock band gig, not even to the new multi-screen cinema on the edge of town. She'd had no real boyfriend. And now, until she started university, she had to work – on supermarket shelves and checkouts, petrol station forecourts – anything to add to the miserable grant (at least she would get the full amount) and any loan she might feel unwillingly bound to take out. But look what the future held!

The future held Julian.

She'd known, deep down, that this was *it* as soon as she saw him. There had been a few unsatisfactory men already. She was beautiful: without false modesty, she knew it. But she kept attracting prats.

Whatever else he was, Julian was no prat.

Disagreeing with him, puncturing him, became a delightful sport. In many ways it was unreal.

Until one night.

Julian had made a speech at the Oxford Union. Though Grizelda had disagreed with every reactionary word he said, it was a brilliant effort (so it should be: she'd helped him put it together) and she'd loved him all the more as he was speaking.

But after the debate and drinks with the distinguished guests and the President of the Union, he'd walked her back to her college, plainly high on excitement and success. It was a dark, cloudy night with drizzle starting. As they walked along St Giles, Grizelda had a sudden feeling they were being followed.

She said so to Julian.

"Nonsense," he replied.

Nevertheless, she turned to look.

A tramp, a down-and-out, a ragged outcast, lurched after

them, head down. As she turned, he straightened and stared levelly at her. It was no bearded, grizzled, old man's face that she saw. This was a young, dark-haired fellow no older than she was, who returned her look fearlessly.

She turned back and went on. Julian was unaware of the stalker. The entire sighting lasted no more than seconds. But she tightened her grip on Julian's arm as she thought: *There but for the grace of God go I!* And then: *What am I doing with this man who would have nothing but contempt for the person following us – and contempt for me also had things been different?*

The sight returned as she sat. Yes, she had pulled herself up to a high ledge which seemed secure. But below her was a monstrous abyss. She could so easily fall back into it. She shivered on Julian's chair and was suddenly frightened.

Light came in through the curtains. London was waking up.

Was that why she would stay with Julian? Because he was a passport to security?

Never. That was contemptible. She *loved* him, she *did*, she *did*! Though she could leave this very day.

But she knew she wouldn't.

There was much defining still to be done. What did she really feel? Time would tell. Meanwhile, she wouldn't talk to him just yet.

She quietly washed, dressed, prepared some cereal and coffee and slipped out of the flat at six-thirty, to start a very long day at Speakeasy Television.

Part Three

Julian

Chapter One

Julian, in dressing gown and not yet shaved and showered, made toast and coffee. In the sitting-room, the carriage clock left him by a doting great-aunt struck eight. The flat was empty. He had heard Grizelda slam the front door more than an hour ago.

Julian was not worried. She'd gone to work early: no more than that. Though she had behaved weirdly these last few days. "Time of the month," he had told himself. It had started when she had first come home from her escapades in God knows where at the behest of the fat, freakish deviant she worked for. It seemed rather soon after the last time of the month, but then, he thought, the sooner it was, the sooner it would be over so the familiar relationship could carry on.

There was still work to do on Grizelda before she would pass as the loyal helpmate to parade at constituency selection committees. But there was plenty of time: the career outside politics had to be fully cemented before he took on anything seriously political – that is, if a political career looked worth the candle. Still, Grizelda had a mind of her own. He liked that in a woman. As long as. . .

His thoughts were interrupted. The post came through the letterbox. Bills, junk mail, a Wine Club selection, letters for Griz, and three for him – including a blue envelope addressed in firm, elegant, feminine handwriting.

He'd know it a mile off. His mother.

He should go to Mockbeggar House more often and take Grizelda with him. Three years together and his mother had only seen Grizelda four times. On two of those occasions his father hadn't been there. Still, now he was *Sir* William Claverhouse, Mockbeggar House saw him almost as seldom as Julian. So, though this was hardly the dutiful son sharing his life with the parents, it didn't seem much like the dutiful husband sharing his life with his wife any more. Still, *Lady* Claverhouse... He knew his mother would put up with a lot for that title.

He opened the envelope. The crisp, embossed paper, unvaried for as long as he could remember, and the indefinable but unmistakable scent carried with them a sudden and sharp reminder of childhood. His mother disliked the telephone for any messages of substance. Letters from her were regular, on the same paper, but never before had he felt such a keen tug of nostalgia. Sadness was not an emotion much known to Julian. But he was close to it now as he read.

My main reason for writing is to give you news about someone who may mean nothing to you now, though you may recall her from when you were very young. Dear Mrs Brady, who used to come in three days a week to do the heavy cleaning, is dead. In rather desperate circumstances, I'm afraid. It seems she took her own life. She lived in one of those maisonette places on the big estate on the edge of Wycombe. There's been an inquest. I saw it all in the local paper and I felt so sorry I sent a wreath to the last address I had and a little note saying that I would help in any way I could if they liked to ask me. But you know what these people are like and I don't suppose I shall hear anything.

I always had a soft spot for Mrs Brady, though. Do you remember the terrible trouble she had with her son Gary? You were about the same age, I remember. When you were very little and she brought him round with her when she came to work, you and he used to play together. I thought it would be good for him and Mrs Brady was so grateful.

I didn't go to the funeral, of course...

Julian read no more. As unreasoning as the sharp nostalgia was the mixed anger and contempt, fresh as childhood itself, which suddenly flooded him. He put the letter on the table next to his third cup of coffee and felt his heart beat and his head spin. He sipped coffee and calmed down.

What was the matter with him? What association deep in his mind had been triggered by his mother's news? And why, now he thought of it, was he not so surprised? Why did it seem inevitable, as though all that had been thought and spoken between him and Grizelda over the last few days was somehow preparing him for it? For the anger he was feeling now was of the same quality, the same nature as he had felt when Grizelda had attacked him over what he – quite rightly – thought about this ghastly oik she had found and was making such a fuss over. And it was raised by those same ghosts he had seen for just a moment – before Grizelda told him about Teddy and all was well again.

He finished his coffee, washed up (he would give Grizelda no cause for reproach when she came back), shaved, showered and dressed. Then he went downstairs to the

BMW and drove, deep in thought, to the Lombury Hazards Bank.

His mind was peopled with indistinct figures. He must find out who they were. But he mustn't spend his whole working day in a dream.

The first person he saw was Piers. He had spent yesterday avoiding him after the dinner party. Piers spoke loudly. Was there a touch of malice?

"Great dinner the other night. I say, Grizelda put you in your place all right, didn't she? No bad thing, old son. You need it."

Julian smiled weakly. Grizelda, the arguments, his mother's news – all were bound up in a way he was going to have to sort out.

There were days when Julian did his job on auto-pilot. He read the *Financial Times* (which he classed as work); he sat in meetings round a big oak table; he held quick confirmatory or dismissive conversations in his office or that of a colleague; he composed letters into his dictating machine for Mrs Burden, his secretary, to word-process; he booted up screens full of figures on his computer, scanned them and saw their significance at once; he drawled news down the telephone to people who would be made or broken by what he said. But today his mind was invariably somewhere else. There were ghosts peopling it: his mother's letter had called them up. But Grizelda hovered with them, tantalizingly, sometimes sliding away so that he had to snatch her back with conscious desperation.

Just as he realized he might have to do in real life. For her crisis, and these ghosts visiting him, were connected. He was sure of this. And there was a long trail which they had followed to reach him. He had to retrace it himself – even if what he found at the end was not to his liking.

It was coincidence that his mother's letter had arrived when it did. But then, *of course*, it was coincidence. Life, he was sensitive enough to realize, proceeded entirely by coincidences. There was a word – Grizelda sometimes used it when she talked happily about the way they had met: "synchronicity". To her – and she was a superbly *unsentimental* creature – it described what she thought of as the fateful good fortune of their first meeting at the party in Frobisher College. He would never tell her that he had seen her in Broad Street coming out of Blackwell's bookshop a fortnight before, taken a good look and then said to Teddy, host of the party, "Find out who she is and get her for me, will you?"

As for the faces mingling in his mind now, he'd not said to his mother, "Get them for me, will you?" No, she had provided them without his asking for them by writing that letter. And he wished she hadn't.

He stood and walked to the window. Outside, on a fine and sunny day dulled by a pollution haze, traffic bludgeoned its way through Bishopsgate: cars, vans, double-decker buses.

Julian's eyes were drawn to the buses. He could not remember ever having been in one. What were they but institutional mass transport for people he cared nothing for? He had applauded the deregulation of the buses by the lamented last government; saw splitting up the monopoly in London's transport as a triumph for freedom and commercial wisdom and hoped that the old government's successors would have the sense to leave well alone. But approval of how the buses were now organized wouldn't make him go on one.

So why was he looking at one now – an old red Route-master – with such fixity? Because somehow it had made the mists clear. He began to recognize the ghosts...

"See who's come to play with you, Julian."

"Who, Nanny?"

Nanny bends down to me. She smells nice. She has always smelt nice.

Lots of people look after me. First of all there is Nanny and there is Mummy. I do not know which I love best. Nanny is always here and plays with me, feeds me and smacks me sometimes. She takes me out for walks, not in the pram any more but in my pushchair sometimes and now on my bicycle because I can nearly ride it. Mummy comes in the morning when I have had my breakfast and am washed and dressed and have done the things I have to do every day. Sometimes she takes me out in the car and I go to nice places and see other children who I do not always like. She comes in the evening when I go to bed and plays with me and reads to me sometimes and she never smacks me but always talks nicely to me and cuddles me and brings me lovely things.

Mummy has a funny name for Nanny. It is "Wander". I know what "wander" means because in the stories they read to me sometimes people wander over the hills and far away and Nanny never does. She is always here.

Then there is another one who laughs and talks to me and sometimes when nobody is here she shouts at me and I cannot say her name properly yet and it is "Ing-id".

And there is a lady who comes into my room sometimes when I am not there. She has a mop and she takes all the bedclothes away and pushes the noisy hoover. She is a Mrs. And her name is Duffy and that makes me laugh.

Then there is my daddy. I do not see him much and when I do he tries to be nice to me but I am frightened of him because he is big and bristly.

And today there is someone new.

He is a boy and he is as big as me. And his clothes are not nice like mine and he does not say anything. Nanny says he is called "Gary" and I must play with him because his mummy has come to help my mummy. He is poor and does not have lovely toys and games like mine and I must be nice to him.

I do not want to be nice to him because there are poor people in the stories Nanny and Mummy read to me and on the television sometimes and I do not like them.

But then Mummy says I must be nice as well. So I will try.

Total, unexpected and quite irrational recall of when he was three and Gary first came to the house. And the bus outside had been the trigger.

I have a big nursery with lots of toys and games and nice trumpets and whistles to blow and keyboards to make tunes on. I have a big model railway that Daddy bought. I have aeroplanes and boats and bicycles and lots of things to dress up in like tin helmets and greeny clothes and toy guns so I can be a soldier. I have boxes with things in them I can put together to make toys with and then pull apart. I do not like putting them together much, so sometimes Nanny and Ing-id do it for me. But I love pulling them apart.

Because Gary is here today, Mummy knows I will be upset because there have never been any other children in my playroom. So she has bought me a new present to make it all right.

It is a box. It is called Lego. I like Lego because you can stick all the bits together how you like and then pull them to bits again.

On the box there is a picture. It is of a big red bus and it is made of Lego.

I do not care about the bus. I do not care about Gary.

Nanny says, "Say hello to Gary, Julian."

I will not. I do not want poor people to be here.

There is another lady in my playroom. She is Gary's mummy. She says to Gary, "Isn't it nice of Master Julian to let you in his playroom? Say thank you to him."

Gary does not say anything. Nanny talks to Gary's mummy.

"Don't worry, Mrs Brady. I'll look after him. They'll play nicely together."

I will not let Gary play with my toys. He is nasty because he is poor. I will not talk to him.

I open my new box of Lego. There are wheels in it and lots of Lego bits. I stick a few together. Then I throw them all up in the air because that is what I like to do with them and I go away to play on my own.

From over the years, as he watched from his office window while the Routemaster edged its way down Bishopsgate, feelings of overpowering resentment came back.

No, I will not play with Gary. I will not talk to him. I will not even look at him. I will play on my own like I always do, with Nanny and Ing-id to find things for me when I lose them.

But I look at Gary. He is picking up all the bits of Lego that I threw in the air. He is looking at the bus on the box.

He is silly. He is poor. He does not talk. He does nothing.

I play with my trains. Then I put my jungle-green battledress on and my helmet. I take my sub-machine gun and crouch behind my big toybox. I am going to ambush Gary and kill him.

I creep up on him. He takes no notice. What is he doing?

There is no Lego on the floor. He sits back.

There is a red bus on the floor, made of Lego, just like the one on the box. How has it come there?

I run to Gary with my gun. I pick up the bus. I do not care how it got there. I am going to throw it in the air, break it in pieces again.

But then Nanny sees me holding the bus.

"Why, Master Julian!" she says. "You are *clever."*

I do not break the bus up after all because Nanny is so pleased with me. Now I remember making it while Gary watched me. Gary is only a poor boy and so he cannot do clever things like that.

*"I am going to take this away and show it to Mummy,"
says Nanny. "She* will *be pleased."*

Mummy is very pleased with me indeed. She hugs and kisses me for being a clever boy. Gary does not say anything at all.

In the afternoon, Gary's mummy comes for him and takes him away. I am glad. He will not be here tomorrow because his mummy does not come every day. He will come the day after, though. I will not be nice to him.

In the evening, Daddy comes up to see me. He looks at the bus. He cuddles me.

"Well done, old chap," he says. "I'm so pleased with you."

And I am pleased that he is pleased. That night, after Nanny and I have watched television, Nanny has read me a story and I am tucked up, I sleep all night without waking once.

The Routemaster had gone. The phone on Julian's desk was ringing. He shook his head to clear it, then took the call. It was a matter he dealt with in two minutes. He put the phone down.

Why was the red bus so important? He knew now that it was a kit meant for older children and he should not have been able to make it. So what had happened that morning?

A phrase rang through his mind, strong enough to be a motto to live by: *poor boys are not clever enough to do things like that.* He was clever and Gary was not.

Which was as it should be, wasn't it? So it always was and it would always stay that way. And so it should!

Oh yes, he could well imagine the conversation when Mrs Brady came back from her duties to take her son home.

"How has he been, Miss Gates?"

"Oh, no trouble at all. Such a quiet little boy. Perhaps too quiet for his own good."

Would Mrs Brady have said then, "Well, he makes enough noise for two when he's at home." Or, "Yes, I know. He always has been." Did it matter?

And then Wanda would have said, "Of course, Master Julian was very kind to Gary. Why, he built a bus out of Lego for him, which is *extremely* difficult for a child of three. I think Gary's going to learn a lot by coming here. It will be very good for him."

Mrs Brady, suitably submissive, would answer, "I'm sure we both appreciate it, Miss Gates. Thank you so much."

And they would be gone, only to be back two days later. For as time went on and memories solidified, Julian pondered on more.

That last conversation was in his imagination, made up now as he looked over crowded Bishopsgate. But he knew it must be close to reality. A pattern was established and now he was trying to sort out the truth behind it. More Lego models would be made – difficult, exact, intricate. Some would be seen by Wanda with cries of, "Look, Gary! *Isn't*

Master Julian clever?" And Nanny was infallible. With a shock, he realized that she was infallible to him then and even now she *still* was.

And then there were drawings in chalk or crayon – of buses, planes, cars, animals, people. How good they were Julian had no idea now. If Nanny found the models before they were broken up, the Playdoh animals before they were squashed or the pictures before they were scribbled over – and that must have been Gary's doing – she kept them and, when his mother came in, would say, "Look what Master Julian did today!" Then his mother would kiss him and his father would come up later and see them all and say, "Well done, old chap!" and remark quietly to his wife, "You know, he really does seem quite extraordinarily able."

That phrase! One to savour. He had lived by it ever since.

The phone rang again. He jerked out of his reverie to answer it. Grizelda.

"Darling, I'm sorry about last night. We shouldn't argue about things like this. We can agree to differ, can't we?"

With an effort, Julian recalled the night before.

"Well, I did go over the top a bit. I'm sorry."

Grizelda went on. "Because I'm not stopping the work I do, not for you or anybody."

"No, no, that's all right. I wouldn't want you to. Only..."

"Only what?"

"It's just that..." He remembered what she had said: *"Something about this has really got to you, wormed its way under your skin."* Were this morning's obsessive thoughts anything to do with that? Griz was right, he had to admit, though he wouldn't say so over the phone. What he did say sounded lame. "I've just been fairly tense lately. Big things happening here. They can be a worry."

"I know, my love. Take care. Don't let mere work get you down. It's not worth it. I'll be home the usual time tonight. Let's go out to eat."

Julian put the phone down and went back to the window. He had lost track of his thought. He spent a moment putting it together. Of course he knew what he was seeing – the earliest foundations of his future life, a metaphor for all that he had believed in ever since. He had welcomed a poor boy to him, had helped him, seen the fruits of his help broken in his face. Destructive and inarticulate – that's what Gary had been, even then. Like them all. But what had *he* been at the same time? "Really quite extraordinarily able", of course. The die of life had been cast in the playroom. It was true, true, *true*! A little *oik* (oh, that word, so beloved at school for any outside its bounds!), illegitimate, raised in the gutter on baked beans or whatever these people ate, pathologically unable to speak, had been brought to him as a playmate – he, Julian, destined for school, university, a great career. "By their fruits ye shall know them." His fruits were ripening, maturing, bred in the bone and nurtured by environment. They were his birthright.

But why had these memories come *now* with such holographic clarity? It must be because of Griz and this delving into the sewers queer Quentin was making her do. That and his mother's letter. Well, there was no need for it. Griz was wrong when she said he was taking everything personally. He was not. He was angry on behalf of what was *right*, God-given, unquestioned for centuries until the barbarians assaulted the walls and only the vigilance of people like him and his family kept them out.

Yet there was something deep, tucked away, unexpressed, *wrong*. Did he fear it? Should it not speak its name?

The phone rang again. Piers. Nothing about last night's dinner party this time but strictly professional. Julian looked at his watch. Time was slipping by. There was a meeting in the afternoon and a report to prepare. He had better set to work, fast.

As he sat down, sentences from his mother's letter came into his mind. *Dear Mrs Brady . . . is dead. In rather desperate circumstances, I'm afraid. It seems she took her own life. . .*

Before shutting his mind to everything except bank business, he allowed himself just one question.

Why?

Chapter Two

"Do you plan on seeing your performing oik again?" Julian said.

He had delayed reference to the previous night's row until coffee. Obviously, Grizelda had resolved to do the same. They had skirted the subject – and anything important about each other – like shy teenagers in a fifties' film on their first date. Very different, Julian reflected, from their actual first date.

"I don't see how I can," Grizelda answered. "He's disappeared."

"He can't just vanish."

"Can't he? Tommy Trefoil's the only name I have. I've rung every agent I can find, every club, every pub. Nobody's even heard of him. It's as if my whole trip away was just a strange dream."

"So what will you do?"

"Quentin says leave it. The man will turn up. Nobody can resist being on television, especially born show-offs like pub entertainers."

"Is he right?"

"Well, ordinarily, I'd say yes. Except that Tommy Trefoil doesn't strike me as a born show-off."

"What is he then?"

"I wish I knew."

Julian nearly said, "He's scum and not worth the time of

day from you," but he choked it back. He wouldn't start another fight.

They left the restaurant. Julian wanted to go to a club, to dance the day's strange visions out of his system. Grizelda didn't.

"Please, no, Julian. I'm seriously tired. I hardly slept last night."

Julian felt shame. His own righteous indignation last night was so strong that it hadn't occurred to him that Grizelda could be devastated by it. Perversely, the shame was replaced by a touch of pride. A sleepless night, no less. And all on *his* account!

That was childish. He fought it down. But then, today had been full of childish thoughts.

They took a taxi back. The atmosphere remained quiet and strained. Julian was still preoccupied by his own thoughts.

Shall I tell Griz about what's been bugging me today? After all, it has something to do with her. If it hadn't been for these last days I wouldn't have taken any notice of the news in my mother's letter.

The idea was intriguing – even tempting. The words were on the tip of his tongue, but they never came out.

No. The letter – and the memories, no matter how vivid they were – don't have anything to do with what Griz said. It's just that they caught me off-balance, a tad vulnerable. All I'll do is cheapen myself in front of her. I won't *do that.*

The corollary to that last sentiment lay unformed in his mind because he didn't need to think it – *nor in front of any woman.*

So they sat quietly, companionably, knowing the coldness would soon end, consuming a leisurely bottle of wine and listening to CDs. Gradually, mutually, they felt warmth return. And then they went to bed.

Now Julian found sleep difficult. The day had posed a question. He worried over it for hours. By morning a response had come. Over breakfast he let go his one positive idea.

"Do you fancy a trip to Mockbeggar House this weekend?"

"But we haven't been there for months! You never even seem to think about it."

"Just a thought," he said lightly. "I'd quite like to."

Grizelda looked at him narrowly.

"Julian, something's brought this on. You usually have to be dragged there." Julian said nothing. Grizelda continued, "Are you sure you want me there? You know I'm not your parents' ideal source for the widening of the Claverhouse gene pool."

Ideally, Julian would *not* like Grizelda there. If he was going to ask his mother about matters of long ago and especially about the sad fate of an ex-domestic, it were better he went alone. Yet a little nudge at the back of his mind told him that Grizelda *ought* to be there. However indirectly, she had brought this on and it might be that the outcome would affect her very much.

So he said, without even a nanosecond's hesitation, "Of course you must. I want you to. And she really is fond of you."

"If you say so," said Grizelda.

Julian took that answer to be both consent to going and acceptance of his mother's approval.

* * *

Friday morning at the bank was hardly frenetic. People were thinking more about their weekends than high finance. Julian had a stress-free day. No hassles with clients or colleagues, no sudden crises in Frankfurt or Singapore to make his head burst. During the day he rang his mother. They would drive over on Saturday morning and stay until Sunday afternoon, if that was all right with her.

"Your father's in Stockholm," she said, by way of an answer.

Somewhat irritably, Julian replied, "I don't give a damn where he is. It's you we're coming to see."

"And Grizelda's with you?" said his mother.

Julian knew the question veiled her meaning. *If your father were here, better if you did not bring Grizelda. She is not the sort of partner he has in mind for you.* So his answer of, "If that's all right with you," concealed the riposte, *Well, sod him then!*

"Of course it is," his mother replied.

As the day went by, Julian began to wonder whether he ought to be a little more up-front with Grizelda about why he wanted to go. His mother's letter was in the top drawer of his desk. He took it out and read it yet again.

No harm could be done. He would show the letter to Grizelda that evening. She would see there was a perfectly good motive for the visit – without letting her in on more disturbing issues.

But he should have forecast Grizelda's straight-to-the-point questions. She read the letter, her forehead wrinkled. Then she looked Julian full in the face and said, "So this is why we're really going to Mockbeggar House?"

He nodded.

"Well, Julian, you grief-stricken about a cleaner who I

don't suppose you've given a moment's thought to in your whole life till now shows a completely new side to your character. You'll tell me next you want to be chief mourner at her funeral."

"Of course not," Julian replied, stunned. "But Mother's plainly a bit upset. I thought we could cheer her up."

"Your mother? *Upset?*" cried Grizelda. "She's about as upset as if the bathroom taps dripped." She waved the letter. "'You know what these people are like.' What a sentence! It says it all."

Julian knew better than to protest. Grizelda was in full flow.

"It shows what your mother thinks and what you think as well. At least she didn't say 'scum' or 'oik'."

Julian saw the hard-won reconciliation slipping away again. "That's not fair, Griz..." he started. But Grizelda hadn't finished.

"I bet you always presented me to your parents as the once-rich girl down on her luck through no fault of her own."

Julian didn't answer. Of course he had. And was equally sure his father had investigated the circumstances of the rise and fall of the Grissom Green Advertising Agency.

"Well, let me tell you," said Grizelda grimly, "the fact that my father started off a broke ex-art student, became a millionaire, and lost the lot and his own life into the bargain has nothing to do with me. I might have started out at a really snazzy school but it was from 'these people' that I came and it was back to 'these people' that I went when my mother was left picking up the pieces and I had to make Oxford by my own efforts. So when you talk about 'scum' and 'oiks', *you talk about me as well.* Got it?"

Julian was speechless. At last he managed, "So you don't want to go?"

Suddenly Grizelda laughed.

"Of course I want to go," she said, throwing her arms round his neck. "It's just that you need educating."

Jullian listened to this, looked at the flashing greeny-blue eyes, mobile mouth, shoulder-length, rather carelessly swept back dark gold hair, the lissom body whose language alone spoke volumes and thought: *I am in complete thrall to this girl. I cannot envisage life without her. I, Julian Claverhouse, who played the field at Oxford, whose forebears would have demanded "droit de seigneur" with every farm and working girl of the class from which Grizelda undoubtedly springs. No wonder my mother is condescending, my father absents himself. And I must look forward. Would Grizelda one day transform herself into a loyal constituency wife? Or might we – extraordinary fantasy – end up the first husband and wife to fight each other at an election? I doubt if Griz could ever compromise her fizzing brain enough to join any one political party. But she might, just out of devilment. Well, the times they are a-changing – in fact, they've changed beyond my father's recognition already – and the only thing wrong with such an election prospect is that one of us would lose. This is the important relationship of my life and while I'm not daft enough to let it block the path laid out for me because I value that as well, I'm certainly going to trim that path, adapt it in ways my father might not like and my mother would not understand. And I can only hope I take Grizelda with me. But there's a long way to go yet.*

He kissed her, feeling obscurely that the relationship had moved on a little.

They arrived at Mockbeggar House for lunch. Georgina was, as usual, gracious towards Grizelda, but for the first time, Julian saw a patronizing edge. He knew that Grizelda was perfectly well aware of this.

Only after lunch, when they were walking in the garden on a warm, clear day with an autumn breeze putting a chill in the air, did Julian broach a difficult subject.

"I was sorry to hear about Mrs Brady."

"Very sad," said Georgina. "Overdose. She must have been dead a week before she was found in her kitchen. Poor woman. Do you remember her, Julian?"

"Very clearly," he said.

"It was a long time ago," said Georgina. "I didn't think you would."

Grizelda spoke.

"What was the trouble with her son, Gary?"

They were walking away from the house, across lawns, through shrubberies and an orchard.

Georgina did not answer directly.

"Do you remember Gary, Julian? Mrs Brady used to bring him. She had nobody to leave him with. Well, of course I was very pleased that she should. Though I didn't dare tell your father. But it was not a success, I'm afraid. A surly, nasty, spiteful boy. You did your best for him, Julian. You were very attentive, even though you were only three. You made him things, drew him pictures, tried to show him how to do things for himself. But to no avail – he hardly said a word all the time he was here and sometimes he was very destructive, no matter how wonderful you were to him."

Julian was aware of the look of complete disbelief on Grizelda's face.

"Did you see all this, Mother?" he asked. He could not

remember her ever coming to the playroom during the day.

"I had no need to," Georgina replied. "Wanda let me know everything that happened. Oh, Wanda Gates, that *treasure!*"

They had walked to the top of the garden. Its boundary, beyond a screen of trees, was a brick wall, made of small, dark red bricks, very old, repaired in places by larger, modern bricks.

"Sixteenth century, this wall is," Julian said to Grizelda. "It bounded the immediate grounds of the Tudor house knocked down to build this one. My mother's family's land once stretched way beyond it but it was all gradually sold off."

From the other side of the wall traffic passed on a main road. They stood in a clearing: horse chestnut and sycamore trees one side, the smaller trees of the orchard stretching back towards the house. Beneath their feet was grass – an unexpectedly close-cropped lawn.

"Do you remember what used to be here, Julian?" said Georgina.

Julian wrinkled his forehead.

"Not really," he said. Then, "Wasn't there a big shed or something when I was *very* little?"

"Big shed?" said Georgina, slightly indignantly. "No, it was a lovely summerhouse. Your great-grandfather built it. He loved it, I remember. Well, he needed an escape hole from your great-grandmother. He did a lot of writing there in peace."

"I remember now," said Julian. "It was certainly here during one holiday. Then I went back to school and when I came home for summer it had gone. I didn't notice for some time and when I asked nobody seemed to want to tell me. So I forgot about it."

"We didn't think you needed to know," said Georgina. "It was, I'm afraid, Gary's downfall. One night he actually crept over the wall from outside and set fire to it. He was hardly eight at the time. The first of several such arson attacks. Not only was he silent, destructive, a clear mental defective, but he showed very early on that he was a criminal as well."

"Where is he now?" said Grizelda.

"I have no idea," Georgina replied. "Of course, he wasn't old enough to be found guilty of criminal intent. Had he been, we would certainly have pressed charges *most* strongly. No, he disappeared into whatever lenient process our nanny state uses to cosset the evildoer. But it was the beginning of the end for his mother, who was having trouble anyway, so I was told, with her appalling husband."

"Wanda Gates told you, of course," said Grizelda.

Julian looked at her sharply.

"Of course," said Georgina.

"So why did Mrs Brady commit suicide?" said Julian. "This was a long time ago."

"Well, her only child was in care, a young offender, subject to psychiatrists' reports, regarded as a dangerous young menace. Her husband was in and out of work, off to Germany and Saudi Arabia, wherever the money could be found, too shiftless to find work in his own country" – Grizelda forbore to comment on the contradiction there – "and then finally disappeared altogether. Is there any wonder?"

"How do you know all this, Mother?" said Julian. "Did you go to the inquest?"

"Of course not," Georgina answered indignantly. "But I did read the local paper and I listen to the gossip of the domestics."

"So not Wanda Gates this time?" said Grizelda softly.

"Wanda Gates left my employment many years ago," Georgina replied stiffly.

Julian stood at the edge of the clearing and tried to remember the summerhouse. It rose in his mind as a mysterious structure which was not there any more one summer when he came home from prep school. Still, life for an eight-year-old was full of unexpected, unexplained events. He thought – looking back on it, straining to recapture childhood thoughts and feeling none of the amazing total recall of Thursday – that until these last few days he had probably forgotten Gary as well.

He was suddenly aware of Grizelda's next question.

"Where is Wanda Gates now?"

Give it a rest! he wanted to say aloud. Why so interested in Wanda? You're not researching for Quentin now. But he wasn't going to break their new rapport in front of his mother.

"I've no idea," said Georgina. "Back in Ilford, I expect."

"It sounds as though she left under a cloud," said Grizelda.

"I valued Wanda," Georgina replied. "She served me well. But then she let me down. Like all her class, she was undependable in the end."

That ended all reference to Gary, Wanda and Julian's early childhood. The rest of the weekend passed amicably enough. Julian noticed that, after those few dangerous moments by the site of the old summerhouse, Grizelda and his mother seemed to get on well. Georgina talked much about family and friends – though nothing about husband – who meant little to Grizelda, questioned Julian about work, Grizelda about her own work, both of them about London. Grizelda launched into an account of her project with Tommy Trefoil. Julian noticed that his mother was, quite unexpectedly, deeply interested.

Julian was also surprised to notice that Georgina had hired staff to cook dinner, a more elaborate meal than he had expected. Was this to show Grizelda's importance to the family or to impress – and even intimidate – her? If the latter, his mother did not understand his tough-minded partner.

On Sunday morning, Georgina went to matins at the parish church. It was obvious she wanted Julian to go with her. He didn't think it even worthwhile asking Grizelda. To his amazement, she said, "What about me then?"

"But you don't..." he started.

"If she's going to play the great lady in front of the awed townsfolk, I want to be there to see it."

So they went, with Georgina driving the Range Rover. Apart from a marked absence of awed townsfolk, it was as Grizelda had forecast. They performed a stately walk to the reserved pew at the front of the church which Julian remembered from years back, and afterwards they all shook hands with the vicar and Grizelda was graciously introduced as "Julian's friend from London".

They left after lunch. Grizelda sat back in the front seat of the BMW and said, "So ends my weekend in the country. Not quite Bertie Wooster but you can see the resemblance."

Julian did not answer. But he saw a look which told him he had not heard the last of Gary, the summerhouse and Wanda Gates.

Chapter Three

They were home. Julian felt a sense of relief as he unlocked the front door of the flat.

They spent the rest of the afternoon with the Sunday papers. Only after a quickly rustled-up supper did Grizelda start on him again.

"Your family isn't *quite* up there with the blue-blood, is it, Julian?"

"I never said it was," said Julian, defensively.

"But your mother wishes it were," Grizelda continued. "That was a good duchess-worshipping-with-the-plebs act this morning..."

"So was yours," Julian said, more spiritedly than he had meant. "You *really* put it on."

"Ah, but I knew I was hamming it up. I don't think she did. No, I'm no threat to your father's standing, whatever that is. Squires – that's what I think you were. Farming squires who did well in the eighteenth century, kept out of trouble in the nineteenth when the Corn Laws ruined most, made some good marriages, got a bit of land together while others went broke, sold it and made a pile."

"That was my mother's side," said Julian. "The Claver-houses got rich in India, with tea. There've been three generations of us in the City. My father's the first one ever knighted."

"I mean, how can you be kosher aristocrats? Where's the

faithful old family retainer? Where's all the army of servants in black suits and white pinnies?"

"They've never been there. A nanny, cleaners, hired staff for big occasions, that's all I remember. No butlers – not since before the Second World War, anyway."

"Yes, nannies," said Grizelda musingly. "The mysterious Wanda Gates."

"No mystery," Julian replied. "She dominated my life. Even more than my mother."

"Anyway, you were wrong thinking your mother was upset about Mrs Brady. What was your *real* reason for going?"

"Should I need reasons for seeing my mother?" said Julian, stiffly.

"Of course not. That's why giving me one seemed so odd. But that was a fascinating story, about Gary and the summerhouse. It's as much worth following through as Tommy Trefoil's. Where did Gary go? Where has Tommy been? Two unanswered questions. They make a nice balance."

Julian said nothing.

"In fact, if Tommy Trefoil stays missing..."

"Oh no," said Julian firmly. "You lay off."

"There's more to it than meets the eye. A young child burning down a place like that – that takes a brain. Did the Bradys live in?"

"Of course not," said Julian.

"So where did they live?"

"On an estate at the edge of Wycombe. Ghastly place – there's always trouble there."

"How far away?"

"About five miles."

"So an eight-year-old child travels five miles on his own at night to set light to a particular building. Does he ride his little bike? Does he hitch a lift? Does he come on a bus? And he goes home unharmed and undetected, having done a very efficient job."

"How do you know that?"

"Your mother said it was the first of several arson attacks. So he wasn't caught for a while. He must have got careless."

"What are you trying to say?"

"I'm saying, Julian, that it doesn't add up. Your mother said Gary was a silent mental defective. Those were her words. Real severe learning difficulties stuff. Well, as I see it, the two Garys aren't the same: Gary the playroom thickie and Gary the infant criminal genius. It doesn't make sense."

"Does it matter?" said Julian.

Grizelda laughed. "I love the idea of you as the selfless child paragon. All the little toys you made for him, the lovely pictures you drew – and that little toerag destroyed them all in orgies of breaking up and scribbling. Oh, how terrible that must have been for your tiny, sensitive soul, my darling!"

"Oh, shut up," said Julian uncomfortably.

"Well, you've certainly changed," Grizelda continued. "Doing the Fauntleroy bit when you were a mere infant and then becoming the scourge of oiks and working-class shysters – what a personality change! Perhaps it's because you were so righteously enraged at seeing your benevolent efforts thrown back in your face that you believe all the rubbish you talk. Perhaps it's not bred in the bone after all."

"None of this is fair, Grizelda," said Julian. A small, sharp sliver of anger was finding its way into his mind and he was trying hard to suppress it. "I don't remember any of what mother was talking about."

Ah, but I do, his brain told him.

"Of course you won't, my love. It's all on the say-so of the all-powerful Wanda Gates. I'd love to meet our Wanda and ask what really happened."

"Well, you won't," said Julian. "I've no idea where she is."

"Ilford. She's gone back to Ilford. That's what your mother said. It shouldn't be too difficult."

"You *dare*!" shouted Julian.

"Or perhaps I don't have to." Grizelda was at her most teasing. "I can work it all out for myself. Let's think. You were this wonderful little boy, this acme of generosity, helping your playmate by making nice things for him, and he was so awful, so nasty, that he smashed them all up in your face. You're *far* too young to remember any of this, so whose testimony do we accept? Why, the excellent Wanda Gates, the nearest I've found so far to the faithful old family retainer in the Claverhouse ménage. Only she got booted out later, for unspecified crimes against the State."

"That's what they say, so leave it there," Julian muttered.

"I can't. It just doesn't add up. I don't know much about arson, but I always thought that, unless it's really criminal, getting vast sums in insurance or making away with some-one you know is inside at the time, it's a sort of protest."

"Protest at what?"

"It's a 'look-at-me' statement. An 'I've tried but nobody listens' gesture. This is the only way I can get through."

"People who set fire to other people's property are either criminals or lunatics." This was so obvious to Julian it should not have to be stated. "I'll have no truck with this psychobabble rubbish."

"Ah, but you must, my sweet." Sometimes she riled him

so much he could hit her. "You must. Nothing else makes sense."

Julian spoke slowly, loudly and clearly.

"Gary Brady grew up into a young thug. He started early and, from what I've gathered today, paid the price early."

"Ah, but you don't *know*. What if it's not like that at all? And what if dear, enigmatic Wanda is the key?"

"I don't know what you're talking about."

"Let's turn the whole thing over on its head. What were the secrets of the playroom Wanda ruled? How many children besides Gary ever came into it?"

"How should I know?" Julian snorted. "Don't be stupid, Griz."

"I don't believe any did. You were an only child and you were brought up as one, uncontaminated by the outside world."

"I bet I saw *lots* of children when I was young," Julian said indignantly. Instantly, he regretted it. Why be *angry* over this rubbish? Why show himself *rattled*?

"And your mother and Wanda wanted it that way. Until Gary, of all people, turns up. Of all your possible first companions, why him? The least likely, the most unsuitable I would have thought. Why, his presence even has to be kept from your father. In comes Gary, silent, destructive, by all accounts thoroughly nasty. Why didn't Wanda have him booted out at once as a complete misfit?"

"That's her business," Julian muttered.

"I wish I could ask her," said Grizelda. "But then, it would only be to confirm what I'm beginning to think."

"And what's that?"

Grizelda seemed to draw back from the brink of speculation.

"Oh, it's impossible. But it's Wanda who says what goes on in the playroom. Nobody questions her. She can invent reality. She's a one-person George Orwell Ministry of Truth. I'd *love* to talk to her."

Julian was angry. "I won't hear any more of this," he shouted, getting up to stalk out of the room.

But Grizelda caught him by the arm and pulled him back. There was sudden concern in her face and her voice.

"I'm not getting at the *now*-Julian, who thinks and does things that infuriate me and yet I still love. What you see is what you get with you and I really am happy with that. I wouldn't want anybody poking about into what I did when I was little. I bet I was *swinish* to little Barnaby when he came along. It's Gary I want to understand."

Julian sat down again, partly mollified.

"But the way you're talking," he said, "you can't sort Gary out without sorting me out as well."

Grizelda looked at him.

"That's very perceptive, Julian," she said quietly. "I've said too much. I'll shut up."

"Oh no." Julian was very sure about what he said next. "You've gone too far. You've got to finish now."

"If you want me to." Grizelda seemed less sure of herself now. "Well, think of this. Back in his miserable little home, Gary has nothing: no Wanda, no toys, no wonderful things to keep him occupied and stimulated, just a harassed mother and a deeply unpleasant father. In fact, didn't your mother say he was a stepfather? But the baby Gary doesn't fit there. He's bright, has natural curiosity, but nothing's pushing it on, bringing it out. Probably by the time he came to you he was bursting with something he didn't know was frustration. And then he finds himself with all these wonderful things that he never knew existed. Now I don't know what happened then. Neither do you. Why should you? Neither does your mother. Wanda does, though. But it suited her not to let on. In fact it was *essential* for her not to let on."

"Where's all this fantasy leading, Griz?"

"Whoever came into the playroom at three years old could, by the age of eight, work out and then put into practice a careful and successful campaign of arson. *That's no thickhead, Julian.* What happened?"

"How should I know?"

"Can you begin to imagine what he might have felt, pushed out of his depth into a strange place with you, Wanda and an au pair girl?"

"No. And I won't bother to, thank you very much."

"Well, I think I can. I might get somewhere near Gary from my own experience. Only a little, though. It upset me at the school I went to, all innocent, after Dad was dead. I didn't like being called a female boff and have good things trampled on in front of my eyes. And it's no good me saying, 'Where are the ones that did it now? Trapped like Gary's mum, I expect,' because it hurt then and it still hurts now. So just think what it could have been like for little Gary if I'm right. Millions go through what happened to me and much, much worse. Not so many end up reacting to it all like little Gary."

Julian still said nothing. He wasn't going to let Grizelda know that had he known her then he would probably have been one of her tormentors.

But Grizelda didn't seem to notice his silence.

"It's uncanny," she went on. "It's synchronicity again. Here I am, surmising about what happened to Gary, and it's so exactly like the sort of thing I was sketching out to be

Tommy Trefoil's story that I'm really quite gobsmacked. Two identical oddballs in a week. Amazing!"

"Look, let's drop this, shall we?" The feeling of being put in the dock became too much to bear. "I've been very patient. I haven't got angry. I know the good old phrase 'the politics of envy' annoys you but it seems a perfectly sensible one to me and it's behind everything you've said tonight. The world's divided between 'haves' and 'have-nots' and the difference is that the 'haves' did something about it which made them 'haves' in the first place. And do I have to remind you that you're one of the 'haves' now? And a pretty fortunate one as well."

Grizelda was suddenly fiery. "That's ludicrous. 'The politics of envy' are your last refuge. You're selfish and blind, like all your sort. There's no point in trying to change you."

Now Julian did snap.

"Don't push your luck. I can kick you out now if I want to."

"Go on then. I dare you," Grizelda said, angrily but evenly.

"My God! My father was right. What are you but an oik yourself?"

As soon as the words were out, he wanted to call them back.

Grizelda said softly, "It's happening again, Julian."

Julian said, as if his fire had been doused in water, "Yes, it is. I vowed it wouldn't."

Grizelda shivered. They looked at each other. They did not touch or come closer.

What really goes on in her mind? I don't know what's going on in mine. Except that more ghosts are rising.

* * *

Julian woke in the small hours. Grizelda breathed easily, one arm across his chest. He smiled. He remembered how they had looked at each other with the same thought: *Why are we letting this happen again?* Then he remembered what they had together and what made it seem certain that, chalk and cheese though they so often were, parting was inconceivable. He lay on his back in the darkness. Sleep was far away. The new ghosts which had mutely risen were taking shape. He was in almost total recall again: a time not long ago, when triumph was accompanied by niggling doubt, like a death's head placed before a king. But now he recognized the niggling doubt. He could see the death's head and know it for what it was.

Chapter Four

Oxford had been perfect. From his rooms overlooking Merton Street, Julian organized himself a social and political life which was completely satisfying, like a living work of art. Now, in his third and final year, there was a wonderful woman to go with it – different from the usual: clever and beautiful, not a frumpish bluestocking or a bimbo on the make, but witty and unafraid – even disconcerting. She was puzzled, even awed, by much that surrounded him (which was nice), but able to puncture it, douse it in cold water (which was good for him).

For instance, when she had seen the big, gold-embossed invitations on his mantelpiece from the Apsley Club, she had said mockingly, "You aren't with those reactionary aristos, surely?"

The Apsley Club. An exclusive dining society with aristocratic connections, admitting old boys of only about three public schools, with champagne breakfasts and private dinners full of venison and roast swan and swilling with old port, where opinions of antediluvian extremity were held as gospel. Teddy had proposed him for membership. Julian saw it as his *real* passport to greatness.

"I can't believe you're in that High Tory crap," Grizelda said.

"It's the most influential gathering in the university," retorted Julian indignantly.

"The Apsley Club!" she repeated scornfully. Then, "I can't understand why you name it after south-west Hemel Hempstead."

"Apsley House was the Duke of Wellington's London residence," said Julian stiffly. "The Duke of Wellington, as the nation's saviour, great general and then great Prime Minister, signifies all the values we hold dear."

Grizelda sat in the leather armchair by the window overlooking Merton Street and laughed and laughed.

Julian was never able to take the Apsley Club seriously after that.

But there was more to Oxford. Of course he took his PPE course seriously. Politics, Philosophy and Economics – though he could have done without the Philosophy bit – were important to both his assured banking and probable political careers. He rose high in the political clubs: that was important as well, to be known and watched for the future. He realized now that he would not be President of the Oxford Union, which was a blow. But there could be only one President at a time and Oxford, like all universities which didn't know which side their bread was buttered, was very anti-government at the moment – both dons and undergraduates. So people with unsound views, including (God help us!) women, kept getting elected. Ah well! The Party talent-spotters would realize the circumstances. This partial failure would not be held against him.

Nevertheless, a big debate at the Union – that juvenile clone of the House of Commons – was coming up and Julian had a central part in it. The debate was a public occasion where influential people from the outside world gave the main speeches and undergraduates seconded them. But Julian was to second the motion "This House holds dear the

141

principle of independent education". The main speakers were from Westminster: a member of the then Conservative Government – not quite Cabinet – and a member of the Labour Opposition – *definitely* Shadow Cabinet. He would be seen, he would be known, he would be separated from the ruck by his scintillating epigrams and his remorseless logic.

Once upon a time, he was told, such debates were broadcast on BBC radio. Once the entire country had been shaken when this House voted not to fight for King and Country. No longer. But the public gallery might be full – attracted to this wordfest of the nation's brightest and best.

A month had passed since Teddy's procuring job for the party had been done. Julian was still suffering the seismic shock of that first meeting with Grizelda. This relationship was not just a pleasant means of whiling a term away. He was *hooked*. But one thing he was sure of: Grizelda had not attempted to get her hooks into him: unlike most women he had known and quickly escaped, she seemed neither impressed by his family and his class, nor contemptuous of them. She was just herself, expecting nothing, experiencing everything. If he had to describe the state she was in, he might have said something like, "besotted and watchful".

So here she was, helping him with his speech in the rooms looking out on to Merton Street. Helping? If she had been speaking, she would be on the other side. Part of him wondered if this might store up trouble for the future if they stayed together. Yet he was also delighted. If his speech could get past her, it could get past anybody.

Julian's speech-writing method was not scientific. On the table was a pile of paper. Dotted round the room were wine glasses, eight in all, a pair in each corner. On the mantelpiece were four bottles, open and breathing, of a rather good red wine from the College Buttery. At the start of the operation that Sunday morning, the paper was empty and the glasses were full.

At ten o'clock, Grizelda entered. Julian's first thought was, *Sod the speech!* He said as much. But Grizelda wriggled away with, "Much as I agree, you said you'd put this crap together today and you can't leave it until the last minute. I thought Thursday night was important to you."

She was right, of course.

"I can see you're going to be really good for me, Grizelda," he said, and wasn't being sarcastic in the least.

He explained his method.

"Those glasses put there," he said, "mark each stage of the speech." He took a white postcard, wrote START on it and propped it against the wall behind one of the pairs of full glasses. Then he waved his hand at each of the pairs of glasses in turn.

"Over there is MIDDLE. By the window is END. Here by the fireplace is SPARE BITS."

He labelled three more cards and put them in their places.

"We make up good points and write each one down on a separate piece of paper. Then we decide if each point is start, middle, end or spare bit, and put it by the right glasses. When we've decided which it goes in we allow ourselves a swallow of wine each from the section where it's gone."

"Most people work out an argument first," said Grizelda.

"This isn't an argument. It's a speech."

"That says volumes," said Grizelda. "I'm the very last person to help you with this."

"You're devil's advocate," said Julian. "And you can decide where all the spare bits should go. You can tell me what you think the order should be of all the bits in each section. You don't have to agree with it to do that. Don't worry if we get through all four bottles. I've got plenty more. I can send out for some lunch. Are we ready?"

Grizelda nodded.

"Right. First point. Independent education means freedom of choice."

"Absolute rubbish. Freedom for who?" Grizelda said at once.

Julian didn't answer. He wrote it down, dashed to START, took a quick swig from a glass, ran back to the table, wrote the same point out again, took the paper to END, turned to Grizelda and delightedly said, "That's a very important point. I'll start and end with it."

"But it's just not *true*," said Grizelda.

"Better and better," said Julian. "I'll know what the opposition's going to say."

Grizelda shrugged her shoulders, then marched to START and END and took her own swallows from the glasses.

They stuck to their task with great discipline, even though Julian had to open two extra bottles. By evening, START, MIDDLE and END were fat wads of paper, with all the SPARE BITS incorporated. Grizelda, after saying, "I'm doing this as a logical exercise, not a search for truth," had arranged the contents of each section in some sort of consequential order. Julian, glass in hand, watched her. Then he looked out of the window and saw long evening shadows darken the mellow stone of quiet Merton Street, thought of the changelessness of certainties and felt both peace and a welling pleasure and anticipation for all that he could expect in his life.

"Finished," Grizelda said, "as far as I can make sense of such antisocial drivel. You'll have to write it up yourself."

Her hair gleamed in the subdued light of the reading lamp. Yes, the task was done. Now the day would *really* start.

The debate was on Thursday evening. Grizelda was in Julian's room early to make sure his dinner jacket hung well, his black bow tie was straight and his white shirt creaseless and immaculate.

Then she kissed him.

"You're on the wrong side tonight and I could never vote for you, my love. But what's a vote beside everything else we've got?"

For the second time, Julian was on the point of saying, "Sod the speech!" But Grizelda, who looked radiant, firmly propelled him through the door, down the staircase, through the quad, the porters' lodge and into the street. Here they started their walk to the Union building, with its galleries, its portraits, its busts and overpowering atmosphere of male Victorian complacency.

By the time they reached it, Julian was on a high. His heart beat fast; every sense was alert. This was a significant night, to savour and live to the full. For the rest of his life he would return to it as the time his destiny was truly shaped. He knew this with complete conviction.

It was good to meet and eat with the other speakers first. The proposer of the motion knew his godfather well. Julian felt this was one up to him even before they started. He and the woman from the Shadow Cabinet talked about Westminster with a sort of conspiratorial friendship which sounded nothing like the broadcast rows in Prime Minister's

Question Time. Julian noticed how good Grizelda was here – her instant rapport with the Shadow Cabinet lady, the appreciative glances from the Minister. *She is so good for me*, he exulted. *Everything is perfect. I stand on a peak in the foothills and look down in glory. Great Alps and Himalayas rise above me. We will scale them together for there is nothing we cannot do.*

Dinner was over. The speakers filed into the chamber. The President of the Union rose and tapped with his gavel for quiet. He announced the motion and the speakers: "Proposing the motion, the Right Honourable Charles Hailey-Repton, Queen's Counsel, Member of Parliament and Minister of State for Education. Seconding the motion, Mr Julian Claverhouse of Frobisher College. Opposing the motion, the Right Honourable Angela Craig, Member of Parliament and deputy spokesperson on education for Her Majesty's Opposition and Mr Ray Short of St Catherine's College."

The debate commenced. Charles Hailey-Repton spoke epigrams in an off-hand drawl: if his aim was to epitomize any superiority of the independent system, he was certainly concentrating on one aspect – laid-back, entirely confident of his audience. Mostly, they loved it. Julian listened and watched. The inflection of voice, exact body language, knowledge of when to make his audience laugh and wait: Julian stored it up in his mind for the future. Tonight, though, he would be himself and no other.

He had an eye on his own text as he listened. Sometimes he wrote in an extra phrase – "As my honourable friend has already indicated", "To expand on a point made earlier by my learned colleague". He had to demonstrate co-operation and continuity.

Charles Hailey-Repton was finishing: a persuasive call on the forces of tradition, continuity, order and established values. The applause rolled from many who had felt their inmost convictions justified in the face of guilt at their good fortune.

Angela Craig followed. She was punchy, direct, pouring scorn little short of contempt on the previous argument. Julian detached himself from the content: there was too much in it for him to grapple with. But he listened to how she said it, admiration filling his mind despite himself. Yes, here was another way and he would have to master it as well. He looked at the two parliamentarians, still young, surely both destined for high office, and noted their respect – even half-concealed friendship – for each other. And he thought: *This is the glory of how we live in our land: dissent without rancour, disagreement without murder. It is our way: government by assent, opposition by reason – a nation in which all have their place and their stake and where peace and reason rule. I am part of it now and will be even more so.* He surveyed the chamber and its eager, absorbed faces and felt elation at being one item in a greater whole.

But a significant item. Why, one day he might be a new member of a government when Charles Hailey-Repton was Prime Minister.

But even as he felt at one with his world and his destiny, a niggling doubt entered his mind. The time would come (and perhaps as he lay remembering on his bed it had come already) when he would look back on this moment and know it was his real, his only, peak and everything afterwards would be decline.

Angela Craig had finished. The applause grew and waned. Julian's turn. The President introduced him. Julian rose. Adrenalin pumped round his veins in litre dollops.

"Mr President, honourable guests, ladies and gentlemen. My learned and illustrious friend has already..."

A sea of faces, featureless, blurred. No, not all blurred. One, unaccountable choice from that multitude, stood out. His stomach contracted: his heartbeat quickened even more. A veiled blackness descended into his mind. One face, like a questioning spectre, hovered there in the public gallery. His words did not falter: he had been over them too many times. But there was *something* out there, among the unknown faces.

No, not unknown. Grizelda's was among them, quizzical, enigmatic, with him and yet against him. And so many friends. Teddy. Old Dr Raeburn.

And someone else.

That face in the high gallery, fixed on him with anger, burning resentment, which he could feel scoring his skin like a laser.

Silly. Nerves. An emotional reaction to the strain of waiting and now *standing up* in front of these people on such a night. And there were, he knew, plenty there who were envious, saying, "Why aren't I one of the main speakers tonight?" They had stinging barbs ready to aim at him when the debate was opened to the floor.

He collected his wits and proceeded.

"Surely it must be realized what a profound effect on our constitution, our learning, wit, polity, the great public schools have had? Surely it must be accepted that in no other institutions are those qualities fostered which are so characteristic of our island race: fairness despite temptations to greed, fair play, magnanimity to the vanquished and steadfastness in the face of disaster?"

The words themselves called out a separate wave of antipathy. *People from state schools won't like that*, he thought. But the mixture of "Hear, hears!" and derisive laughter he heard from all over the chamber were part of the game, the reaction he expected – in fact, wanted. Not this other feeling, like a little spine of ice projected into his heart from far away.

As he spoke, his eyes roved the gallery. No, still the undifferentiated mass. The speech must go on, though the glory was gone. Julian stuck to his task until the ringing sentence that he was so proud of: "And so, ladies and gentlemen, I ask you to support this motion, which characterizes the life-blood of our nation, which is so apt and self-evident in principle, so absolutely demonstrated over centuries in its practice. Thank you."

He sat down. The resounding clapping should have been like nectar to him. But he hardly heard it. His eyes were searching the chamber again. Was there someone who was *not* clapping, but burning with hostility?

There. In the front row of the gallery. Someone sitting apart, next to the exit. Unmoving. Now the face and body began to stand out. Why had he not isolated it before? A thin face. Dark eyes staring unblinkingly. Lank hair. The more Julian looked, the more he was sure those eyes were the source of the fury. Why?

Ray Short, from a comprehensive in Liverpool with a mind Julian respected and slightly feared, rose to second the opposition. He was not a friend: at first Julian had patronized him; now he was aware Ray did not so much dislike as scorn him. He found this both puzzling and unsettling. But Ray was no blind hater.

Julian peered again at the face. It meant nothing. Yet

there *was* something stirring a chord, something...

He shook his head. *It doesn't matter. Some twerp off the street out of his depth. Oxford's streets are crawling with them. Why don't the police clear them away?*

He looked out again as Ray's flat voice with Scouse overtones piled up daunting statistics. Grizelda was listening carefully – and with obvious agreement – to the rival speech. He smiled at her; she did not notice.

He looked up again. The place where his silent tormentor sat was empty.

He never afterwards mentioned this to Grizelda. Why should he? Perhaps it was an illusion brought on by his heightened state of awareness. Perhaps it had...

Perhaps what? Been the first step down from the peak? The manifest hint that nothing would be the same again, that every triumph would now taste like ashes? Often now, in both waking and sleeping moments, that face came to him. He saw it as he had then, unrecognizable but unmistakeable, especially over the last few days, since Griz had come back from her expedition and they had argued so explosively.

When he was about eight or so, Julian had read a very exciting spy story. A British Special Operations agent dropped behind enemy lines was alone in a wild, rocky valley with a river flowing along the bottom. He tried to get some rest as the moon rose and then set about working out his next move. He recalled his landing place. Was there any sign of the enemy? Were they invisible but near at hand? He reconstructed, purely from memory, a complete picture of the scene. Then a detail he had not registered at first came clearly to mind. In one corner of his mental picture were fresh tyre tracks in the mud by the river. At once he knew he was known and probably being watched.

Julian had been very impressed by that. How did the man know it was not just his imagination? Could the mind *really* store away information like that and bring it out when necessary? Many times he tried it for himself. He could not do it. Either agents sent behind enemy lines were given incredible training or it was just a bit of author's licence to keep the story going.

He remembered this now, lying sleepless next to Griz – and realized with a shock that after all these years it *had* worked. For the features of that face coalesced into detail – the black hair, strangely sensitive mouth, eyes not just dark but burning. And everything that had happened in the last days combined to tell him who the angry watcher was. This was no wild hunch or inspired guess but completely assured conviction.

As he lay in bed and the girl to whom he would commit his life breathed quietly beside him, he admitted the truth. The face which haunted him was that of a grown-up Gary Brady, unrecognized that night of triumph but unmistakeable now.

Chapter Five

Another letter from a parent came on Monday, this time for Grizelda. She opened the envelope, read it, then looked at Julian.

"Are we doing anything this weekend?" she said.

"We're invited to a Conservative dinner and dance on Saturday."

Grizelda gave him a look of some incredulity.

"No, I thought not," he said.

"How about a quid pro quo? If last weekend was with your mother, then the next one's with mine?"

"Any particular reason?"

"It's a special do for her Townswomen's Guild. She's organized it."

"Why on earth would we be interested in that urban Women's Institute? For God's sake, Grizelda!"

"Listen. This is their annual big meeting. They all make exotic little dishes, meet in the Corn Exchange and sample each other's wares, saying how good they are..."

"... and spitting cats at each other, no doubt," said Julian.

"Not fair,' said Grizelda. "Anyway, when they've supped their full, some performer they've hired entertains them..."

"Sounds even more exotic," said Julian.

"Shut up!" said Grizelda. "It's a singer or a comedian usually. It's my mother's job to arrange it."

"And your mother thinks we'd like that, does she?"

"She thinks *I* might."

"Why?"

Grizelda pushed the letter across, pointing at a paragraph halfway down.

As you tell me you've been scouring the country for entertainers to interview, I thought you might be interested in who we've got for our social evening. I thought I'd arrange for a Country-and-Western singer to come. She seemed quite enthusiastic, not that we could pay her much. But last week she rang to say she couldn't make it.

Grizelda interrupted his reading.

"I wonder if the singer was Darlene Nash?"

"Why should she be?" said Julian and carried on reading.

I was at my wits' end to get anybody any good at such short notice. Then, on Thursday morning, the phone rang and a man's voice said he'd been told we'd been let down, that he was a London agent and had a great new act available for next to nothing – a conjuror we'd one day know a lot more about. The Amazing Artistico, he's called. So I booked him there and then. I remembered what you told me about going miles to find hopeful artistes, and anyone willing to do an obscure function for a few middle-aged women deep in the sticks seemed to be right up your street.

"Well, it might be more fun than eating rubber chicken and listening to some thwarted hopeful's bid for power," said Julian.

"Are you afraid I'd be rude to him?" said Grizelda.

"Yes," said Julian. "I am."

Besides, he thought, following Grizelda's wishes and not his own might not be a bad idea in present circumstances.

"OK," he said. "Why not?"

Julian's new working week was busy. By day he forgot about Gary Brady, doubts about himself and friction with Grizelda. During the evenings there were two theatre visits, a dinner party and a Bow Group meeting where *proper* political thought was exchanged. Only when he woke in the small hours did memories of the playroom return, with Gary and Wanda – and the au pair Ingrid, probably now a Scandinavian matron made melancholy by winters of ever-lasting night and surrounded by a clinging, flaxen-haired brood. But what actually happened in those memories was still cloudy, beyond interpretation.

And the Union speech. *Was* that Gary's face he saw? Was it likely?

Julian had a dull certainty that it was – a foretaste of nemesis.

A weekend with Mrs Grissom would not be riveting, but it would please Grizelda. At the moment that was reason enough. And he might at last get a full night's sleep.

Their destination was rather different from Mockbeggar House. Now that her own parents were dead, Wendy Grissom owned the three-bedroomed semi she had moved into after Larry's death. She had never remarried, though Grizelda often wished she would.

As the BMW turned into the road of identical houses, Julian felt a sinking of the heart, which he knew would lift when he was actually in the house.

154

"Can you imagine what it was like when we came here? Two grandparents, Mum and the four of us shoehorned in here with them?"

No, Julian couldn't. Such proximity to other humans was worse even than boarding school – like living in a perpetual rugby scrum.

But trust Grizelda to put the boot in.

"Then how can you begin to understand inner city families in rundown flats or homeless people repossessed and shoved into bed and breakfasts?"

Julian said nothing. This was no time for another argument.

This weekend, though, would be bearable. Barnaby was still at university reading Fine Art, Joel had a room of his own, and Amy was staying over with friends, so Grizelda and Julian could share her room with the rock posters and the hi-fi. Julian was painfully aware of the difference in atmosphere between here and Mockbeggar House. With Wendy Grissom there was no constraint, no half-conscious condescension. Once, Julian knew, she had looked on him with suspicion. That was long gone. He just hoped he would never give her cause for it in the future.

To Julian, Wendy did not look like someone who had suffered such a terrible double blow as losing her husband and every material thing. But that was – what? – eleven years ago now. She had adapted well, he thought – and to the deaths within a few months of each other of her parents. Except when he saw tired lines around her eyes and the wrinkled forehead of one who has taken on complete responsibility. Seeing Wendy sometimes made him half ashamed of the roots he was usually so proud of.

How I have changed since meeting Grizelda! he thought. And then, *I like it here.*

As they left for the Corn Exchange, Wendy spoke to Grizelda.

"Perhaps you'd like to talk to the Amazing Artistico afterwards. I'll find you a place somewhere."

"We'll see, Mum," Grizelda replied. "But I can't see him as anything but a poor substitute for my lost Tommy Trefoil."

Julian drove Wendy and Grizelda to the Corn Exchange in the middle of the town. Inside, in one of their two hired rooms, the food was ready. Julian was charmed by what he saw. A table covered with dishes, each one topped with a little cardboard flag.

"You see?" said Wendy proudly. "We thought we'd have an international evening. Everyone's made a national dish from another country. We've got Swiss fondue, Spanish gazpacho, Mexican tortillas, Austrian Wiener schnitzel, Danish pastry..."

Julian listened to the catalogue. Going round sampling all this was well worth the drawback of being introduced to a score of strange ladies of a certain age. Still, if he ever got into Parliament, there would be years of this, so he had better learn to like it. "Grizelda's boyfriend she met at Oxford. Yes, I expect they *will* get married one day, but that's up to them, isn't it?" How many times did Wendy say that? And how many times did he smile and say stereotyped sentences about the lovely food?

Grizelda made a face at him and muttered, "I wish Mum had stuck to painting. She's wasting herself."

After an hour he was quite replete. His offer to help with the clearing away and washing up was politely refused. So now he looked forward to an undemanding time watching an unknown magician. He needed no prodding when Grizelda took him by the hand and led him to the next room. Here, rows of chairs had been laid out in front of a little curtained stage. Soon the room was full. Wendy came to the front and spoke.

"We were all very worry when Darlene Nash couldn't be here after all..." ("I was right," Grizelda whispered to Julian) "... but by a great stroke of good fortune we've managed to secure a really first-rate substitute. I'd like to introduce to you a young magician who I am sure is going to go a very long way. The Amazing Artistico!"

There should be a great fanfare here, thought Julian. Instead a succession of rather dreamy chords played by the strings of an orchestra sounded through the loudspeakers. The Amazing Artistico stepped from behind the curtains to polite clapping. There he stood, in red cape, white tie, black suit and shiny top hat. He took off the hat with a flourish and gave a low bow. Before replacing the hat he straightened up again.

Julian saw clearly the thin face, the dark, deep eyes, the lank black hair flopping either side of a centre parting. He felt Grizelda stiffen and heard her gasp, "It's Tommy Trefoil! I should have known."

But Julian was watching him with fascination ... was it horror? Was it the feeling that the last fortnight was *bound* to end like this, that he had actually known it all along, that he couldn't be surprised, that now there would be consequences which would either release him or damn him for ever? For he also found himself speaking out loud, words which made Grizelda look at him in a way *not* altogether surprised.

"It's Gary Brady."

Grizelda whispered, "Deep down I think I knew."

Julian had no answer to that.

The Amazing Artistico performed alone to his music. After a few minutes, Grizelda whispered, "I'm sure this is his accompaniment to 'Stranger on the Shore'."

No assistant meant he brought on his own props – few enough. Two packs of cards, the flags of all nations, florid handkerchiefs, but no doves or other expected stock-in-trade of the conjuror. Once he called a volunteer up. Wendy took the challenge. He performed the same trick that had impressed Grizelda in the Jolly Angler.

"You see?" whispered Grizelda. "He has no patter. He doesn't try to make us laugh. He doesn't distract us from what he's doing by what he's saying. He just lets the tricks speak for themselves."

Julian watched silently. He was thinking – oh, he had no idea what he was thinking. Muddles, fleeting scraps funnelling themselves to a fearful point – *I'm coming to a crisis. Does he know me? Would he remember? Shall I just introduce myself and say, "Hello, Gary. Remember me after all these years?"* Why *had this encounter come?*

The Amazing Artistico gave his audience just half an hour of magic. They clapped with genuine appreciation. Grizelda whispered, "Three out of ten for presentation, ten out of ten for technique. He's a lot better magician than comic."

Wendy rushed to the front and said her thanks. As the other townswomen of the Guild rose and walked chattering out, she came over to Grizelda.

"I asked him if he minds you talking to him. He's pleased. He wants you to."

The Amazing Artistico was behind the curtains packing his gear.

"Hello, Tommy," said Grizelda. "So I found you."

He looked up.

"Oh, no," he said. "I found you."

"What do you mean?"

He resumed stowing his gear and would not answer.

Julian was looking at him bemused. Yes, here were the lineaments of the tiny face of childhood; here was the actual face which had stared him out in the Union. His stomach knotted. He knew he had to speak.

"Gary," he said. "Do you know me?"

The Amazing Artistico stood up straight and looked Julian full in the face.

"Yes, of course I bloody know you," he said. "But I won't speak to you. You're not worth the effort. You're scum."

Part Four

Tommy Trefoil

Chapter One

Gary stood in the dark condemned street outside the door of the squat and watched the tail-lights of Grizelda's Calibra disappear into a more welcoming world.

He looked back over the evening at the Jolly Angler. It was a disaster, except for *her*. Well, one thing he knew: either he dropped the comic bit and built up the magician bit, playing his flute just for busking money, or he worked on it hard.

He could still hear Reg Welsted, remarkably affable considering the fiasco. Only, though, because he'd bullied the Rocket Ravers into an extra stint. "You're crap, lad. I'm docking twenty-five quid." Still, the rumpled twenty-pound note and the fiver, added to the loot picked up in the shopping centre, made a good day's haul in this dump. But he'd conned his way into the Jolly Angler, so he couldn't grumble.

And there was a bonus. More: a lightning bolt. He had no licence to busk in the shopping centre. He'd been there for a fortnight and nobody had moved him on. He'd worked two days just to earn the fine when it came. But it hadn't. That cold, bitter, windy morning, though, he'd been sure his luck would change for the worse. It had been cold on the pitch, but he wouldn't put a coat on to hide the black singlet with the lightning and flame motif. I AM WHAT I AM, he would continue to tell everyone.

He'd set up the gear, run the tape, been through the numbers on it. No shoppers stopped. The coins in the battered black flute case were not accruing into a vast pile.

"Stranger on the Shore" came up. He had a momentary loss of concentration. He missed his lead. So he waited a bar and came in with the melody four beats late.

Well, why not? It would sound in tune and none of this lot would notice. Press on, get done, don't make the same mistake in "Greensleeves".

But why had he lapsed? He never did that. One thing he could do, better than most, was concentrate.

Something had made him. What?

The melody was established. He could play it in his sleep. So he looked up and scanned the shoppers.

One of them had stopped, approached, and was listening. Their eyes met.

Yes, his subconscious mind had given him advance warning of what he would see. That was why he had missed the lead. Even so, the shock nearly made him stop there and then. He looked away, then back in a double take.

Still the same.

His heart lurched inside his thin chest. It was *her*.

Just once before he had seen her – that night in Oxford, that night he'd resolved to leave the streets and doorways and *do* something, so that one day he could ... whatever it was he did not know, but he knew what he wanted out of it.

But could it really be her? He'd hardly seen her for a second. Yes, without doubt it was the same face – that unattainable sort of face people like him either yearned for in fantasy or wanted to smash.

And that night in Oxford she was with *him*, with *Claverhouse*!

Well, that had been a sort of triumph as well. Begging in a doorway, invisible as a human being, he had suddenly seen his scourge, the reason for being where he was – seen him and recognized him with certainty. Claverhouse had grown up, filled out, was a man now. But he *knew* – Claverhouse was unmistakeable.

He had followed. Claverhouse entered a college. But if *he* went further than the porters' lodge, he would probably be arrested – turfed out at the very least. He waited, thinking. Then an Oxford tour went by, with its guide pointing out landmarks. Certain that he would be spotted because he looked so out of place, he tagged on the end as the group entered Frobisher College, with the guide checking first at the porters' lodge. Nobody noticed him, so he walked safely round the level green lawns of the ancient quadrangles.

Now he kept his eyes open. No Claverhouse to be seen. Had he made a mistake?

No. At the foot of each staircase in the old buildings names were painted in white on a black background. They must show who lived there. And he saw it. Fourth in a list of eight.

MR J R D CLAVERHOUSE.

Now the fantasy which had ended in a hot, burning summerhouse became real again.

He'd watched all day. He'd seen the girl go in the college: who could fail to notice her? They had come out together. He had followed them, seen them enter a building and disappear. What to do now but wait?

Dark came. He was cold. It would be rain tonight: this expedition meant he would probably lose his sheltered doorway.

More people had gathered. Some were going into the

building. Well, Claverhouse was inside already, so why should he not be too? Once again he slipped behind a knot of people. He now felt less noticeable. These were students: some looked as unkempt as he did.

He followed them upstairs to a gallery. Here he could look down to where smarter people sat. No Claverhouse, but he saw the girl.

And then Claverhouse entered with four others. The man of the moment.

Claverhouse spoke. The last time on the very fringes of his memory that he had heard Claverhouse's voice, it had not broken. That superior tone telling lies. Nothing had changed. Claverhouse had not changed. Claverhouse would never change. *But he would make him change.* He stared him out. Claverhouse never wavered.

He wouldn't listen any more to Claverhouse's laughable hypocrisy. Only one person in this whole room knew what Claverhouse really was and what he had done. And that person had seen enough.

He slipped outside again and waited. The rain was near. But he'd been out in worse.

The wait was long. The others in the gallery came out first and disappeared, talking animatedly and laughing. He waited on.

The two appeared again, the girl leaning on Claverhouse's arm. He nearly rushed out at them there and then – to do what?

Stupid. Just follow again.

They walked now along a wide street going north to where the Woodstock and Banbury roads divided. Their footsteps echoed on the wet pavement. He was getting too close: he dropped back.

And then she turned. She looked at him, full on. His heart beat fast, the hair on the back of his neck tingled. No, in the presence of *that face* he could do nothing to Claverhouse. But the sight was stored up indelibly in his mind.

Claverhouse never turned round. After a few seconds, the girl turned back and they walked on undisturbed.

What now? Follow? What was the point? He was powerless, fated to rage unseen.

There was a hand on his shoulder and a voice in his ear.

"Keep your eyes off, my lad, and stop thinking rude thoughts. We've had our eye on you. It's a night in the cells to look forward to now."

So the filth took him away and, rather than waste a magistrate's time on him, kicked him out of Oxford next day.

He had left, vowing change. I have *power*. I *know* I have. Find out what it is. Use it. What I want to happen *will*. It *must*.

He remembered all that even as he played "Stranger on the Shore" a bar out of sequence. He looked at her again. She looked back. She put money in the case but showed no signs of recognizing him. And then she was gone.

He kicked the ghetto blaster in frustration. What could the likes of him, prisoners of their own lives, do?

But then came the evening *and she was there again*, wanting *nobody but him*. He was still reeling from this.

It was cold here on the steps of the squat. He felt through the letterbox for the string with the key on it, opened the door and locked it behind him.

He had much thinking to do if he was to turn this new sensation to his advantage. He felt for matches – electricity was long cut off – and lit the old hurricane lamp.

By its light he saw a folded piece of paper with GARY written in black felt-tip. He opened it and stared at the words: YOUR MOTHER HAS TOPPED HERSELF.

He blinked uncomprehendingly. He said the message slowly out loud. Then he sat down on an old chair picked up from the local tip.

Another rush of memories swept over him. With them was a grief stunning in its force. Then guilt. It was so long since he had seen her. *Topped herself. Because of me?* Then a sort of relief. *Surely not* just *because of me?*

Then something took grief's place. *Who could have sent this? Who knew where I was? Might it just be a cruel joke?*

Some instinct told him it was true. Enough had happened on this momentous day already. Why this rocking shock at the end?

What could he do? He *had* to go home, *now*, whatever the hour. He owed it. He would have gone one day – but he was proud of how completely he'd disappeared and could come and go and be seen when he chose. Yes, he had to go.

He felt his way upstairs to where three bodies sprawled out on old mattresses emitting breathy snores of exhaustion. For a moment he longed to throw himself down beside them, but he couldn't.

Such scanty goods as he travelled with he snatched up and threw in his old backpack. First went his props, which he would leave for no one: his tape player and flute, his cloak once worn by a nurse, collapsible top hat and packs of cards which constituted his magician's outfit, the suit he wore for both magic and comedy. He nearly put the suit on for the journey – but no. For the open road and hitch-hiking he should travel in jeans and singlet with an old jersey over the top. In his sock he made sure he tucked the army knife which in the past he'd had to use to defend possessions and earnings. He found a piece of cardboard and a felt pen and wrote WYCOMBE on it.

He stole back down the creaky stairs and out of the front door. This he closed behind him and pushed the key on its string back through the letterbox. The others would ask no questions. He had come for two weeks, paid his way and now he'd left.

He walked cautiously, watchfully, through deserted night streets in this run-down place. He mustn't be stopped by the police, whatever happened. Not that the place exactly crawled with them. He picked his way across waste, derelict ground towards lights. Soon he reached a road leading out of town towards the motorway. Now was the time to try for a lift.

He stopped near the slip road, took the cardboard out of his backpack, held it up and waited.

He was lucky. Within ten minutes an old ERF truck stopped.

"Hop in, mate. I'll take you to the next services."

Well, it was a start. He clambered up into the passenger seat in the hot, shaking cab. Once inside, as the lorry butted through the night, he lay back and let his mind fill with memories of all the early years with his mother.

Chapter Two

The first picture – something magic. He wasn't yet four. Now, grown up, sitting in the cab of a lorry, scenes drifted in and out of his mind like a television programme half-watched by one drifting into sleep.

There was a box of red and white things, like tiny bricks. Gary had touched them with his hands and they had metamorphosed into a lovely red bus, just like the one he and Mummy came on.

The little bus which appeared under his hands was as wonderful as the big one he had sat in. The big one he sat in was *truly* wonderful. It brought him from a nasty place where he was sad to a lovely, light place where he was happy.

What made him sad? He did not know what sad was till he came to a place where he was happy.

He was sad because of the big dark man he called Daddy even though he knew he was not a real daddy. He knew he wanted to do nasty things to this man who had a sharp smell he did not like and who Mummy was afraid of. This man never hurt him, never hit, never kicked him. But Gary, with three-year-old instinct, knew he would like to and one day might. Mummy was frightened of this man. *He* wasn't frightened because nothing ever frightened him. But Mummy was *very* frightened. Mummy loved Gary. Gary loved Mummy so much that one day when he was *very* little he had done something so she need not be frightened of Daddy any more and would only love Gary. What it was he could not remember now. But Gary would love Mummy much more if she was not still frightened of the man who was not his daddy.

Now there was the lovely place he came to on the big red bus. There were things to do, to play with, to see which made his head nearly burst with joy. So *much*, so very *much*. He was left here with nobody near him except a lady with black hair who left him alone. So he found out about these new, wonderful things – like the little bricks which changed into a bus under his hands. There it was in the picture on the box – and there it was under Gary's hands, real, that he could hold and push and look at. Then he knew he had really seen – and done – magic.

He was in a little paradise that Mummy had found for him by going on a red bus.

Gary knew, though, with all his three-year-old experience of what sad must be, that every paradise had its serpent.

This serpent was golden-haired and no bigger than himself. This serpent took his lovely bus and broke it up into little bricks again and ran away laughing.

Gary watched his foe as fixedly as he watched the man he called Daddy, saying nothing, doing nothing, just watching.

Then he picked up all the little bricks and in a few minutes the bus was magically reconstituted.

Gary now, in the hot, moving cab, knew again what he had known then in his tainted paradise: nothing was permanent, nothing would last. But Gary would put things together again, time and time again, with the patience of a slow-moving lizard in the desert who conserves his energy and grows almost without sustenance.

* * *

When Gary had first seen crayons, felt-tip pens and lots of creamy paper in his new wonderland, he had seen the point of them at once. He made his first mark on paper. Then he made another mark. Two lines which met. Then he made a third. He looked at his bus. Then he drew it. There it was, on a piece of paper, another bus that he had made (Gary was not to know that what he had done, both in drawing and in constructing a far from easy model kit, was quite remarkable for a child of three). The surge of happiness was not like anything he had known before. Even now, twenty years later, Gary still felt it, sharp, something barely known since.

But then came his blond enemy, ripping his drawing into little pieces and running away laughing.

Was that a real memory? Or was the mind, which could be a terrible cheat, making it up for him, to feed his anger? But he did remember what happened next, because it happened many times.

He cried. The lady with black hair came in. She saw the pile of torn paper. She shouted at him. Gary cringed. He could not see what he had done wrong. His foe was not there. Soon the lady, having swept the bits up with a dustpan and brush, went over to another lady who had yellow hair and who was reading to his enemy, who was now very quiet.

So, with his dogged persistence, Gary set about building his bus again and then drawing it. For a long time there was no sound in the playroom except for the yellow-haired lady's reading. Gary worked on.

Then the black-haired lady called out something. Gary did not know what it was. He looked up. The reading had stopped. His enemy had crossed the room to look at what he was doing. Was he going to break it all up again? No. The black-haired lady stood by him. She spoke. Twenty years on, Gary still heard her voice. "Just a minute, Julian."

She bent to the two buses, one built, one drawn. She picked them up and looked at them. Then she looked at Gary, a long, searching look. Then she took his two little triumphs away and put them out of sight, and safe so nobody could get them.

The grown-up Gary could still see this sight, clear and shocking and re-enacted many times.

Other children cried at being deprived of what they had done. Not Gary. If he felt anything, it was that they were safe with the lady: no enemy would tear them up and break them before his eyes.

Only as years passed and he had long spaces of time to dig to the roots of his personal catastrophes did he realize that they might have been taken by a still greater enemy.

Then Mummy came. He sat on the bus looking at the fields and trees outside, snuggled against her, and felt very protected. Then they were home again.

The man he called Daddy was waiting. Gary knew all his mother's happiness dropped off as they entered. Even at not yet four he knew he was in a place of depression and defeat.

But tonight, this daddy person was not sullen. He was happy. He was even nice to Gary. He had packed a big case which stood in the middle of the floor. Mummy made something to eat which was nicer than usual. She made herself look pretty again. She and the man called Daddy went out together. Mrs Pike came in and she and Gary watched the television together until the picture went funny, like it kept on doing. Then Mrs Pike read little stories to him, just like the two ladies in the playroom had read to his enemy.

Then she put him to bed, after an amazing day.

Gary had had years to brood over that first day, to rebuild it from scraps which might have been. Later, when everybody thought he was thick and a criminal and he had tried to find words for what it was really like, he had dredged his brains to sort out what had happened to him to do as he did. This first day was what he kept coming back to, time and time again. At first it seemed beyond the reach of his memory: gradually he put it together again. It might not have been true, but he believed it. He had made wonderful things and felt magic, only for what he had done to be destroyed before his eyes. It was that which started the build-up to his explosive anger.

One undimmed vision about that day was the big suitcase on the floor. Because next day the hateful man called Daddy had gone away.

Next morning, Mummy held his hand as they stood looking out of the window, watching Daddy walk away carrying his big case.

"Daddy's going to be away for a long time to get us a lot of money. And now I'm getting some money as well so everything's going to be *lovely*."

Gary must have asked if he would ever come back.

"Yes, he's coming back one day with lots of money and we'll all be very happy."

Gary would not have been old enough to say, "I'll believe that when I see it."

Even so, the next months spread out for him like a little lifetime in which he was sometimes truly happy. Gary often recalled this time, relived it, like a lost kingdom. Three times a week, Mummy took him in the bus and left him in the magic playroom. Here he explored the marvellous things – the different construction toys, plasticine, Play-doh, jigsaws, toys and animals, crayons, felt-tips – everything his enemy had been given but did not seem to want.

He was used to his enemy breaking and tearing now. He could avoid it. He knew who his enemy was. His name was "Master Julian". Gary thought he was spiteful and nasty. But Master Julian could not spoil things for Gary – and Wanda, the black-haired lady, was always keeping his nice things safe for him. So that was all right.

Now that the daddy-man was out of the way, the flat became a sunny place. Mummy took Gary for bus rides into town where all the big shops were and lots of people bustled round him. Sometimes he felt frightened because there were so many. Sometimes they went to places where there were only fields, trees and hills. She took him for little walks and they had picnics. But sometimes he felt frightened here because it was so lonely and deserted and if Mummy had not been with him he might have run off and hidden and never come out again. Once or twice she took him to the cinema and he saw lovely, coloured cartoon films and he was never frightened even when he was supposed to be because he knew he was only watching in a seat. Mummy got someone round to make the television set right again. Sometimes she read little stories herself instead of Mrs Pike, but Gary never liked them much. They were silly.

She bought him his own felt-tip pens, a colouring book and some plain paper. Some few of the glories of the play-room at Mockbeggar House came home. How he loved it. All the pictures in the colouring book were filled in with patient care, with no colour going over the lines. On the plain paper he drew flowers, trees, cats, dogs and people.

They looked real, not just stick creatures. And cars, trains, planes and ships. And buses. Lots of buses.

Mummy looked at these things and one day, when Gary had been four for a long time and the man called Daddy would soon be home again, she spoke words which he remembered still because he knew now they shaped the great paradox by which he had lived the rest of his life: "You do lovely things, Gary. Why can't you do them when I take you to work and stop upsetting Master Julian? It's only because Wanda is so nice and puts in a good word for you that Julian's mummy lets you stay there. You'll get us both into trouble. Please try to be good, Gary."

He said nothing. This was his first day of insight. He knew without drawing breath that to say, "But I am good, Mummy," would have been quite useless.

One summer day, when Mummy took Gary to the big house, Master Julian was not there, but Wanda, the black-haired lady, was. Master Julian had gone many thousands of miles away, to a lovely place where the sun shone and the sea was blue, where Gary could never go. Gary knew all about the sun but even though he was four, he knew nothing about the sea. Julian's mummy and daddy – whom Gary had never seen: indeed, he had supposed his enemy had no daddy – had taken Julian and the lady called Ingrid, with yellow hair.

So Gary had the paradise to himself. It was perfect. He played on his own, wanting nobody, utterly happy all the time. Black-haired Wanda – though he never called her "Wanda", or anything else for that matter – sat in the playroom ignoring him, reading and writing letters.

She never let him take his pictures or things he made

away with him. Instead, at the end of each day she made him put all the bits back in their boxes. She took all his pictures and put them carefully away in a cupboard.

Four-year-old Gary never wondered why. But Gary in the cab of the truck travelling down a dark motorway knew exactly why.

Master Julian and the man called Daddy came back on the same day. Gary's happy world crumbled at once.

Julian was brown and full of energy and had come back with lots of new toys. Gary wanted to show him what he had done while he was away, but Wanda had taken it all. So he waited empty-handed while Julian burst into the room with Ingrid following. Wanda sat him down and Ingrid said, "Tell Gary about all the things you did when you were on holiday, Julian, please."

And Julian had said, for the very first time, "Shan't. I'm not talking to a nasty oik."

Wanda had said nothing and Gary returned to the Lego, suddenly certain that he would never be allowed to finish anything ever again.

When the man called Daddy arrived, Mummy was happy at first. But, like Julian, this daddy-man had come back from abroad with new things for himself and for Mummy but with nothing for Gary. When Mummy showed him Gary's colouring book and his pictures and all the felt-tip pens, he was not pleased. Instead, he shouted, "I'm not having you spend the money I earn on that little sod. Right?"

Though Gary imagined he was turning the bundled, kaleidoscopic impressions of when he was three, four and five into a connected sequence, he couldn't be sure. So many times, during all the long years, had he turned them over and over in his mind, trying to find the root reason, the ultimate cause for what he did and what happened afterwards, that he feared he might be making a story where none was. But about one thing of which he was certain he had never wavered.

The person who had put him where he was, was that same Master Julian.

In the dark, the notice "Services, 1 mile" loomed up.

"I'm stopping here for a bite before I leave the motorway at the next exit," said the driver. "Do you want something to eat?"

"I don't reckon," said Gary. "Drop me in the lorry park. I'll keep on my way."

Three minutes later, Gary was saying "Ta," swinging himself to the ground and standing in sudden cold in a puddle.

The next lift was harder to come by. He stood with his sheet of cardboard by the exit to the truck drivers' section of the services but no one seemed to be biting. He wondered about trying the car park. But getting a lift from a private motorist these days was almost impossible. Every hitch-hiker was supposed to be a serial killer.

So he left the services altogether and stood under a sodium lamp just where heavy lorries had to pause before coming on to the main slip road. For some time he was still ignored. The big articulated trucks with valuable cargoes swept past him.

But just as he thought his ears would be full of the throb of diesel engines and the scream of fast traffic on the motorway for ever, his luck changed. An older, smaller lorry, belching black fumes, lucky to be still on the road, stopped. He opened the passenger door.

"OK, lad," said the driver, a man in his fifties with a grey, grizzled beard. "I'll take you some of the way. I know what it's like waiting there."

Gary got in, settled back in the worn seat and was soon lost in memory again.

Chapter Three

Two things happened as Gary's fifth year passed. First, Master Julian was often not in the playroom. Gary could not understand this. Only later did he know that Julian was now at the kindergarten more days a week instead of just two, so he could mix all the time with children of his own sort.

Second, Mummy suddenly stopped taking him to Mock-beggar House. She went on her own. Gary had to stay at home with the man called Daddy. Except he didn't want to call him Daddy any more. So he called him nothing. But he thought of him with the name Mummy gave him – Kieran.

Only years later did he find out that this was because Julian's mother would not let him be there and had said that, now Kieran was at home and not working, he should look after him if Chrissy was to keep her job.

Gary's whole life caved in. He was an exile from two lives. Now Kieran was home, there was no more fun with Mummy. She was forever trying to keep him out of Kieran's way. The felt-tip pens disappeared; the stories were no longer read. When Mummy had gone, Kieran would push him into a chair in front of the television and shout, "Just keep quiet, you little sod, and don't bother me."

Often, Kieran would go out, leaving him there. Sometimes Kieran would be back quickly, with the *Sun* and cans of beer. Then Gary was frightened because soon Kieran looked as though he would hit him. But he never did.

Though often, after many cans were emptied, Kieran would squat in front of him, breathe into his face and say, "I hope you die, you little bastard! Don't think I don't know what goes on in that evil head of yours. Don't think I don't know what you did to me and my own kid. 'He's only a baby, he didn't know what he was doing.'" This last in a hideous, high-pitched voice which Gary knew was supposed to mimic his mother. "You knew all right. I don't care if you weren't two yet, you did a murder and you meant to. You killed my baby and your mother can't have any more."

At first, Gary didn't know what he meant. Then he recalled that funny feeling he sometimes had that once he had done something to stop Mummy being frightened of Kieran. Well, that was it. But Mummy was still frightened of him. Kieran was cross so now Gary was frightened of him as well. All Gary could do was not flinch and not say anything, but not saying anything made Kieran crosser than ever so that he had to put his hands firmly in his pockets and swing off outside again, slamming the door and leaving Gary on his own.

But Kieran was always in when Mummy came home and Gary watched them together and made huge efforts of will: *Go away, go away for ever. Leave Mummy and me alone and don't come back.*

Even now, in the night's second cab, Gary felt the anger, fear, frustration, loss, sheer blinding, numbing boredom of these days without Mummy in the flat. Time slowed: the days felt like slices of eternity. But he was learning fast. He was very, very patient: he could sit silent, eyes hardly blinking, like that lizard in the desert who could live without water and who would still be crouched in the land when everything round it was charred stump and white skeleton –

181

but whose tongue could flick out and dart with deadly speed when nobody expected.

"Were you a good boy while I've been away, Gary dear?" Mummy would say when she came in.

He would nod, carefully not speaking. Once Kieran burst out, "He's thick, that boy of yours. He never says a word. He just stares hour after hour and I don't know what he's thinking. He gets on my bloody nerves."

"But Kieran," Mummy said fearfully, "it's what you wanted. You said, 'Shut him up or I'll shut him up for you'."

"Oh, my fault, is it? *I've* made him a bloody zombie? Well, he's nothing to do with me. He takes it from you and his sodding lunatic father."

"You know nothing about his father!" Mummy was shrieking.

"No, and I don't bloody want to. Bad blood. That's what it is. And it shows."

Another time, after Mummy's "Were you a good boy, Gary?" Kieran's answer was, "I couldn't give a toss if he's good or not. I'm out of here. Got a job in Saudi Arabia. Don't worry, I'll send you the money."

At the time, Gary only heard shouting. Only over the years did he reconstruct the connections. But one thing he was quite clear about: Kieran was going away.

Gary felt sudden, secret joy. He had wanted Kieran to go and now he was. Gary was strong after all and could will whatever he wanted.

Master Julian had long holidays, like big boys who went to proper schools. Gary knew that soon he would go to a school himself. He wondered if there would be other Julians there who would be his enemies. Looking back, Gary realized there was something strange about his years before school. He had never been let out on his own. Mummy had no friends outside who had children he could play with. So he had met none but Julian. Without that, he would never have known anyone of his own age at all.

Now, though, things were familiar. Kieran had left, the flat seemed bathed with light and Mummy was nice again. The visits to Mockbeggar House started once more. But now Gary only sometimes went into the playroom. Now he was bigger and Wanda seemed to have so many other things to do. He spent a lot of time with Mummy as she hoovered, dusted in awkward places, pulled sheets off beds and put them in a big washing machine. It was not as nice as before.

Sometimes Mummy took him outside. They crossed lawns, walked past flower beds, pools and trees. On one side, far away, were fences and on the other were buildings called greenhouses and others called stables and sometimes Gary heard horses neighing, which he knew from television. At the very end, when Gary looked back, the house seemed miles away and the garden like a whole world on its own. They reached another house. It was small and made of wood and inside was furnished with chairs and tables made of cane.

"This is the summerhouse," said Mummy. "Mrs Claverhouse wants it all nice and clean again so people can use it."

It was bigger than their maisonette and Gary said, "Can't we live here?"

Mummy sighed. "Wouldn't it be lovely? Just you, me and Daddy."

"No, Mummy," said Gary. "Just you and me."

Mummy didn't answer but got on with her work.

Wanda was nice. She gave Gary picture books of Julian's to look at while Mummy was working in places he could not go. But then Julian's mummy, whom Gary had hardly ever seen, came through and noticed him with them. She called Wanda.

"Are those books ours?"

"Yes, ma'am."

"Take them off him, please, and put them back where they belong. You know how destructive he is."

"Yes, ma'am."

Wanda took the books away. He did not know then what "destructive" meant, but he missed the lovely pictures.

That day, Julian was back. He saw Gary but pretended not to.

"Aren't you going to say hello to Gary, Julian?" said Wanda.

Julian looked at him as if for the very first time, studiedly up and down.

"No, Nanny," he said in his clear voice which Gary, sitting in the old lorry butting through the night, could still hear as if next to him, "I won't. I mustn't speak to people like him because he is scum."

He walked away like a young gentleman five times his age.

"Master Julian, that's not very nice," said Wanda. "Come back and apologize, please."

Julian took no notice.

When they got home, Gary asked Mummy what "destructive" meant. When she told him, he puzzled over how it could apply to him. When she asked why he wanted to know and he told her, tears started out of her eyes.

All these happenings stuck in his mind, like evidence.

School was noisy, shrieking, and he could not cope with it. Where had all these children come from? He drew himself into a corner and became more like an invisible lizard in the desert than ever before.

The room he was in was full of things he wanted to touch, shape, draw with. It was nearly as nice as the playroom at Mockbeggar House. But there was not one potential enemy here – there were twenty. They milled uncontrollably, threateningly, round him. If, before, one person had torn up everything he did, what was the point of trying if twenty were here to do it?

Mummy was outside the school gates every day to meet him (afterwards he found out that her hours had been adjusted).

"What was it like today, Gary?" she always asked. "Have you made any friends? What did you do in school?"

Gary could never answer any of these questions.

One day, as they walked home surrounded by other children, noisy and jubilant, and their mothers, Chrissy burst into tears.

"Gary, why won't you *speak* to me? Surely Kieran isn't right about you after all?"

Perhaps Kieran was. For all the dead years between then and now, Gary had tried to recall exactly his state. There seemed a sort of glass wall between him and everybody else which he could not break through. He wanted to join in with the other children but something stopped him. He wanted to talk to the lady who was called the teacher but, however nice she tried to be, he only rarely managed this. He would have tried to write or read or draw for her if he was sure nobody could come near and see or hear him. But with these scavenging, marauding invaders close, he could do nothing.

The lorry chugged on at a steady forty miles an hour in the inside lane. Everything overtook it. The driver never tried to make conversation. The radio blared, the motor shrieked. But even through the noise and heat, Gary's thoughts were staying clear.

Mummy wasn't saying much to him herself now. She wasn't as nice as she used to be. He wanted to say, "Love me, still, please, Mummy. I can't help being quiet and I don't want to be. I want someone to help me."

But nobody ever offered, not even Mummy.

He knew with terrible certainty what it would be like when Kieran came home.

"Told you, didn't I? Get rid of him. Let someone else take him on. I'm pissed off with it all."

Gary saw his angry face, felt the force in his body. The hitting was not far away now.

Kieran bought a car, an old Austin Allegro, rusting but still able to go. It meant that on some days at least, Mummy might not have to catch the bus to Mockbeggar House. Kieran often took her there and met her when she finished. At first he did it with bad grace, then he seemed to look forward to it. Sometimes in the school holidays he left Gary at home either with the now frail Mrs Pike or on his own. But Mummy was cross then. So sometimes Gary sat in the back seat.

It was odd going to Mockbeggar House in a car, driving in at the side entrance instead of walking through, and sitting waiting outside the back door Mummy always went through rather than going in with her. It made Gary sad to be so near. At first, Kieran never got out of the car; when they arrived he just grunted "Goodbye", and accepted a kiss on the cheek as if it were his due; when they left, he moved off the moment Mummy had shut the door.

One morning, the car would not start. Mummy was very agitated. Kieran put the bonnet up and fiddled, then tried again. Shakily, the engine fired. They were ten minutes late.

When they arrived, a black-haired lady was waiting outside, looking cross. Gary's heart leapt. It was Wanda. Perhaps she was waiting for him, to say "We've missed you, Gary" and take him to the playroom again. He waved to her.

She never saw him. But Kieran saw her. He jumped out and spoke to her, smiling and earnest. Wanda's face softened. They seemed to have a lot to say for people who had never seen each other before.

After that, Kieran always got out of the car. Quite often, especially in the evening, Wanda was waiting outside as they arrived much earlier than they needed to. She and Kieran would talk and laugh together. This was funny to Gary. He had never seen Kieran laugh while he was talking to Mummy.

Gary always hoped that Kieran was telling her what a nice, quiet boy he was and how he missed the playroom. What else could he be talking about?

Wanda always went back into the house before Mummy appeared and Kieran was his sulky self again straight away. How Gary wanted him to laugh like he did with Wanda. But no. Not ever.

He wondered about it then and he wondered again in the old swaying cab, just as he had for the years and years between. The same thought always came: *I can't believe it. But it must be true.*

Soon after Kieran and Wanda had started talking to each other, Gary's peace at home was broken for ever. He was used to silence. Only Mummy talked to him and when he didn't answer, she cried and walked away. How he longed to call after her, "Mummy don't cry! I want to talk. I love you." But he couldn't. Something stopped him, though he thought the words – just as at school something was still stopping him saying all the words on the pages of the little books the teacher tried to make him read to her, although he knew perfectly well what they were. Oh, he *wanted* to, but he couldn't, and he watched helplessly as the teacher's patience cracked. His mind was full of old things he had once made and drawn and seen destroyed before his eyes and he was too afraid to risk it again.

But alone with Kieran, even if he could speak, he wouldn't. After he first saw Wanda, Kieran began talking more when Mummy wasn't there. He would start as they drove home from Mockbeggar House. Kieran's happy mood vanished the moment he returned to the car. Gary would be on the back seat, hunching himself into a corner. Kieran's resentful voice soared over the noise of the engine. He seemed to need to complain about his lot and only Gary was there to listen.

"Keep your nasty eyes off me, you little bugger! I know what you're thinking. Evil little sod!"

Gary pushed himself even further into the corner.

They reached home, got out of the car. Kieran pushed him upstairs and through the door.

"Get in there. What's happened to me, trapped here with your idiot mother and lumbered with a dummy like you? You'd get on anybody's bloody nerves, you would."

Gary looked at him, paralysed with fright.

"Say something, can't you? I don't care what. I know you're not bloody dumb. So *speak*, for Christ's sake!"

Gary stared at him, transfixed with fright.

"I'll *make* you speak, you little bastard."

He drew back his right hand and brought the flat of it hard on the side of Gary's face. Gary staggered backwards.

"Now *speak*!"

Gary stayed silent.

"*SPEAK*, I said."

The left hand came hard on the other side.

"Next time it's fists."

Gary had fallen in a heap on the floor.

"*SPEAK!*"

Still silence.

Kieran drew back, panting.

"Why don't you ever bloody cry? You're unnatural. Son of a madman. Yes, and a madwoman as well."

Gary made himself stand up. He faced Kieran and looked straight at the red face, angry, bloodshot eyes and working mouth. He was not brave. It was just that he *couldn't cry*.

"*I'll make you sodding cry.*"

Now Kieran bunched his fist. The blow caught Gary in the chest. The shock winded him; pain shot through his ribs. Once again he fell backwards. His spine hit the wall and he was dazed, head spinning, half-lying, half-sitting against the skirting board.

He opened his eyes and looked up at Kieran.

"Oh, sod you!" Kieran said and strode out, slamming the door.

Gary heard the car start. He would be alone till Mummy came.

* * *

The driver turned the radio down and shouted to Gary.

"I'm going all the way up the motorway. You'll want the next exit. I'll take you off it and drop you on the slip road. I can get on the motorway again over the roundabout, no trouble."

Gary nodded.

Three minutes later he was clambering down on to the ground and watching the lorry lumber off. Light rain fell; he was cold and he had to scrabble in his backpack for something to slip over his shoulders. The sky was well lightened in the east. Day was here and the last lap of his journey had started.

Chapter Four

Seven miles to go. Get off the big main road into town. Take the B road which goes past the estate. No point in trying for a lift before the turning. Walk half a mile and then try.

Made it. Wet and miserable. Too tired to walk any more. Just wait here in the rain. Something will stop.

The memories now were very clear. Gary no longer felt he had to try to piece a patchwork into a story. He never went inside Mockbeggar House again. With most children, the house would just be a fading memory. For Gary, as his sixth and seventh birthdays passed, it stood like a lump in his mind, mocking him. A great pleasure dome where true happiness could only be found – yet also an enemy fortress, the evil wizard's castle; a magical place of chambers and gardens of delight but also a terrible region of dungeons and torture. Mockbeggar House, always there, solid and immovable, stuck in his head like a great dam.

Kieran had not hit Gary again. The lumps and bruises had healed before school began and no teacher would report suspicions to social workers. Kieran had made sure he never came near Gary. Mrs Pike was entrusted with him when Mummy was at work. But she was old now, and wandery, and Mummy was frightened to let her into the maisonette. Soon it had to stop. Kieran shut him in the bedroom when he was at home. If he went out he let Gary into the living room and kitchen but locked the front door behind him. So Gary spent whole days as a prisoner.

It was while he was alone that Gary began to look carefully at the matches as first inklings entered his head. If he were to light one and hold it to the curtains in the living room, wouldn't Kieran be angry? Yes, but wouldn't Mummy be sad? Regretfully he put them back.

Gary knew the teachers were worried about him. Each school day passed like a great panorama which he watched but hardly took part in. Yes, in the end he had made himself read to the teacher, because he knew he should and things might be bad if he didn't. Yes, he did, unwillingly, copy the big letters on the board and join them up and write as much as he had to. And, yes, he could do the counting and work with numbers and shapes and write it down even if he did not say anything. He realized that if he wanted to remain a spectator and not take a central part, he would have to. He had long ago realized that as long as he was allowed to keep it all to himself, most of the things they wanted him to do at school were so *easy*.

But make it so that the children round him could be treacherous destroyers, invading him like his enemy at Mockbeggar House, was something he would *not* do.

Oh, they tried. They laughed at him, goaded him, called him "dummy" and "dickhead", hit and kicked him. But he was so good at taking no notice and looking at them with a contemptuous lack of interest that they always tired of it and left him alone.

Gary knew the teachers tried to tell Mummy. She would hug him sometimes and say, "Gary, *why* won't you talk at school? The headteacher says I ought to take you to a doctor. They keep asking if there's anything wrong at home. There isn't, is there, Gary? Not now? Kieran didn't hit you again, did he? You haven't told anyone, have you?" She looked at his unmoving face and said, "No, of course you haven't."

She went on.

"They keep saying they'll refer you to someone very high up to give you tests to see if you're all right. You don't want that, do you, Gary? Say you don't, love?"

Gary kept looking at her. He still said nothing, but shook his head.

"That's all right then, Gary. If you hadn't shown you could do all your reading and writing and maths as good as anyone else, they would do. And I *know* you're a clever boy, Gary. I *know* you're not nasty and destructive like people say."

Which people said he was? Gary did not understand this. He wished suddenly he could say, "No, I'm not. Who says I am?"

But, as the message from his brain reached his vocal cords, the door slammed shut and he said nothing.

For half an hour, Gary had stood in steady drizzle by the roadside. His cardboard sign was limp and smudged. Traffic was sparse here. The morning rush hour into town hadn't built up. The feeling of travellers bonded together which had seen him all right on the motorways had gone. What was the time? Nearly seven. He had been on the road for five hours and had covered about a hundred and twenty miles. Not bad. Pity to stick over the last five.

Though there was no pavement, he walked on the left, with the traffic, instead of facing it as he should, because he wouldn't give up hope of a lift. As he walked, his mind still dwelt on the childhood story which had determined what he was and what he would be.

Kieran. How he hated Kieran. How he wished Kieran would go away and leave Mummy and him alone. Kieran had hit him only once. Afterwards, when she had seen the bruises, Mummy had cried and punched with her fists on Kieran's chest, but he had caught her by the wrists, thrown her back and shouted.

"Don't worry. I won't touch him again. He's not worth doing bird for. Neither are you."

Then, he had swung off out and was gone until the next evening.

After that, Kieran had been less in the house. Gary knew he wasn't going to Germany or Saudi Arabia because one night Mummy was crying and gasping words in between the sobs: "I wish you were away and all I saw of you was money sent home," and Kieran had answered: "What makes you think *you're* going to get my money any more?"

Then one day the shouting shook the maisonette. Mummy was crying so much it sounded like laughing. She tried to punch Kieran again. Kieran had packed his big suitcase, but he'd not said anything about going to work again.

No. But he was roaring at Mummy. "I've *had* it with you and your evil little bastard. I've been a sodding *saint* to stay this long. There's *nothing* for me here any more. You can't give me *anything*. I don't *want* you. I'm *out* of here. I'm off where there's a *welcome* for me."

Gary cowered in a corner, out of the way, where Kieran wouldn't notice him. Kieran going? This was too wonderful to be believed. When the shouting stopped, they'd be on their own again. Wouldn't Mummy be pleased?

But no. She clung to Kieran, screaming. He pushed his suitcase out of the front door, turned and shoved her away so she staggered backwards across the room against the opposite wall.

"*Fuck off!*" he hissed, quietly but worse than the shouting.

The door slammed on Kieran for ever. Gary heard him outside sawing away at the Allegro's starter, which made great retching noises and then was silent. Gary thought the car would never start again and Kieran would never leave. But it fired, roared, then quietened as Kieran drove jerkily away.

Kieran had gone but Mummy was not pleased. No, she threw herself on a chair, leant her head on the arm and pummelled with her fists on the seat and cried and cried. Gary, watching dispassionately, went towards her, touched her on the shoulder. She looked at him with a ravaged, tear-stained face, then pushed him away so he staggered backwards and hit the wall just like Kieran had done to her a little while before.

"It's all your fault," she gulped and resumed her crying.

Gary crept away to let the storm blow itself out.

Mummy didn't go to Mockbeggar House any more after that.

He must have been walking for half an hour. Daylight was here. So was the traffic. He did not have long to wait now.

A white Ford Transit van drew to a halt. He saw the sign on the side: EVANS ELECTRICAL CONTRACTORS. Gary rushed up and slid the door open. There was plenty of room in the front for the driver, his mate and Gary.

"We're going right past it," said the driver when he mentioned the name of the estate. "As long as you don't mind a little detour: we've got to pick someone else up."

Gary sat back in more comfort than for the whole of the journey so far. Who cared about the detour? Suddenly, he wished the journey would last for ever. For almost the first time since he had left the squat, he said to himself: "*Why am I going to a place where nobody lives any more?*"

The two tried conversation with him: how far had he come? Was he looking for a job, because there were none here?

Soon they left off. Gary's short answers showed he didn't want to talk. His private saga had to be got through before he reached what was once his home.

Gary was seven now. Life with Kieran gone, never to be heard of again, saw him turn in on himself completely. Mummy didn't care about him any more – or anything or anybody. She didn't work, she only got money when she went to the Post Office with her book, she smoked sixty a day, there was hardly anything to eat and the maisonette got dirtier and dirtier.

People from the Social Services kept coming round. Gary looked forward to them: only then was the place a bit cleaner and he had something slightly nicer to eat. Most of the time he was on his own, with no parents, no friends, nothing to do but live with his thoughts.

Sitting now in the van, Gary knew this had been a very important time. He did not know it, but it was a preparation for the rest of his life.

He spent hour upon hour motionless, like the unblinking lizard in the desert he could become whenever he wanted to.

The questions rolled round his mind and the answers he came to determined everything. *Once I did lovely things which made me joyful, made me happy with a searing pleasure I can remember like it was now but which I can't have any more. Why can't I do these things now? What stops me? Who stops me?*

Once I had a mummy and a man I called Daddy. He's gone. Good riddance. Is it all his fault? No, it isn't and he's gone anyway.

So is it Mummy's fault? No, it isn't. It's Kieran's fault Mummy isn't like a mummy any more. But Kieran never threw me out of paradise. Kieran never knew I was in it, and if he did he wouldn't care.

So who threw me out? There was a lady called Wanda. Sometimes she was nasty to me. Sometimes she was nice. She never threw me out. There was a yellow-haired girl called Ingrid. She wouldn't throw me out. There was another mummy there. I hardly ever saw her. How could she throw me out?

So who was it?

The same answer kept coming. The little golden-haired serpent who laughed and destroyed and spoke words which curled and shrivelled his soul inside him.

Yes, that first stinging shape that ruined all he did: that grew and was bloated, detestable, hateful in his mind and was called Master Julian. It was *he* who had Gary thrown out of paradise. It was *he* who stunted him and thwarted him and brought him to where he was.

Gary now, in the Fort Transit, knew well that little seven-year-old Gary brooding in squalor had inside his head a fifteen-year-old brain which could give clear shape to all these musings. And now, on his way guiltily late to wherever his mother lay dead, he almost cried aloud for the waste of it all.

For he knew that the moment Kieran left, the obsessions started. Who ruined the few glimpses he ever got of a lovelier, more expansive life? Who stamped on his fingers every time he tried to scramble over the lip of the precipice to the level, green ground? From the red Lego bus onwards, who was the only cause of all his misery? Gary's brain ached, his fingers itched at what he *could* have done. Frustration settled on him like a high spring tide, drowning his mind.

But the tide had gone out, leaving him clear and purposeful. He was destructive, everyone said so. Well, now he would be. He remembered the matches, he remembered how easy it would have been to set the curtains alight and how *wonderful* to watch the orange flame, feel the sudden sharp heat, know the solid object was consumed.

Gary seldom dreamt. But now he started to dream every night. He dreamt of fire. Yellow flames reached into the sky, consuming, scouring, leaving dirty places clean of all but elemental ash. He woke after such dreams feeling intensely satisfied.

He never thought of setting light to the flat. That would be trivial: the few miserable flames he could make, whether of curtain or furniture, would mock his dreams.

No, if these dreams were to come true, they must come true completely.

He had the dreams several times before he connected them with Julian.

One night the dream was slightly different. Before, the fire had left pure and scoured the remains of he knew not what. This night the fire was not just *burning*, it was burning *something*. Even in his sleep he felt sudden excitement. What was it burning?

Two dreams later, he knew. The fire was not burning *something* but *someone*. Not Mummy, not Wanda, not even Kieran. It burnt Master Julian. Blurred, then clearer, Gary saw the golden hair catch light and flare, blue eyes pop, nose and mouth fall in, face dissolve.

The first time he dreamt this, he woke more elated than he could remember. Oh, if only...

Soon the dream was so regular he could not imagine sleep – deep sleep, no surface dozing – without it.

Fire engines sometimes came into the estate. Nothing spectacular: chip pans in flames, bonfires out of control, paraffin heaters falling over and catching light. Chrissy had acquired a couple of old paraffin heaters years before: they provided most of the warmth. The smell and drowsy atmosphere they made was part of winter life to Gary. There had never been an accident with them, though.

One night there was a serious fire in another house. Gary saw it from the window. Flames burst through an upstairs window nearly opposite: there was a sort of crumping roar. The smoke made black, drifting fog. Gary heard screams. Two people with fire coming out of their backs jumped from the burning windows and lay very still on the ground. Three fire engines arrived. The sirens, lights, ladders, hoses, water, foam, scurrying people who all seemed to know what they were doing, were intensely exciting. Gary's heart lifted in a way he had never known before except when something new, model or painting, used to grow under his fingers.

Helmeted firefighters put ladders up to the window,

disappeared into the smoke. They emerged carrying black objects the size of small children. Crowds had come from all the houses to watch: Gary heard a collective sigh as the objects were laid on the ground, people in green overalls ran from the ambulances and then the objects were covered in blankets.

Next morning, he knew that a whole family – mother, father, two toddlers and a baby – had died. A cigarette left on a chair had caused the blaze and the killing fumes. Although he lived so near, Gary did not know the people. He felt no shock, no sorrow, just deep awe at fire's power and excitement at what it caused. For a few days, the real thing made his dreams disappear. But they came back eventually – this time with a thought: *I can do it.*

Nights passed and thoughts changed – from *I can* to *I will.*

Chapter Five

Gary hadn't noticed where the detour had taken them. They had gone out to a village where a third man waited who was quite happy to scramble in through the rear doors and sit in the back amidst the tools.

But now the Ford Transit passed through country that was familiar. He had a strange feeling he was in a time-warp. He was all attention.

On the right was a brick wall. Over it, trees showed. Behind the wall, he knew, were extensive grounds, beautiful gardens, a huge, imposing residence. How strange that the timing of his thoughts had brought him to the very place where the great finale of his first life had been. For behind those walls was Mockbeggar House.

"You OK?" said the driver's mate. "You look a bit peaky."

"Fine," said Gary.

Little Gary had resolved: *he would do it.* He would burn down Mockbeggar House with Julian inside it. He would watch the flames leap up, see the wreathing, poisonous, black choking fog, hear screams, see Julian brought out – a shapeless object laid on the ground and covered up. He would feel the joy of six hundred Lego buses built at once. His scourge would be gone for ever. First Kieran, now Julian. Life would be wonderful at last for him and Mummy.

How? Matches, paraffin to make the fire spread, seat

covers which made fumes which killed even before the flames consumed.

He would choose a nice night with no rain. He would pour paraffin out of the can into a lemonade bottle, so nobody would know it was gone. He would take matches and money out of Mummy's purse. She wouldn't mind when she knew why he was doing this. But he mustn't *tell* her, not yet. Then he would catch a bus to Mockbeggar House, steal unnoticed inside, do his worst and creep out before anyone knew he had left them inside a blazing coffin.

One hot afternoon in July, when he thought Julian should be home from school, he decided that night would be the one. He waited in a silent ferment. Mummy went to bed early nowadays, with five aspirin to help her. When she was breathing deeply he had to work fast.

He wished the glug-glug of winter's leftover paraffin coming out of the can into the bottle weren't so loud. He wished the box of matches didn't rattle like dead bones in the wind. He wished he did not have to push squeaky drawers to find the spare key he needed.

But he did all these things unheard and soon, clutching his cargo in an old plastic shopping bag, was waiting at the bus stop.

Twenty minutes later, he got off at the turn for the lane where the main entrance was to Mockbeggar House. He walked past silent hedges on one side, the worn brick wall on the other. He reached the big iron gates, open on to the wide drive. The floodlit shape of the house was etched against the deep blue of clear sky in late dusk. The smooth front lawn was bathed in white light. Sleek cars were parked on the drive in front of the house.

His nerve failed. How could little Gary Brady get into

that lighted fortress and, once inside, fight to bring down the entire hated Claverhouse family? He crouched up against a brick pillar and cried with frustration and defeat.

What could he do? Go home, tail between his legs, and forget about it? He'd have to.

He picked up the plastic bag, in which the paraffin sloshed in the lemonade bottle, and trailed back to the lane and to the bus stop. It had been so easy in his thoughts, so impossible really.

He walked to the end of the road. The bus stop stood on the other side.

He stopped. Why was he giving up? He could do *something*, surely?

He racked his brains. Then he remembered: the summerhouse. Like a little wooden cottage on its own, where he and Mummy could have stayed if the Claverhouses had been nice.

But they weren't nice and the summerhouse would be easy to fire – all that dry wood, all that cane furniture.

And, who knows? Master Julian might *just* be sleeping there, as a summer treat.

He ran along the brick wall, looking for a place where he could climb over.

He had sat astride the wall, unseen by firemen and watchers, full of elation even greater than when he saw the house on fire from his window. *He* had done this. And he could do better. Next time he *would* get into Mockbeggar House; now he remembered the difficulty, he would work out how properly. Tonight had been just a first go.

Time to be off. He slipped lightly to the ground and started walking. No bus: his eight-year-old legs felt as though they would carry him as far as China, no trouble, not just to the miserable estate.

So, what next? A few practice goes: out most nights to see how things burned and how you got at them and into them unseen? Yes, that was it. A careful preparation for the final assault on Mockbeggar House. Night after night he would choose a new target – small at first, gradually bigger. And he would take money from the purse for his own paraffin and matches.

A week later, from the shelter of a hedge, as he watched a toolshed on the allotments flare and felt his own soul flare with it, a strong hand clamped suddenly on his shoulder.

"Got you!" said the policeman. "Before you burn the whole town down, you little bugger."

The Transit van was on the outskirts of Wycombe. Gary startled himself into attention, still in the time-warp. He was staring out at his childhood.

To the right was the road into the estate. Time to stop.

"Drop me here," he said. "And ta very much."

He watched the van dwindle away to whatever job the three were doing and then looked round. Except for a pedestrian crossing with lights nearby he could detect no change over the years. He crossed the road protected by the little green man and stared at the shabby houses, some boarded up, graffiti-laden garage doors and worn grass.

His mother would never walk that way again. And suddenly he felt shame, hot tears, for all he had done, all the pain he had caused her.

He couldn't go any further yet. He had to prepare himself before he went to that empty, misery-laden maisonette.

After six hours on the road, he had no idea what he had come for.

On the edge of the estate was a greasy spoon café. He entered it, unbelievably hungry, and bought a mug of tea and a bacon sandwich. He looked round. Every person at the tables and behind the counters was a complete stranger.

Chrissy's face, worn and weary, lived suddenly with shattering clarity in his mind. She had not known where he was these last few years. He'd meant to visit her, to say, "Look, Mum, I'll be all right. I've got things to do, things to give. I'll *make* it. And when I have, I'll be back." But he never had. What if that rat, the man he hated, had come back? Even as he thought, Gary's hand strayed to his knife. No, surely he'd not be around. Perhaps that was why she had topped herself.

He finished his tea and bacon sandwich and sat for a while. Then he got up and finished his journey.

Here it was, the desolate building holding two maisonettes, surrounded by scrubby grass and broken rubbish. What should he do now?

He walked up concrete steps to a nearly paintless front door and knocked at it.

No answer. But from behind the door of where the Pikes once lived came the scrabble of chains and locks. It opened a couple of centimetres and a woman's voice said, "Yes?"

"I'm Gary Brady."

"Too late. She's dead. The funeral's today. Half-past ten in the crematorium."

The door closed again.

Three minutes before ten-thirty, Gary stood alone at the

back of the small, draughty chapel. A bus had dropped him at the entrance; he had waited for a funeral full of weeping strangers to clear away before he entered the building to get out of the thin drizzle which had set in for the day. He waited in silence.

A clock outside thinly struck the half-hour. Faint recorded organ music started. A lugubrious male voice sounded from outside – "Man that is born of woman hath but a short time to live..." The coffin, two small wreaths on top, was wheeled in on a trolley by a black-suited man followed by a surpliced minister still chanting the funeral service.

There were three people in the short procession. The third was a woman in a dark grey coat. From the rear, the blackest, most funereal thing about her was her hair: unnaturally black, newly dyed. As she moved into a pew at the front, she turned.

Even after so many years, Gary knew her at once. It was Wanda Gates.

Eleven-thirty. The ceremony was over. Chrissy Brady had taken her last journey through the curtains to the hidden furnaces. Gary had looked at the two wreaths before the undertaker took them away. He had cursed himself for forgetting even to pick a few flowers. There were two cards on the wreaths. One said *From your friend Wanda*. The other, to his amazement and anger, bore the inscription *With deepest sympathy, Georgina Claverhouse*.

Wanda and Gary, still reeling from yet another confrontation from the past, sat in a pub opposite the cemetery, Gary with a small lager, Wanda clutching what looked to be the first of many gin and tonics of the day.

"Well, you came, Gary," she said. "Too late, but you came."

"I don't know why," said Gary. "Nobody knew where I was."

"Didn't they?" said Wanda knowingly.

"Who could have left me the message?"

"Perhaps there were some who didn't want you to disappear."

"What does that mean?"

"You dropped out of sight after you were let loose again into the world. Your mother was grief-stricken. She thought she'd see you again. Well, you came. But then you went again. You seemed to have gone for ever. Then you were recognized, busking."

"Who by?"

"A friend. It doesn't matter."

"A friend of my mother's?" This puzzled Gary.

"A friend of *mine*, Gary. Your mother had no friends. Except me."

Gary ignored the last sentence.

"Where's my—" He suddenly didn't know whether to say "father", "stepfather" or "Kieran". None would fit on his tongue. He wanted to say "that bastard" but remembered those days at Mockbeggar House – Kieran in the Allegro, a young Wanda talking, smiling, giggling – and didn't want to antagonize her just when he might need her most. So he finished the question with " – he?"

"That bastard?" She had said it for him, with real rage. "Gone. In his own coffin now."

Gary did not ask further. There was something more urgent to find out.

"But how could *you* be my mother's friend?"

"Life plays strange tricks, Gary," she said. "No one should know that more than you."

True. He'd been victim of so many. Now, almost for the first time since he had read the note in the squat, he remembered the most ironic – that the news had come just as he was planning how to see Claverhouse's woman (if they were still together: how come he'd not considered that possibility?) on his own terms and in circumstances of his own choosing, to gain the advantage over Claverhouse himself. And the shock had pushed the most important thing in his whole life right out of his mind.

But of that he said nothing.

"Mum really topped herself, did she?"

"Gary, you know *nothing*. There's been a post-mortem, inquest, everything. And a week to track you down. I got the funeral delayed while we looked for you."

"You're right. I do know nothing. And I still don't know what *you're* doing here."

"Gary, listen to me, will you? I'll open your eyes."

So Gary listened. By the time she had finished he was even more certain that he had to find Claverhouse's woman and get to Claverhouse himself.

Part Five

Reckoning

Chapter One

The Amazing Artistico stood up straight and looked Julian full in the face.

"Yes, of course I bloody know you," he said. "But I won't speak to you. You're not worth the effort. You're scum."

Grizelda was expecting rage, a contemptuous verbal lashing from Julian before he stalked angrily out of the door and slammed it behind him. But nothing like that happened. He went pale – something Grizelda, usually worried by his high colour, had never seen before.

There was silence. Faintly through the door came the sounds of Townswomen from the Guild laughing as they cleared up their buffet of all nations. The Amazing Artistico still glared fiercely, unafraid, at Julian. Against all probability, he had the upper hand. Grizelda felt she was watching a taut tableau stretched beyond reason: an explosion was imminent. Well, why shouldn't these two, locked together in ways she could not yet understand, settle it now? But it was too soon. She knew things must run their course. So she spoke, to break the tension.

"I don't think that's fair, Gary," she said. "Julian hasn't seen you since you were both little boys."

The Amazing Artistico turned on her.

"He tells you everything, does he? Who says he's got to see me for me to see him?"

Grizelda changed the subject.

"Is it coincidence that we've all met tonight?"

The Amazing Artistico almost spat at her.

"You lot think people like me are thick, don't you?" Grizelda squashed the urge to say "Of course we don't"; she daren't be patronizing. "Not only have I seen him, I've seen you two together." He forestalled Grizelda's obvious question. "Doesn't matter when or where. No, tonight isn't coincidence. Remember Darlene at the Jolly Angler?" How could Grizelda forget? "She told me about this date here that she'd rather do without – she's beyond peanuts like this. She told me where and who was organizing it. Then you gave me your card with your ma's address and number on. I recognized it from what Darlene said so I rang her to ask if I could do the gig instead. She was chuffed to get out of it. I rang your mother and that was it. I'm here and Darlene's not."

"Putting on your famous agent-imitation again?"

For the first time, the Amazing Artistico allowed himself a half-smile. "Reg has been talking to you, has he?"

"Why not just get me in London if you wanted to talk?"

"And see *him* on his own ground?"

"But he's here now. You couldn't have known that."

"Oh, wouldn't it scare you if I did. 'He's psychic,' you'd say. 'He's got sixth sense.'" The Amazing Artistico was savagely sarcastic. "No, I never thought I'd hit the jackpot like this, with him at a disadvantage. I just wanted to keep in touch. Your mother was a good start."

Grizelda forgot Julian. Quentin and her job were coming first.

"You mean you *will* do the programme?" she said.

"It's not you I'm bothered about," said the Amazing Artistico. "It's *him*."

"What does that mean?" said Grizelda.

"I'll talk to you. But I don't want *him* anywhere near."

Grizelda looked at Julian. She half expected him to say something oafish, like "Talk to that oik on your own and it's over between us."

But he said nothing. There was a look in his eyes she had never seen before. Could it possibly be *pain*? Not for the first time Grizelda marvelled at the change in him since she had first seen Gary as Tommy Trefoil.

Well, if Julian's not to be there, then so be it, she thought.

"Not now," she said. "How about tomorrow morning? Where are you staying?"

"B&B," was the short reply.

"Is there a pub where we could meet?"

"Always pubs," said the Amazing Artistico. "That's what I mean to you, isn't it?"

"There's no room in my mother's house. And we need neutral ground."

"The Cross Keys in the High Street," said the Amazing Artistico. "I passed it coming here. It looks quiet enough."

"Eleven-thirty?"

"Don't bring *him* with you."

It sounded like a threat.

"Don't you mind?" Grizelda said in the car.

Julian didn't answer.

"Say *something*. Even if it's 'You disloyal bitch. Get out of my life.' You've not spoken since he called you 'scum'."

Still no answer. Grizelda waited. Then, hesitantly, in a way she had never heard before, "He haunts me, you know. He's right. We have seen each other."

"When?"

"He was in the Union gallery the night of the education debate. He stared at me all the time with gorgon eyes. It's a wonder I could carry on."

"You knew him then?" Grizelda said. "After all those years?"

"No, it was the eyes, the hatred in them, that got me. It only clicked who he was years later, after we'd been home and talked to Mother."

Grizelda gasped.

"That's when he saw *me*. And I saw him. He was following us down St Giles. I remember now. But I didn't connect that with the Jolly Angler or tonight."

Julian drove on saying nothing.

"Julian, I'm not being disloyal, am I? I need to follow this up. It's my job. This programme could be big for me."

Again, no answer.

She tried again.

"There must be something deep in your mind which you're unconsciously covering up."

At last, Julian spoke. "Thanks a bunch."

"Look, I'll scrap all this if it's going to upset you."

Julian still said nothing. His mouth was working: Grizelda knew he was travelling in what must be for him uncharted territory indeed – a mental struggle. As they approached Wendy's house and he slowed to park outside, he spoke at last.

"No, go ahead. The more you find out, the easier the ghost will be laid to rest. Besides, I want to know what happened to him."

Inside the house, Wendy was high on the evening's success.

"The Amazing Artistico's *wonderful!* I'll book him again."

"If you can find him," said Grizelda.

Julian had turned away from her the moment they were in bed. He said little but polite pleasantries to Wendy at breakfast. Nothing was said to Wendy about their plans: when they went out at eleven, she was meant to think they were having lunch together. She merely looked slightly pained that they weren't taking her. Before he and Grizelda parted outside the Cross Keys, Julian said, "I'll be outside here at two on the dot. But I won't expect to see *him*."

"Fair enough," said Grizelda.

Before she entered she turned and watched Julian drive away. Then she stood for a moment preparing herself. She was here to find out what had brought Gary to the point where he was now. She was not here to find out why Julian was *scum*. Not now, anyway.

Her quarry sat in the public bar with a small, half-finished glass of lager. He wore the black singlet with flame and lightning motif that she had first seen in the shopping centre. He was definitely Gary now: not Tommy Trefoil or the Amazing Artistico. She bought herself a St Clements and he accepted her offer of another lager – this time a pint.

He came straight to the point.

"How did you know Claverhouse and I knew each other when we were little?"

"Julian knew you at once."

"Good memory, then." Gary smiled with what seemed to Grizelda deep satisfaction. "Why should he tell you?"

So Grizelda, quite happy to start by being interviewed herself, told him about Georgina's letter, Julian's sudden wish to go there and the revelation about Gary and the burned summerhouse.

"So you know about the fire-raising?" said Gary.

"I know as much as Julian's mother knows."

Gary nodded as if he expected as much.

"Why?" Grizelda said. "You don't seem criminal or schizophrenic to me. You're creative. You *do* things: you don't destroy them."

"Oh, you've noticed, then."

"Don't be sarcastic with me, please, Gary. I'm worth more than that."

"I'm sorry." Gary spoke with what seemed remarkably good grace. "Who knows why? I had all these doctors and psychologists trying to find out why. They never did, so why should you?"

"But *you* know why, don't you, Gary?"

"Perhaps I do. Perhaps you'll find out."

"I think I know already."

"Don't tell me what you think."

There was silence for a moment. The bar was filling up. Talk might soon become difficult.

"The police picked you up, didn't they? After you'd set light to some more places?"

Gary grinned.

"So everyone thought you were a compulsive arsonist. Were you? Would you still do it?"

Gary's grin widened. "Try me," he said.

"Don't play games, Gary, please."

"OK. That's what everyone thought – that I couldn't help it. Nobody cottoned on to the real reason I kept on after the first. And I wasn't going to tell them.

"What was the real reason?"

Gary leaned forward conspiratorially and whispered, "I was in training."

"I asked you not to play games with me, Gary."

"But I was. I was training for the big one."

What did he mean? Or was he just having her on? There was a smile playing on his lips, but he was serious. Something told Grizelda not to follow this line any more: there were strange possibilities that she did not want to think about.

"Gary, tell me what happened after the police picked you up."

"You can take notes now," said Gary. "But no recording."

"I've not got the recorder with me."

"OK. Well, they couldn't do anything."

"You were too young for criminal responsibility?" said Grizelda.

"Of course I was. So the Social Services got in on the act after all. If it wasn't me who was the wrong 'un, it had to be where I lived. They took me away from my mum."

"Did you want that?"

"No. Why should I? It could have been all right now Kieran had gone."

"Kieran?"

"Forget him. They took out a Place of Safety Order on me."

Grizelda looked up from her notebook.

"I've not heard of that," she said.

"Why should you? It's all changed since the 1989 Children Act."

Grizelda looked down again and wrote.

"And don't go thinking, 'Doesn't he know a lot?' I've got quite an expert over the last fourteen years."

"What was this place of safety? A children's home?"

Grizelda thought of all the child abuse revelations that seemed lately to fill the papers. It was a wonder Quentin hadn't done a documentary on them – everyone else seemed to have.

"It wasn't bad, I remember. There were too many people around for any funny stuff. It was an Assessment Centre."

"Assessing you?"

"Yeah. I remember it like yesterday. Doctors, psychologists, social workers – all trying to find out what made me tick."

"Did they?"

"What do you think?"

Grizelda looked at the narrow face, inscrutable dark eyes and eye-bending black singlet and thought, *No, nobody's likely to find out what makes you tick.*

"But they must have found out something."

"Yes. They found out that I might be too young to be a criminal, but I wasn't too young to be a danger to society. So no going back to Mother and no nice foster home for me. No, they sent me off to this boarding school place for misfits miles away in the country. And there I stayed."

"Did you like it?"

"Are you joking? I was supposed to. Everybody tried to make me like it. Well, they did their best. Teaching me, looking after me, counselling me. At least that's what they called it."

Grizelda knew the sort of place he was talking about. "But they're *good*," she cried out.

"Not to me they weren't. No help at all."

She saw the wall of stubbornness in his eyes and knew well that nobody could *make* Gary Brady do anything.

"So what happened?"

"I played dumb, didn't I. I'm good at that. Once, when I was little, it was my only way. I can talk now if I think it's in my interests. Then nobody can shut me up. But mostly I'll just look at people and drive them round the bend. I did it with my stepfather. I meant to."

"You're talking to me now."

"I reckon it's in my interests."

"What about your mother, Gary?" said Grizelda, quietly, daringly.

Gary said nothing for a moment. The wall of stubbornness shifted slightly.

"No, I didn't mean it with her," he said.

"But you did it just the same," said Grizelda.

Gary stood up, threateningly. People round the bar were suddenly quiet and turned to look.

"Don't blame me," he said. "I didn't make her top herself."

Grizelda's question *Didn't you?* remained unspoken and Gary sat down again.

"Did you see her after the police took you?" she said instead.

"Once or twice. They let her come to me. Like prison visiting," he said bitterly. "She looked awful."

Grizelda changed the subject, making a mental note to come back to it.

"What did you do at the school when you weren't being interviewed?"

"Like I said. They tried to teach me. Useful skills. Education for life." The last words were bitter.

"That was good, wasn't it?"

"All they thought I was good for was just coping when I came out."

The same bitterness. *And I was at Anglo-World still and Julian was in his expensive boarding seclusion, both being taught how we'd rule the world*, Grizelda thought.

"And then you did come out?"

"Yeah, they let me go when I was sixteen. Sent me home with a list of people to keep in touch with and made me go to college. More life skills."

"Did you go home?"

"Is that what you call it?"

Grizelda had no answer. She felt a new revelation was coming.

"My mother had lost it completely, given up. The place was a filthy tip. She managed to clean it up a bit before I got there so the Social Services could say it was all right for me to stay, but as soon as I was back it all went to hell."

"Perhaps she expected you to help her keep it decent."

Grizelda wished she could call the words back at once.

"*You know nothing*," he said, venom in his voice and anger in his eyes. He rose again as if to leave.

"I'm sorry. Please don't go," Grizelda begged. "Look, can I get you another lager? Something to eat?"

"No."

He did walk away, but only to the bar. He returned with another pint of lager but, pointedly, nothing for her. He took a swig, looked at her and his mood changed.

"How could you know what it was like for my mother? She was beyond me. I didn't know what to do to help her."

In spite of all these useful skills and education for life, thought Grizelda.

"It broke me up," Gary said.

He had calmed down again, though he was drinking his lager quicker than before. Grizelda waited.

"So I buggered off."

"What do you mean?"

"I stole some money. Did the tills of four shops. Got quite a bit together. Then I hitched to London."

"So as far as anyone knew, you'd just disappeared," she said.

"I wanted to," he said bitterly. "Just get away from the whole sodding lot of them."

"But didn't anyone look for you?"

"Who, for instance? There are thousands on the streets who've just disappeared. Who bothers?"

"But you could have ended up a rent boy, died of AIDS, been murdered."

"So what? Who'd have cared? Anyway, I didn't. Begging, hostels, sleeping rough – you can get by."

"But you don't do that now," said Grizelda. "What happened?"

Gary looked down into the depths of his lager as if he would never answer.

"Something must have happened," she persisted. "There are three positive things, three *good* things that you do now that you didn't before. What happened, Gary?"

He still didn't reply, but turned the glass round.

"Gary?"

As if the words were dug out of him with a spade, he gave an answer which left Grizelda speechless.

"You did," he said.

Chapter Two

Julian watched Grizelda go into the Cross Keys, then drove off, not knowing quite where he was headed. After a few moments he noticed a sign pointing up a side road: HEATHWELL SCHOOL. Where Grizelda had been. On impulse, he signalled right, drove two hundred metres past small houses, then stopped opposite the closed gates and the yellow warning letters marked out on the road outside. Beyond the gates were the school's square, flat-roofed buildings. He got out, crossed the road and looked at them.

Until he had met Grizelda, he could not imagine himself speaking on equal terms with someone from such a school. Even now, he assumed that Grizelda was an exception who had never fitted in there. Whenever they had discussed this and she had said, "It took time to settle but when I had, I enjoyed it. I had good friends. A lot were cleverer than me. It wasn't the school's fault they never went to Oxford," he had dismissed it as misplaced loyalty. No, she should have left it behind. She owed that place nothing.

So he had once assumed. But, like everything else taken for granted before his mother's letter, this thought was now in a melting pot in his brain. His head was spinning from all that had happened: he was in free fall and he knew there would be a collision soon that he could not begin to forecast.

What had he really felt when Gary, come from nowhere in outlandish magician's guise, hissed "You're scum" at him? A fortnight before he would have wheeled away with disdain; last night he accepted it quietly, wondering if it were true. A fortnight before he would have looked at Grizelda and said, "Do you think that sort of person is worth more than a second of your time? Then do without me. It's over between us. I won't be demeaned by you."

So why not now? Why was he afraid of Gary and dependent on Grizelda? What in God's name had happened to him?

Oh, that letter from his mother! *"Dear Mrs Brady ... is dead. In rather desperate circumstances, I'm afraid... Do you remember ... her son Gary?"* From that moment it was as if a door at the end of a long, forgotten corridor had opened: he had peered inside and known something was hidden in the dark which he would rather not see. But it could be kept there no longer. These odd snatches of scenes from childhood in the playroom, clear but beyond understanding. Nanny, Ingrid, Gary, and their encounters in the nursery. Later, Daddy with those words he didn't understand but which became so familiar because they were dinned into him in that proud, complacent voice: "He really is most extraordinarily able."

"Extraordinarily able". Those words had followed him – through prep school, through that great and ancient school by the Thames, to the great and ancient university further up the Thames and into the lovely college in which he settled as if by the Claverhouse birthright.

"Extraordinarily able". That was how everybody had labelled him from the start. So, obviously, he was. Languid, effortless, never working hard until the last minute to complete some necessary piece of work or get through a vital exam, but always managing it even if not as well as he probably could, because he was "extraordinarily able". Why, he'd never had to work, *really* work, until he went to the bank.

And there was his enemy, his opposite, deprived, despised and rejected, from the playroom – Gary. How was he labelled? Thick, inarticulate, destructive, criminal tendencies, *oik*, *scum*. Yet now Gary had returned, in bewildering disguise to label *him* the same. And was Gary not, even just a little bit, justified? Who made the buses? Who got the credit? "Extraordinarily able". Who deserved that most? So he had not squashed Gary like a cockroach underfoot but had watched, helpless, while the most important person in his life negotiated with Gary, treating him – temporarily, surely? – as *her* most important person.

Of course Julian felt bewildered – and powerless, against a fate he couldn't fathom. The foundations of his life were being cut away and he could not understand how or why.

On this Sunday morning, Heathwell School was deserted. Julian tried hard to imagine his Grizelda going in every morning, surrounded by young Gary clones. He tried too hard, as if punishing himself. He saw her laughing, unaware of any world outside these mean boundaries. The anguished question forced itself into his mind: *Which road is she going down? His or mine?*

He couldn't answer. Nor, he was sure, could Grizelda. They would just argue and set themselves in concrete positions again within a minute.

No, only one person could help him answer. Gary.

He would have to bite the bullet and meet Gary face to face. More than his life with Grizelda depended on it.

"You did," Gary said.

Grizelda looked at him, speechless and nonplussed.

"What do you mean?" she said at last.

"I saw you and him together that night in Oxford."

"I know that already. What were you doing in Oxford?"

"I hitched there."

"Why?"

Again the silence. Then: "I told myself I'd treat this morning straight. You're not his woman, you're just someone from the telly. I'm not here to tell you all my innermost secrets."

"Including why you called Julian 'scum'?"

"Right. But I can't avoid it, can I? There's too much going on for me to have a straight conversation with you."

"If you say so, Gary."

"Well, of course there is. Everything's connected. You want to know why I went to Oxford after four years sleeping rough round London?"

"Yes."

"The posh papers make the best bedding," he said. "You don't get much warmth from eight pages out of the *Sun*. And I could keep up with the news as well. One day I saw his name. You know how one word can stare out of a page you're not even reading? Well, I though I saw the name 'Claverhouse' on a page of *The Daily Telegraph* before I sorted my boxes out to sleep one night. I looked. A piece about something going on in Oxford and his name was on it. *So he's in Oxford now*, I thought. Well, that was it. May as well beg in Oxford as here, I thought. Next morning I was on the road. It was an easy hitch. I must have looked like a student. I soon found the doorways in Oxford were just as wide as the ones in London."

"But why should seeing Julian's name do that to you?"

More twisting of the lager glass. Then: "I'd got so used to my life I'd forgotten why I was there. That doesn't mean I liked it. Liking and disliking are luxuries when you're just existing. I'd lived on the streets four years by then. Seeing his name made me remember why. It was like waking out of a dream."

I mustn't probe him too hard now, thought Grizelda. *Let him get on with the story. He might dry up otherwise.*

"I knew I had to connect myself up again. Not by going home. If I could find Claverhouse, could *see* him, perhaps I'd know what to do."

"I don't get that," said Grizelda.

"Neither did I," said Gary. "I just did it."

Grizelda said nothing. She was sure there was something important Gary wasn't saying. But she knew they were near a revelation.

"Well, I saw him. And you with him. I followed you out of the college, to that other place, the Union. I saw you watch him when he gave his speech. I studied the two of you. Him performing. I hated his voice, the way it sounded, what it said. But do you know what I saw when I looked at you? You hung on to every word, as though he was God himself. Well, I'll tell you this: Julian Claverhouse is *not God*. But I found myself thinking, deep down, why can't I hold someone spellbound like that?"

Grizelda listened with amazement.

"Just a minute, Gary," she said. "You're saying that you listened to Julian, watched me and thought I was being hypnotized, and if you could do that you could get any girl you wanted?"

More toying with the glass, almost shamefaced this time.

"Well, in a sort of way. But that makes it sound..."

"You can forget it. You hated his voice and what he said? Well, I might have loved his voice, but I hated what he said as well. Nobody hypnotizes me, Gary, so get that right out of your head."

The toying with the glass stopped.

"It was never in my head," he said. "That's not it at all. What got me was the idea of doing something *for someone* – a speech, a picture, a *thing* of some sort, something I'd *made* – so someone's going to say, 'That's great, Gary. I appreciate it. I understand it. Thanks.'"

"That's what you wanted?"

"More than anything else. It's what I'd always wanted. I knew that then. But I'd never got it."

It sounded so nice, so reasonable. As if she, unknowingly, had claimed a lost soul.

So why did Julian see "gorgon eyes" and feel such waves of hatred?

Embarrassed, she said, "I don't see how we can put that in the programme. About me, I mean."

"Suit yourself," he said. "You're the boss."

His mood seemed to have changed again. Almost sunny. But Grizelda was still puzzled. She framed a question.

So if you made such a good resolution that night, how come you called Julian scum before his face and looked about to murder him on the spot? You should be pleased with him.

She bit the question back. She shouldn't break this new mood.

"I got picked up by the fuzz that night and kicked out of town next day. So I hitched back to London. I didn't mind. I was going anyway. I had to work things out."

"And you did, obviously," said Grizelda. "Flute, magic,

stand-up routines. And a nice little career in the making."

"I said don't patronize me," said Gary, suddenly hard.

"Sorry. But how did these three come about? Did you play the flute at the children's home?"

Gary looked at her scornfully.

"Do me a favour!" he said. "I'd never even picked up a musical instrument. No, I was back in London, south of the river, off the Old Kent Road. Down a side street was this pawn shop. All sorts of junk. In the window was this flute. I stopped. I kept looking at it."

Grizelda had a vision of the flute, gleaming silver, lying in its box in a bed of blue silk, surrounded by rubbish. She tried to see it through Gary's eyes, deprived, frustrated, suddenly with a vague, impossible dream.

She knew what he was going to say next, but she had to ask the conventional question.

"So you bought it?"

"Did I buggery! I nicked it. The old man wasn't even looking."

"We'd better not put that in the programme either," Grizelda said.

"Why not? It's the truth. I'm not ashamed. But I got across the other side of the river pretty quick."

"Then what?"

"I taught myself to play."

Grizelda stared at him in disbelief. She'd started flute lessons years ago at the Anglo-World School. Even with the best teachers, she had found it hard. Making any kind of a sound at all was a triumph.

Yet this drop-out, sleeping rough, taught himself?

"But you must have known something about music?" she said.

"Never," he said. "It was harder work stopping the other dossers nicking the flute off me. Music's obvious. Once you start, it's all there in front of you. You just follow it."

Grizelda didn't know what to say.

"And the magic?" she managed, after a moment of silence.

"I found an old boy under the bridges who'd been a conjuror in a better life. He was doing the three-card trick to some punters as skint as himself. I did a deal with him. If I busked for a month and gave him half what I got, would he teach me all he knew? Well, he would. Two old packs of cards, a month's teaching and I knew the lot. Better than he did. Then he shuffled off, saying they'd do me no good and I'd be back where he was because of them. I never saw him again."

"What about being a comic?"

"That?" He laughed. "Just a try-on with Reg Welsted. I didn't think the punters who went to the Jolly Angler would be into conjuring or flute-playing. Besides, I'd been playing the flute in the shopping centre for a fortnight. No, I heard about the live entertainment there, thought I'd get in on the act, rang Reg up using my agent's routine and he bought it. Pity I didn't do better on the night."

"But the name? Tommy Trefoil."

"Good, isn't it? I thought it up myself."

"Will you carry on with the stand-up routines?"

"Why not? I'll get it right, like I did the others. I do OK busking with the flute. And I get some good gigs with the magic. I do all right."

He swigged the last of his lager.

"Another one, Gary?"

"Not for me. I'm out of here."

"But Gary, this isn't the end, is it?"

"Of this interview, yes. I'll keep in touch, don't worry. I'll ring you at your work number this week. I won't miss my bit of TV fame."

"I didn't mean that. It's not the end for *you*. You want more than busking and conjuring for Townswomen's Guilds, surely?"

He pushed the glass to one side and looked her full in the face.

"Yes," he said. "There's a lot more to come yet. But I doubt you'll find it out on your TV programme." He stood suddenly. "I'll ring you this week."

And then he was gone, picking his way through the now crowded bar.

Grizelda was left on her own. What had that given her? Quite a lot. But nowhere near the complete truth about this enigmatic law unto himself. There was so much yet to be uncovered. He could be a *brilliant* documentary subject.

And more than that. He was, she was sure, extraordinarily gifted. And for twenty-three years nobody had spotted this. Until her.

Nobody?

Memories of that weekend at Mockbeggar House came back: Georgina by the site of the old summerhouse, Julian afterwards angry at her only half-serious theories.

Yes, there was somebody she *had* to find and talk to. Wanda Gates.

Gary kept on walking. There was no sign of Claverhouse outside. Good. He didn't want to see him. Not yet.

He would get out of this town now. There'd be no busking here – it wouldn't be worth it. On Wednesday he'd got a

230

date at a child's birthday – rich toffs in London. Like the Claverhouses? Well, did it matter? Their money was as good as anyone's.

Anyway, that was good. He'd be within easy reach of Grizelda. And Claverhouse.

He walked quickly through the streets to his bed-and-breakfast place. First, he knocked on the landlady's door.

"I'll be off now, Mrs Lyons. I won't need the second night."

He settled up with part of the cash the pleased Wendy Grissom had paid him. Then he packed quickly and was away.

On this Sunday there seemed little traffic southwards, so hitching would be a pain. There was no coach until five. So, unusually for him, he caught a train, then a tube, and then went to see if he could cadge a bed in an overflowing house with people he knew.

On the train he looked back over his talk with Grizelda.

She could not have known how the sight of her had turned his stomach over with that hopeless yearning matched with hatred for Claverhouse. She could not have known how controlled he had been throughout their talk, how measured every answer was. She could never have guessed how his mastery of all he said, his sheer articulacy, had amazed even him, the boy who at one time never spoke.

Most importantly, she could not have known what he was carefully editing out of his answers. For she wasn't there after his mother's funeral, when he had talked for hours with Wanda Gates and had at last found out all he ever wanted to know. Those secrets were not for Grizelda. They were between him and Claverhouse.

Chapter Three

As Gary knocked on the door of a house in Peckham, Julian and Grizelda were on their way home in total silence. Grizelda watched Julian, his still-pale face, his eyes intent on the road. She noticed fine lines round his eyes and at the sides of his mouth: though he had shaved carefully, there was dark shadow across his jowls.

Several times Grizelda tried to break the silence. She was bursting to tell Julian everything. But there were warnings in his face: *I don't want to know*.

We're back in crisis was all she could think.

Only when they were home and he was slumped in an armchair did Julian speak.

"I don't like this, you know. I wish it hadn't started."

"When do you think it started?"

"When my mother's letter came."

"Not before? Not when I met Tommy Trefoil? Or I first met you? Nothing's been the same since then."

Julian laughed ruefully.

"It's true. Nobody's had any effect on me like you have."

"Even Gary?"

"Even Gary. This must all have started when my mother said he could come to the house while Mrs Brady did the cleaning."

"Even before that, Julian," Grizelda said. "It started when we were born, all three of us. It started in our cradles, in the sorts of cradles we had. I'm beginning to think the three of us together make an explosive mixture. With me in a chalk-and-cheese sandwich."

Julian didn't answer. Grizelda went on.

"I've got to carry on with this now. He's a fascinating character. I think he's brilliant. And I don't use that word to mean 'quite good' like it usually does nowadays. I think he is *truly brilliant.* He's got some of the marks of genius in him. He's an unsung, misunderstood, unrecognized, thwarted genius."

Julian's face, she noticed, was full of pain. He spoke slowly, with heavy irony. "I think I get it now," he said. "Who knows what he might have done if he'd had my advantages? By the same token, where would I have been if I'd had his set-backs? Still in the gutter. That's what you think, isn't it?"

"Julian, don't be silly. I think nothing of the sort. You are yourself and I love you, warts and all. But I've got to get to the bottom of all this."

"So you're seeing him again? You know where he's going next?"

"He'll ring me. He'd had enough today. He'll keep in touch all right. I'm sure of that."

"You're determined, aren't you?"

"It's my job."

Suddenly Julian shouted, "Sod your job! Has it occurred to you that he's just using you to get at *me*?"

"I don't believe that," said Grizelda simply.

"You're naïve. Whoever you say you love, I know who you *sympathize* with. But I don't like being called scum and you shouldn't either."

"I don't. That's why I want to get at the truth."

Julian's flare-up subsided as quickly as it had come.

"Then get on with it," he said.

"There's someone else I've got to see," said Grizelda. "Wanda Gates."

"Nanny?" Julian's cry was involuntary. "What in God's name for?"

"She's got the key. She goes way beyond what you and Gary can remember."

And I'm right about her, Grizelda thought. *Julian's terrified – and she's the source of his terror. There's jealousy, rivalry and worse locked away in that nursery, still casting grotesque shadows.*

"Well, don't ask me where she is," Julian muttered. "Mother sacked her and for all I know she went back to Ilford where she came from. I've no idea why she was sacked and I never asked. And don't say, 'Ah, another expendable servant.'"

"As if I would," said Grizelda gently. "But Ilford's enough for a start. I'll take it from there."

She knew now that their relationship was not in crisis but on hold. Together they were about to face the biggest hurdle yet.

She was early at Speakeasy Television next morning. She poured out everything to Quentin about the weekend except Julian's involvement. Then she waited for him to speak. After all, he might axe the whole thing there and then.

"You're really convinced about this, aren't you?" he said.

"It could be a great programme," she said. "I know I'm only a researcher, but I can see how the whole thing could take shape. Following him round his dates. Watching him at

234

work with his flute, performing his comedy act (don't worry, he'll get better), doing his conjuring. In between, interviews. A collage of events and talk. Maurice Cracknell would love it."

"Sounds fair enough," said Quentin.

"And the extraordinary thing is, I seem to be the first to recognize him for the phenomenon he is."

Quentin leaned back behind his vast desk and surveyed her.

"Grizelda, love," he said, "you're a good researcher and I've come to trust your work and your judgement. So I'm giving you a big chance. For this project, you're no longer a humble researcher. You're the boss. Do it. It's your programme."

Grizelda stared at him.

"You mean...?"

"If it works, then in the credits it will say in big letters: *Produced by Grizelda Grissom.* I can't say fairer than that."

Grizelda looked at her boss's fat, red face and gasped, "Quentin, that's wonderful! Thank you so—"

"Now just get on with it." He waved her away. "Bring me a complete schedule by the end of the month and meanwhile, don't bother me."

She couldn't believe it. She'd come straight from Oxford to get her job here, just as a means of being with Julian. She knew if she'd been really serious about a career in broadcasting she should have been a BBC trainee or something. Instead, all she knew about the job came from watching those around her. There would be jealousy to start with and a few snide remarks, but she could cope with that. No, *get this right*, that's what mattered.

First thing – find Wanda Gates.

Wanda from Ilford? It couldn't be so easy. But today was obviously her lucky morning.

The studio library held a set of BT telephone books for London and surrounding areas. It couldn't be just a matter of looking up GATES, W. and ringing all the Ilford numbers? Well, if not, Grizelda was in for a long slog with domestic employment agencies.

She dialled three likely numbers. To the request, "Can I speak to Wanda Gates, please?" the answers from the first two were the same: "There's nobody of that name here."

For the third there was a woman's voice, very suspicious. "Who wants her?"

Yes, it was going to be easy.

"Is she there?"

"She could be."

This could go on for hours.

"Please tell her my name is Grizelda Grissom. I'm from Speakeasy Television and we are doing a television documentary on someone she once knew. Her assistance would be invaluable."

There was silence. For a moment Grizelda thought the phone had gone dead. Then the same voice said, "Where are you ringing from?"

"London. Camden."

"Who gave you my number?"

"Nobody. I was given your name and town so I looked it up."

"Is this to do with the Claverhouse family?"

"Sort of."

"Is it a profile of Sir William?"

236

"No."

Silence. Then: "You have to tell me exactly."

Though the suspicion was irritating, Grizelda did not blame the speaker. She outlined the bare bones of the project, then gave an account of what had been done so far. Her first mention of Gary Brady's name brought a quiet but sharp intake of breath. "Our researches took us to Mockbeggar House near Beaconsfield, where his mother worked. Your name came up."

"From Lady Claverhouse?"

"Yes."

There was a silence. After a full minute, Grizelda shook the receiver, certain now that it really had gone dead.

At last the voice came again.

"You'll have to put all this in writing. When I get your letter I'll think about it and ring you back."

The receiver at the other end was replaced. Grizelda was annoyed with herself. Could she even be sure she had been speaking to Wanda Gates? Now she was dependent on the whims of other people about when they picked a phone up. "Don't call us, we'll call you." The passport to eternal silence.

Her letter went out at once. The embossed and colourful headed notepaper Quentin had designed himself did look impressive. The laser print looked good too. Wanda would surely feel quite proud to get it:

Dear Ms Gates,
Further to our telephone conversation...

It went first class. Grizelda spent the rest of the day doing other people's work, with one ear on the phone waiting for

Gary's promised call. There was no more she could do on her own.

She need not have worried. She was in the studio early the next day, after a quiet night with Julian in which much was skirted round. Her phone was ringing even as she entered.

The same woman's voice as before. But brighter, all suspicion gone.

"That's all right, then. No time like the present, that's what I always say. What about today?"

Grizelda had cleared her diary for the whole week. "Fine," she said. "It's not far. I'll see you in an hour."

After making sure all her calls would go to the receptionist with strict orders to tell Gary, if he rang, to try the next day, Grizelda was on her way, driving along Eastern Avenue.

The Victorian terraced house with bay windows and tiny front garden looked neat, with a brick arch round the front porch and the doorstep picked out in shiny red tile paint. Net curtains in the front windows twitched as she opened the gate. She rang the bell. The door was opened at once.

Grizelda gasped at the face in front of her – thin, lined, heavily made-up with mascara, blusher and very red lipstick. It looked almost grotesque. The shoulder-length, neatly cut hair was jet black with a sheen indicating recent dyeing. Grizelda guessed this meeting had been carefully prepared for.

She was shown into a small sitting-room. A soft three-piece suite faced a large TV and video. On the mantelpiece over a gas fire were two framed photographs. One was old. A couple stared stiffly out in black and white. The other, in colour, was of a man, red-faced, with sleek dark hair combed back and blue eyes.

They introduced each other formally. Wanda must have caught Grizelda's eyes straying to the man's photograph.

"Someone I used to know," she said. "He's not here now. I really don't know why I keep the photo there."

For me to see, Grizelda thought, with sudden intuition. This was the only male presence in the room.

They sat facing each other, sinking into armchairs. Wanda had no objection to being taped but Grizelda took notes as well.

"So it's Gary Brady you want to know about? A TV documentary! My, he has come a long way! But I'm not sure I can tell you much."

Can't? Or won't? thought Grizelda.

"You were nanny at Mockbeggar House when his mother started as a cleaner there and he came too. Was that usual."

"Oh no. But it was necessary. That heavy cleaner job was very hard to fill – such unsatisfactory, untrustworthy people. They had to be dismissed. I insisted on helping Lady Claverhouse – Mrs Claverhouse as she was then – with the interviewing. She just did not know *people*, you see. Always fell for overbearing, slatternly women who were often dishonest for no better reason, I fear, than that she was afraid of them."

Grizelda found that very hard to believe.

"Well, I could see there was only one suitable person. Mrs Brady was neat, quiet, dependable, knew her place. Even with the inconvenience of having her son there, she was the best person available."

For you, Grizelda thought. *I bet Georgina gave way to keep you happy.*

"And I didn't mind the extra responsibility. Gary was no trouble. A lovely little boy."

Grizelda looked at her sharply.

"That's not what we've been led to believe," she said. "Destructive, silent to the point of catatonia, mentally defective, with criminal tendencies culminating in arson – quite a list."

Wanda gave a nervous laugh.

"However can he entertain people in pubs then?" she said.

"Didn't you know any of that?"

Wanda said nothing. Her lips moved as if she were talking to herself. Grizelda suddenly saw, clear beneath the make-up and wrinkles, the skull beneath the skin.

"Did Lady Claverhouse tell you that?" Wanda said.

"Yes."

"Well, perhaps all wasn't well with Gary. It's not surprising considering his background – father disappearing before he was born, then a stepfather, and you know what trouble that can cause."

Was it Grizelda's imagination or did Wanda's eyes flick for a split second towards the man's photograph? What had Gary said?

"You mean, Kieran?" she said.

"Lady Claverhouse *did* tell you a lot," said Wanda.

"There was no love lost between Gary and Kieran, I believe."

Sudden stiffness from Wanda. "I'm sure I don't know," she said.

She's clamming up, thought Grizelda. *I'm too close to something for her comfort.* She changed tack.

"How did the little boys get on together? Gary and – what

was the other one's name?"

The lie dropped from her lips with honeyed ease.

"Master Julian? Oh, lovely. There was never any trouble. Master Julian was *so* gracious. As you would expect."

"And yet Gary was stigmatized as destructive."

"Well, perhaps he was a little rough now and again. It was the breeding, you know."

"Rough enough to burn buildings down?"

Wanda's mouth closed up again. Grizelda thought: *If she doesn't want to tell me, why let me come?* She decided on a frontal approach.

"You see, Miss Gates, I've spoken to Gary and I think he's been straight with me. And it doesn't add up."

No flicker from Wanda.

"Gary's able, creative, self-taught, and he's learnt very difficult things against all the odds. I think that shows an incredibly strong character. It doesn't tie in with being destructive or criminal. Yet Lady Claverhouse talks about him breaking up everything in the playroom. I'm amazed he was allowed to stay there."

Suddenly, Wanda's face under the make-up flushed bright red. Her voice shook with anger.

"Please leave, Miss whatever-your-name-is. I won't be insulted and accused in my own house. I won't *have* it!"

Grizelda stayed where she was. Wanda got up and held the door open for her.

"I'm not accusing you of anything," Grizelda said. "I only want to know what happened."

"Please go," said Wanda.

Outside, Grizelda walked to the car, angry with herself. *I screwed that up all right. But how? What went wrong? What did Wanda think I was accusing her of?*

She sat in the car for a few minutes. Wanda was a bitter, lonely woman keeping up a veneer of niceness. Wasn't that what ex-nannies were supposed to be like – getting their love from other people's children and lost when deprived of it? Well, that was the old cliché, but was there more to Wanda?

What about the photograph? Her eyes had definitely, probably instinctively, flashed towards it when Grizelda uttered the name "Kieran". Was that it? Kieran and Wanda together – and Gary's mother left deserted by everybody? Was it likely? It could be possible.

It boiled down to this: was Wanda Gates simply a pathetic, lonely woman or had she lived by manipulating and deceiving people? If so, she was only pathetic because there was nobody left to manipulate or deceive. *Except me*, Grizelda admitted to herself with a wry smile. Well, which was it? She had to find out. But how was she going to get back into that house?

At last she drove off, back to the studio, to find there had been no phone call from Gary.

Chapter Four

Julian woke on Monday morning with a headache and strange dark spots before his eyes. He shook his head. He never had migraines – nor had he had anything to drink last night. He could have; he had every excuse. Perhaps he should have.

What the hell was going on? He'd woken up different from how he'd gone to bed – like he was before that blasted letter came to make him look into his very soul. Well, looking into the very soul was no pastime for a Claverhouse. He'd had enough. He was Sir William Claverhouse's son, to whom much was given, from whom much was expected. But if much was expected, then much which did not apply to other people was due to him. And one of those things was *not* to be questioned as he had been, because he was *above* it.

Yes, he felt himself again. This last fortnight had been an aberration, a bad dream. He would put his foot down, as he should have done from the start. Brady would be ignored, forgotten. If they met again, he would tread him underfoot like a cockroach.

Julian looked at the other, rumpled side of the bed, still slightly warm, where Grizelda had been. And that was another thing: these last few days they might as well have been in separate rooms. That had to stop as well. Grizelda would have to choose, too. Yes, she was the most important person in his life. Yes, he would find it hard without her. At first, certainly. But she was only a bloody woman, for God's sake!

She'd gone to the pederast's palace in Camden early again – always a bad sign. Not just bad, terrible.

No, don't waver. She can go when she likes. Guilt? What had he got to be guilty about? He was Julian Claverhouse again, and not one to give in to oiks and scum.

There was nothing of interest in the post. Showered, shaved and breakfasted, Julian left for work feeling rather happier.

And what would Gary do? His night was spent in a sleeping bag on a creaking floor. He woke on Monday morning feeling dissatisfied.

His aims were muddled. He had to sort them. But this hard floor did not help. He got up, dressed, went outside. In a vandalized children's play area he stopped to think.

What did he want? That interview with Grizelda had knocked him sideways. What he'd said about seeing her in Oxford, wanting to *do* something, *make* something for her or someone like her was true, shining in on him like a searchlight and, he knew full well, this alone had reclaimed him. Seeing the flute, finding the old card-sharp, had been accidents. He would have seized on anything he found to learn and master. For something deep inside told him he could do *anything*.

But this desire never dimmed that other furnace burning in him – hatred of Claverhouse. He could *kill* him. And not just *could*: ever since the summerhouse burned down, the conviction that in the end he *would* had never left him. He didn't just want Claverhouse dead: he wanted to *do it himself*, even more so after talking to Wanda. Because Claverhouse had twisted and deformed his life almost from the start. In his guts, he knew this before he saw Wanda. The feeling hadn't changed since he was a tiny little boy. And it never would.

But which of the two ways was really him? Gary was perfectly capable of standing outside himself and surveying from afar. He knew well that a battle raged for his soul: a struggle between good and bad, light and dark, life and death. He looked at it another way. The gut-wrenching sight of Claverhouse and *that girl of all girls* together – the battle was between what Claverhouse meant to him and what she meant.

Which way was it to be? He knew what he really wanted.

I don't want to go back in the pit. Not now I've got finger-and toeholds on the sides as I try to clamber out and daylight's overhead.

But Grizelda had said something. How could she know it sent me clattering down to the bottom again? "A nice little career." "Don't patronize me," I said. But she wasn't, was she? She was saying the plain, obvious truth about the best, the limits, of what I'll ever achieve. Suddenly the daylight seemed not worth struggling into.

But what did I expect? I don't know, but it has to be better than "a nice little career".

He kicked a tin-can savagely. Life was organized to stop him winning. It played tricks designed to keep him in the gutter.

What should he do today? Illegal busking in a tube station? He trailed back to the house. Sod it – the batteries in the cassette player were finished. Was buying new ones worth it? Nevertheless, he took both flute and cassette player with him and left his case locked. He might be staying in a house with mates but he didn't trust one of them.

Then, backpack on, knife out of sight in his sock under his jeans, he left and trudged towards the place where life, bustle and money was. The nearer he got, the more certain he was: *he wouldn't busk again until his fate was clear, either way. Which way didn't matter – except that the unthinkable way meant he would never busk again, conjure, or try to make half-drunk audiences laugh.* And he *was* thinking the unthinkable – but then the unthinkable had always been there, deep in his mind, sometimes hidden, sometimes not, in every waking and sleeping thought.

While Grizelda was having a great day with Quentin giving her a great chance, Julian was undergoing a bad time. His happy feeling had lasted as far as the bank's doors. The walls of the lift seemed to close in on him: when he stepped out on to his floor he felt suffocated. His headache returned. In one corner of his vision was a black, crinkling sensation, as if everything was about to crumple before his eyes. His breakfast had been toast and coffee: it had left an aftertaste of bile, which the black coffee Mrs Burden gave him only made worse. Was he back to the way he was before the letter came? Perhaps he could never be that person again.

He looked out of his window down on Bishopsgate. He imagined that everybody below hurrying past on unknown errands paused to look up at him, accusing and threatening.

He found himself talking to them, angrily.

"I am Julian Claverhouse. I matter. Get out of my sight!"

"I beg your pardon, sir?"

He turned. His secretary had entered with the post.

"I'm sorry, Mrs Burden. Take no notice. Leave them on the desk."

She did so and left, studiously not looking at him.

I'm ill, he thought. *I shouldn't have come in today.*

But he had to, because the thought of loneliness in the flat was what he couldn't stand. Neither could he stand loneliness in his office with only his work and a ringing telephone for company. He switched his phone through to Piers's number and walked to where his friend, feet up on desk, was talking down his own phone.

Gary stood outside a tube station. He could get batteries after all and take up a pitch by an escalator. He could make quite a lot and forget this awful inner struggle.

No, he couldn't. Not today. Not ever. His mind raged with frustration. He took Grizelda's card, now dirty and crumpled, out of his jeans' back pocket. Should he ring her now? The prospect of TV coverage was still alluring. There were payphones in the station.

No, he wasn't ready. He had nothing to say. And those other, darker thoughts were always getting in the way.

She'd be at work now. So would Claverhouse, wherever he went. He itched to dial *something*, to do *something*. Why not try the other number – her private London one? No one would answer. Would they?

He found a vacant payphone and rang. Four rings, then silence. A hiss. *An answerphone*, he thought. *Put the receiver down.* Then came a woman's voice, which made him slip his ten pence in the slot at once. Grizelda. Why hadn't he thought of that? Then Claverhouse spoke. Then the tone. Should he leave a message? No. Just listen to the silence for a moment, then quietly put the phone down.

Their phone had rung in the place where they lived together. Where was that? Suddenly he wanted very badly to know. If only he could find a London phone book. The only place would be a public library.

A search now, through remembered streets.

Ten minutes later he was sitting in the library reference section. He found the right book, the name and the number and looked at the address.

Of course. He might have known where Claverhouse would live. Well, he'd go there. Just to see. It was *something*: an imitation of action.

An imitation of action. Yes, that was it. He would keep going while his mind whirred around, resolving the conflict, discovering what it would finally tell him to do.

Back to the tube station. Half an hour later he stood outside a block of flats, solid and elegant, showing the world that the people inside weren't short of the odd pound coin.

Piers was no good. He only made braying, stupid remarks: "Griz still giving you a run-around? Better watch she's not two-timing you with a horny-handed hewer of wood, old son." After an hour of looking out of another window at the same scene he got from his own and trying not to scream at Piers to shut up, he left for his own office again.

He answered his mail. He lost himself in this quite successfully for a while and spoke coherent replies into his recording machine. Half his mind was sufficient. The other half was in a sort of limbo. His time with Piers had taught him yet again that Grizelda was the only one to whom he could talk sensibly and from whom he would hear the truth.

How could Gary find out more about Claverhouse without

ringing Grizelda? He knew what these expensive blocks of flats were like. There'd be a commissionaire or concierge or whatever they were called downstairs paid to rid the place of scruffs like him. Even if he did get past, security deadlocks would be way beyond his simple lock-picking skills.

Anyway, what did he want to break in for? That wasn't part of any plan, however vague. No, he had to step back and consider.

He knew where Grizelda spent her working days. Where was Claverhouse during the day? He had no idea. Shouldn't he find out? The more he knew about his enemy, the better. But how?

He could go into the entrance hall and ask the concierge. *Do me a favour!* He looked down at his torn jeans, knew the weight of his travel-stained backpack, felt the knife's steel against his leg. Go in there like this and police and security guards would bundle him out in a moment. And quite likely recognize him as well. No, Julian and his sort wore smart dark suits to work and to get into that place you had to look the part.

I've got a dark suit. Doesn't matter that it came out of an Oxfam shop. And a white shirt. I do magic in them. So what if I go back and put them on? Not the cloak, though. He'd ring the funny farm if I did.

But why go to this trouble? Well, he could *just about* pass as a friend of Julian's anxious to contact him. Was it all worth the trouble and risk? Yes, if it cleared his mind further about Claverhouse.

He'd try it. It wasn't much but it was something: it kept up this illusion of action which, at the moment, seemed all that was keeping him going.

*   *   *

What's wrong with me? What crisis seems poised above my head? Strain from the past fortnight? Or a weird foreboding of the future?

Julian had lunched alone, then attended a meeting in which he would normally have said a lot but today had said nothing. He felt as if he were not really there but looking down on himself going through the motions, like some out-of-body experience.

Perhaps he should go home early.

Gary slogged back across London. He changed in the gloomy, creaking room where he had slept. A couple stretched out on a bed watched him without comment. He locked his whole backpack away in the case, together with his jeans and singlet. The knife, though, was still inside his sock.

"Trust us," said the girl on the bed. "We'd never nick your gear."

"Not you," said Gary. "But there's..." He never bothered to finish the sentence. The suit was on and so were the black leather shoes he also wore for the act. They were reasonably clean. But the bow tie would look stupid. He counted out his money. Nobody here would have a tie to lend him. He would have to find a Tie Rack if there was no secondhand shop nearby. The cheapest tie he could find would do.

No, don't go home yet. You'll draw attention to yourself.

Julian stayed, looking uncomprehendingly at his computer screen, answering the phone on auto-pilot.

Another trek west. Here was the road, here the flats.

250

Suddenly he felt outlandish and conspicuous in his greasepaint-stained, shabby suit and cheap new maroon tie. There was a chill in his stomach now that he was breaching the enemy's defences. But then, to survive he had to comport himself on the enemy's terms. He was like an escaping prisoner of war in a hand-dyed overcoat impersonating a Nazi officer.

He took a deep breath and entered. "Excuse me."

The man in the uniform reading a paper behind the desk looked up. "Sir?"

Do his eyes see through me? Will he throw me out now?

"Could you tell me, please, if Mr Julian Claverhouse is in?"

The man looked him up and down. "Who shall I say is calling?"

"An old friend," said Gary. "Mr Brady."

He could have bitten his tongue off. He didn't want Julian to know and this man would undoubtedly report to him. The man touched a button and waited. Then: "Nobody is in. Can I take a message?"

"He'll be at work. I can contact him there."

Gary was putting on a very convincing voice. He was finding mimicry easy. It crossed his mind that here could be another act.

If, when this is over, I ever perform again.

The man returned to his paper.

"Actually, I seem to have lost his work number. You wouldn't have it, would you? And the address? I could meet him there." Gary laughed. "I seem to have Miss Grissom's but not Mr Claverhouse's." He hoped that would sound convincing proof of innocent intimacy.

"Lombury Hazards Bank, Bishopsgate," said the

commissionaire. "I'll write the number down for you."

"Thank you," said Gary graciously.

At five o'clock, Julian thought he could leave the bank without it seeming out of the ordinary. He got into the BMW and drove out of the underground car park, worried lest in that echoing place he was being watched. Once outside in the open air he was sure he was spied on, his every movement recorded. The crowded drive west was even more trying than usual.

When he entered the flats, the concierge called.

"Mr Claverhouse, a friend of yours was looking for you today."

Why should an icy hand seem to grip his heart?

"Friend? What friend?"

Julian had many friends. Why should one be significant?

"Gave his name as Brady. He said he'll contact you at work."

Dully, Julian said, "Thank you for the information."

"Not at all, sir."

Brady knew where he lived and worked! What had Grizelda told him?

As he opened his front door, he straightened up. *You're paranoid. This person cannot harm me; I cannot account for his hatred. I have done him no conscious wrong. And why, if I had, should I even think twice about it?*

Even so, he slumped into a chair, unable to do anything except wait for Grizelda.

Gary looked at the tall, imposing building of the Lombury Hazards Bank. He knew little about merchant banking but could see that nobody was going to get in there without a firm appointment.

But the sight of these two buildings, flats and bank, was having a decisive effect in his mind. Even more than Frobisher College they showed a plane of existence way outside his imagination. And now he knew, with a dull but inevitable shock, down which of his two separate ways they were pulling him.

All Julian knew was that while Gary's reappearance was pushing him down to unplumbed depths, it was propelling Grizelda to new heights. Because of Gary, she was getting her big break.

He had considered saying, "I'm going to the police. I'll have him warned off. Take out an injunction. Bring charges of harassment." As Grizelda babbled on about Quentin, he thought how stupid such a course would be.

But in bed that night, between sleep and wake, he had a presentiment of disaster which he could not keep down. He turned to her and whispered hoarsely, "Help me, Grizelda. Please help me."

Chapter Five

Gary walked the streets that night with the alkies, druggies and drop-outs whose life he once shared. He looked for faces he knew. He was not going to speak or even make himself known. The reason was just beneath the surface, ready to break through like a volcanic island appearing where no land was before. He was on the point of rejecting everything he had done since he had seen the flute in the window: *he was dropping back in.*

He had seen sights today which seared his soul. They showed the numbingly different world lived in by the two who held his fate in their hands.

He had to get this straight.

For the first time since he had met her he was looking rationally at Grizelda. What was she doing but offering him a cup full of poison? Not many people get to be subjects of TV documentaries. But what would it do for him? Would it make him a great performer, in demand everywhere? Or would he end up an oddity, a freak? This programme would not be a talent show. It might even take away his "nice little career".

Oh, how that phrase ate at his mind with sharp teeth!

But the "nice little career" was all he had. Grizelda's poisoned chalice could lose even that for him.

Besides, she was *part* of Claverhouse. Her offer might serve only to prolong the childhood trauma which had left

254

enough hatred in him to fuel the rest of his life.

No, Grizelda's programme was a cheat, a false vision. Reject it.

But now that she had said that awful thing to him, even his "nice little career" could not continue. He might as well throw flute, cards, the lot, into the Thames that flowed darkly past him at that moment.

"Nice little career!" He had worked, aspired, done all he was capable of, only to hear those words coming from that mouth set in the sort of face he could only yearn for: "Nice little career"!

Then she went back to her home, that mansion block, now shining like some heavenly palace, to her unimaginable life with *him – Claverhouse.*

And what would be the end of it all? She and Claverhouse would carry on, undisturbed and safe. How could any threat come from someone having a "nice little career"?

His walk had taken him on to Waterloo Bridge. He stopped, looked over.

How easy to climb up, drop over the parapet and finish it all! Like his mother. What was the point of having Bradys in the world?

For a full minute he wavered. Then he climbed the parapet.

Oh, how happy Claverhouse will be when he hears!

A pull with arms and legs to reach the top. Now just one decisive movement forward.

Or would he? Would anybody give a monkey's? Nobody, now his mother had gone the same way. So what would be the point?

He stood balancing on the parapet, ready to topple over.

If I turn back, there's only one course open for me. I have to finish what I wanted the night I burnt down the summer-house.

He stood still on the parapet, undecided, ready to go either way. The struggle for his soul reached its crisis.

He was finished anyway. There could be no more flute, no more magic. There could be no TV documentary either.

But Claverhouse must go with him. Otherwise there would have been no point to his life.

He was resolved. He clambered down to safety. But he felt no deliverance when his feet touched the ground. A move either way, into water or back to firm stone, signified the same.

He walked away, feeling strangely peaceful. All he had to do now was work out how and where. He knew when. As soon as he could.

Grizelda had hardly entered the studio next morning before the phone rang. A woman's voice, very subdued.

"Can I see you?" It was Wanda Gates.

"When?"

"As soon as you can."

"I'm on my way."

On the drive to Ilford, Grizelda wondered only briefly about this change of heart. Worry about Julian came first. Help him? She had tried. But he was beyond her, in a fatal despondency she hated and could not understand. She had offered him her loyalty, had said, "Look, Julian, I'll scrap this; I'll tell Quentin it's all off, that I don't want any more to do with the programme," and he had answered, "No, I won't hear of it; it's your big break," and she had seen loneliness in his eyes as if he was way beyond her. He had told her that Gary had been to the flats; she never told him about seeing Wanda Gates. It had led nowhere, so why bother?

And she left for work torn, angry with herself, ready to go to Quentin and say, "It's over."

Yet the moment the phone rang and Wanda Gates said, "Can I see you?" she strode to the car without hesitation. That was making her feel the worst traitor of all.

The new day greeted Gary with the whisper, "Do it now. Why waste time?"

Why not? No way could he go back on last night's resolve.

Julian slouched late into the bank and stared unseeing at everything round him.

Grizelda drove quickly. Today there was a space right outside Wanda Gates's house. A good omen?

Wanda opened the door. The mascara and make-up were gone: her hair was dull and fell in knotted, uncombed strands. She looked haggard.

"I had to see you," he muttered. "I couldn't sleep. There's a lot I've got to get off my chest."

Grizelda sat down and waited, recorder on, notebook open.

"Go on, Ms Gates," she said.

"Yesterday I said I'd nothing to say. Well, today I've everything to say. It's a long story. I did some bad things once which I'm sorry for. But bad things were done to me as well." Her eyes flickered towards the man's photograph on the mantelpiece. "And they're all to do with Gary Brady."

"Go on."

Wanda talked low, fast. Grizelda turned the recording level up.

"Mrs Claverhouse, as she then was, engaged me as nanny to Master Julian when he was born. It was my third job as a nanny. I'd had bad luck. One family went bankrupt, the other one went abroad. I wanted stability. And when I first saw Mockbeggar House I knew I wanted to stay there as long as I could."

Grizelda nearly said, "Yes, it *is* nice, isn't it?" when she remembered that as far as Wanda was concerned she did not know Julian. Ah, but she *had* spoken to Georgina, so she would have got away with it.

"It was a big house, but there was a very small staff. A lot of work was required of me besides being nanny. There were au pairs who left quickly because they were worked so hard. Mr Claverhouse would never spend more than he had to. Staff were hired from outside for big events but mostly it fell to the au pair, myself and a cleaner to keep the house in good order. It was I who suggested that Mrs Claverhouse employ another cleaner for the heavy work. I told you that yesterday."

Yes, thought Grizelda. *And made sure the one you could boss around easiest was appointed.*

Wanda continued. "Letting Mrs Brady bring her little boy with her seemed such a small price to pay to get someone so keen and obliging. And I thought Gary would be nice company for Master Julian."

"But how could people like the Claverhouses tolerate their pride and joy having the company of the cleaner's son?" asked Grizelda. Did Wanda detect the irony in her voice? "I wonder Mr Claverhouse allowed it."

"He never knew. Julian had no brothers or sisters. Children of the rich often see few others of their own age. Besides, I had a feeling that Master Julian was not growing up into a very nice little boy. I thought he *needed* Gary's company.''

"And did he?''

"Miss Grissom, you must realize that mine was not a very secure life. I had lost two positions where I was happy and felt I was set for a long time. I did not wish to lose a third. If I supervised the children closely, made them behave well to each other, I thought I would help both as they grew so Mrs Claverhouse would never get rid of me.''

"But it didn't work out like that?'' said Grizelda.

"No. Master Julian was jealous of the new arrival, even more than children are supposed to be of a new sister or brother.'' Grizelda remembered what she had been told of how she had reacted to little Barnaby. "I suppose I see why. Here was a child the same age, come from nowhere, allowed to play with everything as if it were his. No wonder Julian didn't like it.''

"*And* a boy he would be taught to look down on,'' said Grizelda.

"Not by me,'' said Wanda. Grizelda looked at her sharply. "And I don't think Julian was old enough to understand such things.''

"So what happened?'' said Grizelda.

"I'm afraid Julian became very aggressive towards Gary. He was constantly trying to fight him, hit him, get rid of him, I suppose. He certainly tore up and destroyed all the little things that Gary tried to do. As if the fledgling was taking revenge on the cuckoo in the nest.''

"How do you mean?'' Grizelda was thinking ahead fast.

"You'd think it ought to be the other way round, wouldn't you? But Gary seemed to be the quiet, reflective one and Julian the noisy one. I had to spend a lot of time keeping them apart. But then I saw what it was that Gary was able to do."

Wanda's words were catching up with Grizelda's thoughts.

"Gary was so *clever*. He could put together complicated model kits at sight which were meant for children much older. He could draw in a way which I knew would be outstanding for children of eight or nine. Despite where he came from and the conditions he lived in, he was by nature a very clever child indeed. And it was these things which Julian was making a beeline for as if he was consumed with the jealousy of the very young. It was Julian who was the destructive one."

I wondered about this, Grizelda thought, *and I was right.*

Gary entered the telephone box. The morning was sunny but there was a tang in the air. Autumn was here: fogs and the first frosts would soon take over.

He had change ready. He dialled Julian's work number. The blade of the knife was cold against his leg.

Wanda had paused. So far what she said had come out flowing, as if she had prepared and rehearsed it. The next part looked as though it would be more difficult.

"Miss Grissom," she said finally, "I didn't just want to keep my job. I wanted to be indispensable, a good influence. Under me, Julian wouldn't just be happy and no trouble to his parents. They would see that his flourishing was entirely due to me, so they would be pleased – with him and with me."

"So what did you do?" asked Grizelda, knowing the answer.

"I took the pictures that Gary drew, the toys he made with Play-doh and plasticine, the construction kits he put together, and put them aside to show Mr and Mrs Claverhouse, passing them off as Julian's."

"Did they never guess?"

"Why should they? She hardly saw her child during the day; he was either away for days at a time or never home until the late evening. I don't think Mr Claverhouse knew then of Gary's existence. And besides, what was the alternative? To admit that the cleaner's child was cleverer than their own? Too fantastic even to consider." Grizelda noticed the withering sarcasm in Wanda's voice. "I can hear Julian's father now: 'He really is most extraordinarily able.' Wonderful. All the money he would lavish on Julian's education was a good investment."

"And you did that without feeling bad about it?"

"Oh, I felt bad all right. But the alternative was worse."

"Then why not say Gary wasn't fit to be there and his mother had to leave him at home or get another job?"

"But she was good at her work. And it would have been much worse for little Gary. Besides, Julian's parents began to think I *was* some sort of wonder-worker."

"What did the au pair think?"

"Oh, Ingrid kept quiet. She wanted to keep her job as well. Besides, she got some of the praise."

"But didn't you ever think how it might affect Gary?"

"Not really. He was only the cleaner's son." Grizelda did not point out the contradiction here. Wanda went on, "If he could do these things in one place, he could do them in another. He wouldn't suffer."

"But he did."

"I know that now. I didn't know the details of Gary's life then."

"Meaning?"

"It's not just Gary I feel bad about. I've been awake all night. I've got to tell you these things or burst."

"Go on."

"I knew little about Mrs Brady except that she was married but her husband wasn't Gary's father. Then one day Kieran Brady arrived in his car bringing her to work. I saw him and he saw me."

She paused for a moment. Grizelda waited.

"Twenty years ago I was what they used to call a looker. The years haven't been kind to me."

Grizelda looked at the worn face and realized that once Wanda Gates had had features both startling and memorable.

"I'd had a lot of men friends before but my job meant too much to me. The first time I saw Kieran, though, I knew something was going to happen. And it did. The biggest mistake of my life."

"Yet you keep his photograph in a place of honour?"

"More a penance. A perpetual punishment."

What was this morning's interview, thought Grizelda, *but a long self-punishment?*

"I began to see a lot of him. Too much. One day, the terrible thing happened. Mrs Claverhouse found us. Well, you know what that meant?"

Grizelda remembered Georgina, tight-lipped, talking about Wanda's dismissal.

"Yes," said Wanda. "The sack on the spot. What then? Nothing except to come back here. This was my parents' house and they left it to me when they died. I moved back and a month later Kieran moved in with me."

"To Mrs Brady's fury, no doubt," said Grizelda.

"Not with me. She was angry with her husband. She knew he'd gone off with some woman. For years, she had no idea it was me."

"Anyway, you got something out of it," said Grizelda.

Wanda's sunken eyes suddenly flashed with fire.

"Miss Grissom, he was a *swine*! Once he was here and the novelty had worn off I couldn't get rid of him. I saw all too clearly what Gary and his mother must have been through all those years. The irony was, he wanted children. Chrissy couldn't give him any and neither could I. That's why it went sour."

"But he went in the end," said Grizelda.

"You could say that. He was killed in a work accident. It was the happiest day of my life, God help me!"

"And you'd get compensation as well," said Grizelda.

"Neither I nor Chrissy Brady ever saw a penny," said Wanda. "That was partly why I got in touch with her again. She was in a bad way by then: she really needed any money going. We became quite friendly. I think I was her only friend at the end."

"You said 'partly'. What else made you contact her?"

"Gary. I'd seen him."

"When was this?"

"Kieran fell off some scaffolding three years ago now. Gary was already on the streets."

"You mean you and Kieran were together for – what? – it must be nine, ten years."

"Yes. Ten years of hell. Except when he went off on his jaunts abroad. But they got fewer. He was picking up more work locally."

"It was really bad, was it?"

"I understood Gary more from what Kieran did and what he told me."

"But he'd left Chrissy long before Gary started his career of arson?"

"Oh, yes. But hearing what Kieran said, whether it was true or not, made me realize what Gary had gone through. I even began to have some idea of why he'd started burning things down, starting with the Claverhouse summerhouse."

"Go on." Grizelda had found the story interesting enough before; now she realized they were close to the crunch.

"That was the thing which angered me most about Kieran – his quite irrational hatred of little Gary. He even told me some ludicrous story about how, when he was two, Gary had actually murdered Kieran's unborn child. Well, I ask you! How could anyone carry an obsession like that? According to Kieran, it was only because he was almost a saint that he didn't kill Gary himself. He said Gary was so backward as to spend his life almost in a coma. Wherever Kieran went, Gary would watch him. 'Those two eyes, never blinking,' Kieran said. 'They'd drive an angel mad.' He claimed they got on his nerves so much they nearly pushed him to murder. He was very proud of the fact that he only ever hit Gary once. Only once? What a thing to be proud of! I believe that if he did keep his fists off Gary it was only to keep the Social Services out. Besides all that, he said Gary was so withdrawn that he was completely incapable of doing anything at school. Well, I tell you this, Miss Grissom, that didn't tally with the Gary I'd known. I always thought that being withdrawn at school was a sign of ill-treatment at home."

"So you didn't believe Kieran?"

"He kept on about it so much, as if he had a guilty conscience, that in the end I had at least to say I did. Though I didn't want to."

"You and he weren't married?" Grizelda decided she could risk a personal question.

"No. He never divorced Chrissy."

"So you could have kicked him out?"

"Perhaps. I often thought about it, but when it came to the point I couldn't. Besides, when he wanted to he could be really charming."

Silence again. *Keep talking*, thought Grizelda. *It's Gary I want to know about, not Kieran.*

"It sounds to me," she said, "as if you believe Kieran made Gary into what he was."

"I think so," said Wanda. Then, to Grizelda's amazement, she suddenly reached forward and clutched her by the arm. "Miss Grissom, I hope it wasn't me."

Mrs Burden put the call through to Julian. Some sixth sense made her listen, a thing she would normally never dream of doing. When the call was over, she sat for a long time, wondering what she ought to do.

Now we're getting there, Grizelda thought. *There's no point in pussyfooting round this.*

"If you kept taking away all Gary's little achievements without giving him any credit and passing them off as Julian's just to keep your own job, then some of the fault must be yours," she said.

Wanda slumped back into her chair. "I knew you'd say that. Whatever I say about Kieran, I'm really the one to blame."

"Perhaps," said Grizelda. "But isn't it just as likely that Gary saw Julian as the guilty party?"

"How?"

"They were only little boys. From what you say, Julian was pretty horrible to Gary. Could Gary make the connection between Julian and you? Perhaps he thought you were his friend, rescuing his little offerings from destruction. Perhaps the idea that Julian was his enemy got lodged early in his mind and never left. Perhaps it became a sort of trauma, dictating everything he's done ever since."

Grizelda bit her tongue. She'd nearly said more than she ought to there.

"You mean about the summerhouse? Like a revenge on Julian? Or on us all?" Wanda seemed not to have noticed that Grizelda knew more than she should. "You know, I first came to see Chrissy Brady after Gary had been home from wherever they sent him and then disappeared again. By then, Chrissy was in a bad way. I told her I'd find Gary and keep an eye on him."

"And you did?"

"It wasn't easy. He'd vanished. I even wondered if he was dead. I nearly went to the police. But then I saw him busking in London, looking pretty fit and well. Where had he learned to play the flute? After that I kept track of him. When he started doing his conjuring act it was easier. I let Chrissy know where he was when I went to see her, so she was happy that he wasn't dead even if he wouldn't come to visit. I even knew where he was at the time she died. I had friends in the town who found out where he was living. I sent a message about his mother and they left it for him – late, but he got it in time to do something."

"What do you mean?"

"Gary hitch-hiked through the night and got to Wycombe in time for his mother's funeral. I was glad about that."

"When was this?"

"Let me see. It was a fortnight ago today."

Grizelda did a quick calculation. She looked at Wanda in surprise.

"So he was on the road all night right after I'd seen him in the Jolly Angler and dropped him at 1.30 in the morning?"

"That I couldn't say. I'd never heard of you. He said nothing."

More surprise for Grizelda. "You mean you've *seen* Gary?"

"And spoken to him. I told him the lot – about his mother's last miserable days, about Kieran, about how I passed his work off as Julian's."

Gary never told me this, thought Grizelda. *Does it make a difference?*

She looked at Wanda's lined face, white without the blusher.

Yes, it does make a difference. A big one. Gary's had all his suspicions proved. Was there any more to find out?

Grizelda made as if to stand up.

"Thank you very much, Ms Gates. I mustn't waste any more of your time."

To her alarm, Wanda suddenly dropped forward. She was kneeling in front of Grizelda, grasping her wrists.

"No, Miss Grissom. I haven't finished yet. I'm so *frightened*."

"What of?"

"Gary. He means harm, I know it."

"How do you know?"

"He carries a knife. He keeps it down his sock. He took it out while we were talking and felt the blade. I could see how sharp it was. That blade is destined for someone. I know it."

"Not you," said Grizelda. "Not his mother. Not Kieran." There was only one left.

"It's Master Julian," Wanda cried. "I *know* he'll kill him."

"How can you know?" said Grizelda. "Did he tell you?"

"Believe me," Wanda's voice was a sort of howl now, "I knew when we talked after the funeral. I saw where his thoughts were taking him. And, God help me, I made things worse by what I said. I'd fear for Julian if Gary found him now." She put her head in her hands. She was crying. "Oh, Miss Grissom! Both my little boys! What did I do?"

Grizelda's heart lurched. Yes, she realized, she'd really known this deep down as well.

She pulled her wrists away from Wanda's grip and touched her shoulder. She spoke with a calmness she did not feel.

"I haven't been quite straight with you," she said. "But you've been straight with me and you deserve better. I know Julian. I live with him. I love him." She noticed Wanda's gasp of amazement. "If anyone can get them both out of this mess, I can. And I will."

It really was time to go now. She stood up – then, to her own surprise, leaned forward and kissed Wanda on the forehead.

"Don't worry, Ms Gates. I appreciate what you've done. It must have cost you a lot."

She found her own way out. Her last sight of Wanda

268

Gates was as a small figure hunched in the armchair. She started the Calibra and drove off as quickly as she could. A nasty feeling inside told her she had no time to lose.

Chapter Six

When Grizelda reached Speakeasy she rushed to her desk. There had been no call from Gary. By now, though, she neither expected nor wanted one. She rang Julian at the bank. Mrs Burden answered.

"He's gone out. Very unexpected. He's got no appointments for this morning."

"Where has he gone?"

Grizelda had met Mrs Burden. They got on well and she knew the secretary would tell her all there was to know.

"He had a phone call. The caller didn't say who he was but Mr Claverhouse seemed to know him. There was something about the voice – I'm afraid I listened on my extension."

"What about the voice?"

"I don't know ... it wasn't the sort of voice that usually rings here. A man's voice, strained, nervous ... well, I suppose we get quite a few like that ringing us. But there was something else about it, almost as if it was *imitating* someone."

"But he never said who he was."

"No, just that Mr Claverhouse would know him. 'I've been expecting you,' Julian said. Grizelda, he has been rather odd lately, hasn't he? Is he ill?"

"I don't think so. There are a few things worrying him, though. What did the caller say?"

"I remember exactly. 'It's about time we met. We've a lot to sort out together.' Mr Claverhouse said, 'What do you mean?' the caller said, 'You know very well what I mean. I'll be waiting outside your flat.' 'Then what?' said Mr Claverhouse. 'We're going home,' said the caller. Then he put the phone down."

"What happened then?"

"Mr Claverhouse came out of his office. He said, 'Mrs Burden, I'm going out. Don't expect me back today.' 'Is everything all right?' I said. 'Fine,' he told me. 'Don't tell anyone I've gone. If Piers or the directors upstairs ask, say I'm at home not feeling too well.' 'What if Miss Grissom rings?' I said. 'She won't,' he answered. Then he went. Well, I didn't know what to do. It all seemed very odd. I even thought of ringing the police. But Mr Claverhouse would be furious with me if everything was all right. Then you rang. I'm so pleased to talk to somebody."

"What was that the caller said: 'We're going home'?"

"That's right."

"But if they meet at the flats, Julian *is* home."

"It doesn't make sense, does it?"

Grizelda made up her mind.

"Thank you very much, Mrs Burden. I'll sort this out myself. There's no need to tell anyone."

She put the phone down. "I've got to go out again," she shouted across the office to nobody in particular, then half-ran to where she had left the company's Calibra.

It had never occurred to Julian to slam the receiver down. He left the office as if starting on a path laid out for him, though the ending was shrouded in fog.

* * *

271

Gary came out of the callbox near St John's Wood tube station, then looked up and down Wellington Road. Only a short walk to the flats. By rights Julian should have rung the police; they could be waiting for him already.

But Gary knew they would not be, that Julian's BMW would soon be there instead. He was drawing Julian to him as an angler reels in a fish. Their course was pre-ordained and had been since they were three years old.

Julian turned the corner. There, standing on the pavement, was Gary. He wore the black singlet with the lightning and flame motif Grizelda had first seen hardly two weeks before.

Julian drew up beside him. Gary opened the passenger door and got in. Julian could no more stop him than control thunderstorms. All yesterday's thought of injunctions to stop harassment had gone.

Gary put his seat belt on. "Drive," he said.

"Where to?" said Julian.

"Surely you know," said Gary. "There's only one place."

The car stayed where it was.

"No, I don't know," said Julian.

"I said we were *going home*," Gary replied, a dangerous tremble in his voice.

Julian felt something very sharp pierce his jacket and shirt and nick the flesh just above his pelvis. For the time being, he should do what he was told.

Grizelda slammed the car door behind her and ran inside, straight to the uniformed man behind the reception desk.

"Has Mr Claverhouse been in?" she asked breathlessly.

"Not to my knowledge," was the reply.

But he sees everybody, she thought. Nevertheless, she ran

upstairs, scrabbled in her bag for her key and burst into the flat.

Nobody.

She ran out again, downstairs to reception, said a belated "Thank you" and returned to the car.

What should she do? They seemed to have disappeared off the face of the earth.

Well, they can't have. Think!

What had Mrs Burden told her about the telephone call? Something that sounded odd – but needn't be.

"We're going home."

Where in the world was Gary's home? Did he have one? What squat, condemned house, bed and breakfast or cheap hotel, room in a flat lived in by another minor performer, digs in a teeming, unidentifiable street somewhere in this huge beehive called London might it be in?

She rested her head on the steering wheel. It was hopeless.

But then another suggestion.came. He hadn't said, "*my* home" or "where I live", but "*We're* going home." Home for both of them.

There was only one place which could possibly be called home for both of them.

Dare she risk the time it would take to drive there? Shouldn't she just call the police? But if she did, what would she say? "My boyfriend's gone off with a man he doesn't like but I'm not sure where?" Or, "Could you keep an eye out for this BMW, please?" "Why?" they would ask. "Has it been stolen?" "Oh, no, the owner's driving it." "Where might they be going?" "Home, his companion said." "Get lost. Sort your own worries out."

She would have to go herself. If she was wrong, she was

wrong. She started the car and headed off west, towards the M40 and Mockbeggar House.

Julian waited stubbornly for Gary to tell him where to go.

"Keep on towards Uxbridge," Gary said. "Then on to the M40."

"Now I see," Julian replied. His voice had a coldness at odds with the fear welling up in him. "Since when was Mockbeggar House *your* home?"

"Since the day I was brought there. Since the day you tried to push me out of it. Since the day you cheated me out of my talents and sentenced me to silence."

The pain in Julian's flesh sharpened almost unbearably. He was sure blood was flowing under his shirt. He did not turn to look at Gary. He knew, though, that his face was pale and set, his jaws working slightly as if struggling to control violent feeling.

What should he do? Drive so badly or fast that the police had to stop him? He accelerated dangerously past a line of traffic. Someone coming the other way shook his fist in anger.

"*Stop that!*" Gary hissed. "If you get the police on us, they'd *really* have something to see."

Julian felt more sharp, localized pain. He was sure Gary would use that knife properly if he thought he had to. But was there some idea in his head of a fitting, dramatic finale? Julian could not envisage it. Nevertheless, he now drove carefully. Keeping out of trouble for as long as possible was all he could do.

Once on the way, Grizelda had no worries about driving too fast. If the police stopped her, she would just tell them why

274

and hope they would take notice. If Julian and Gary *were* bound for Mockbeggar House, how much start did they have? Would she be too late?

As she drove she thought. Why was she so frightened for Julian? Was it just because of what Wanda Gates had told her? But hadn't she known something like this deep down for a long time now – at least since she was at Mockbeggar House? What would she feel in Julian's place? Well, she was quite sure she would not reject whole swathes of society as if they were a lower form of life and believe they should not tread the same earth as she did. And if she were Gary she would smart at the way she was treated and dearly love to get back at her tormentor.

But then, she could never be tormented in that way because she was not at the bottom of the heap.

She knew what it must be like to be there. Even as she drove, her feelings during her early days at Heathwell swam into her mind. They could not compare with what Gary had been through, but in one jump she'd gone from nearly bottom to back near the top of the heap. That was what Julian didn't seem to understand: a heap had a top *and* a bottom and a few minutes with a spade could turn the whole thing upside down.

So, fair enough, Gary had come for revenge on Julian, satisfaction out of him.

But what had Wanda said?

"I *know* he wants to kill him."

That was ludicrous! Gary must be mad.

And perhaps he was. But why?

There was only one answer. Those days beyond the reach of memory, had been more for Gary than just little boys fighting. They had been nothing less than traumatic. They had shaped every action in his whole life, had brought him to this day and this unknown destiny.

And, deep down, Julian knew this. He must know what was happening. He had been disturbed, *deeply* disturbed ever since the day Georgina's letter arrived, and perhaps even more than – since the night of the Union debate or even further back. Had not Gary had an equal influence on Julian's life? What had pushed Julian on to these so-called great things? Who had made him believe he was the brightest hope for the future, the one to watch, the holder of destiny, master of finance and then master of politics? Nobody but his father, Sir William himself, thanks to Wanda's little deceptions. And would that distant man, obsessed with tradition and influence, ever have bothered with his son if he had not identified promise in the infant Julian – or thought he had? But who had done the things in which Julian's father detected the promise? Gary – the guttersnipe, the object of magnanimous charity who was not supposed to have any ability. That could mean that Julian's entire life was founded on a lie, a delusion.

Did he know this? Grizelda asked herself.

Yes, he must.

Would he admit it to himself?

Perhaps he had. Perhaps not.

If he had not, who should tell him?

She should. It was her duty to him. She loved him so she owed him the truth.

She would tell him.

Ah, but what if he was blind to it?

Worse, what if he accepted it?

Could she love a man whose life was founded on a lie, whether he admitted it or not?

She should have seen all this days ago. She should have known. She should have helped him more.

How? Julian only asked for help when it was too late.

And what if help meant the end of what they had together? Was what they had together worth keeping anyway?

With shuddering clarity, memories of that night in Oxford, the party when they had first met, came back to her. Then, in quick succession, visions from their life together flashed through her mind. Well, some of it was dross, but most had been wonderful.

And when this was over it would be wonderful again. It *had* to be.

Didn't it?

She was on the M40 now. Traffic at this time in the morning was sparse. She accelerated to ninety, stayed here and saw no flashing blue lights behind her.

Julian drove in bright sunshine along the road to Mock-beggar House. It was like scores of homecomings. If he could forget the still, angry figure beside him and the pain and sticky wetness of blood on his side, he could almost believe his parents were waiting and a pleasant, harmonious weekend lay before him.

"Carry on past the gates," said Gary.

He did so, driving slowly along the brick boundary wall. Where the wall turned inward from the road, Gary said, "Stop here. Get the car off the road."

Once again, Julian obeyed unresistingly. Gary got out, walked round the car and opened the door for Julian.

"Out," he said.

The old, worn, weathered wall loomed up two metres high in front of them.

Grizelda also drove along the road to Mockbeggar House, but she turned in at the main entrance and waited as the electric gates slowly opened. She accelerated up the drive and stopped the car with a scrunch of gravel outside the huge front door. She could not see Julian's car. Was it in the garage?

She jumped out of the Calibra and rang the doorbell. A young girl she had never seen before, dressed in a black and white maid's uniform, opened it.

"Who are you?" Grizelda could not conceal her surprise.

"Melanie. I'm Lady Claverhouse's new maid."

"I've never heard of you. You weren't here two weekends ago."

"Lady Claverhouse gave me the weekend off." Melanie was obviously of a chatty disposition. "She's good like that."

Grizelda fought the distraction. Why Georgina did not want her to know she had taken on a maid could wait for another day.

"I'm Grizelda. Has Julian arrived?"

"No, ma'am. Would you like to see Sir William and Lady Claverhouse?"

Surprised, Grizelda nearly said, "Is *he* here?" She managed not to. "I think I'd better," she said instead.

"Climb up the wall," said Gary.

"What?" cried Julian. For the first time he was showing some resistance. Gary produced his knife. It was a wicked-looking dagger, probably an ex-commando knife. Julian only briefly toyed with the thought, *Where did he get that?*

"Climb up the wall," Gary repeated. "And when you're on the top, stay there till I am too."

Awkwardly, scrambling for footholds in the ancient brickwork, Julian did as he was told. Gary held the blade between his teeth and quickly reached him. The grounds of Mockbeggar House stretched before them. Gary took the knife from his teeth.

"Now. On the ground," he said.

Julian dropped, fell awkwardly, picked himself up. Gary, less clumsily, dropped down beside him.

"I don't understand this," said Julian.

"You will," said Gary.

"Who shall I say is here?" said Melanie.

"Just Grizelda."

Melanie knocked on the door of what Grizelda knew to be an opulent sitting-room, from which indistinct voices could be heard. She listened, then opened it: the voices stopped for a second on a questioning note.

"Grizelda is here to see you," Melanie said.

Grizelda had not expected a peal of delight and none came. There was silence, then a woman's voice. Melanie turned and said, "Please go in."

Sir William – expensively suited, pink-faced, smooth-haired – and Georgina sat facing each other in large, deep, leather Chesterfield armchairs. They each held fine china cups and saucers; a small inlaid coffee table was laid with a silver coffee pot and a small plate of pastries. Neither rose. Georgina looked up: Grizelda suspected her glazed eyes and expression of blank boredom had been there for some time.

Sir William never even paused in what he was saying.

"... so you see that if the French remain co-operative then the outlook is really quite good." His voice was a carefully enunciated public-speaking drone, as if Georgina was just another compliant member of the board.

Am I watching Julian and me in a quarter of a century? The thought was terrifying. The answer was comforting. *If we can get through today, I vow it never will be. Or I'll be gone.*

Sir William seemed to have come to a natural break. Grizelda used it to pose her breathless question.

"Has Julian been here this morning?"

Now Georgina did show signs of animation and alarm.

"Julian? No, of course not. Why should he?"

The answer came like a blow. Suddenly, Grizelda was on the point of breaking down.

"But he *must* have been," she wailed. "He can't be anywhere else. He's in danger."

Georgina stood, her face pale.

"What do you mean?"

Sir William's face bore a look of distaste. Grizelda knew that if he spoke, he would say, "You are quite unsuitable for my son. You two should never have met." Mercifully he did not. Perhaps he would later – if there *was* a later.

"He walked out of the bank this morning," said Grizelda. "There's someone with him. Mrs Burden thinks they're coming home."

"Who is he with?" said Sir William acidly, distaste on his face.

"I think it's Gary Brady."

Georgina's hand flew to her mouth. "Mrs Brady's son? That's impossible."

"I do not believe you," said Sir William. "If my son is in any form of trouble, it is my opinion that you have put him there. I must ask you to leave my home."

"It can't be Gary Brady." Georgina's voice was high and fast, like someone in near terror. "Gary Brady was put away. He is a criminal. He was dangerous and then he disappeared."

Grizelda stood and faced them. She looked at Georgina, shaking and about to burst into tears, and Sir William, confident in his own rightness, and thought: *Whatever you think about yourselves, I think you're pathetic.*

"Sir William and Lady Claverhouse," she said, slowly and with dignity, "things which you set in motion years ago have had consequences for your son that you would never understand. I don't fully understand them either, but I do know which of us will be of more use to him now."

She turned and left the room, walking straight past Melanie waiting outside. She opened the front door and stepped with relief into the open air. Once out of that room and away from those people, she wanted to cry where nobody could see her.

She sat in the car and for a full minute sobbed with sheer frustration. If Julian wasn't here, where in the world was he? "We're going home." It *must* be here. The playroom? They could never come into the house undetected and besides, the playroom had been turned into a guest bedroom years ago.

Just a minute, though. "Home" and "house" might not mean the same thing. Apart from the playroom, what place here had changed Gary's life decisively? The picture printed on his black singlet was a constant memorial to the spot.

That was it. She left the car again and ran round the house and through the garden to the far extremities of the grounds near the boundary wall.

* * *

They burst through bushes, under trees, Gary pushing – even steering – Julian. "I don't remember these trees being so high," he muttered. Suddenly they were on a small, well-kept lawn with short, fine grass, open to the side facing the house. The last time Julian had been here was less than two Saturdays ago with his mother and Grizelda, when for the first time Grizelda had heard Gary's name. The last time Gary had been here he was setting light to the old summerhouse before watching his handiwork from the top of the brick wall. By now, though, the trees and shrubs had reached a height sufficient to obscure that view.

"You see?" said Gary. "Here I have to finish what I started."

Julian didn't answer. He stared helplessly at the figure standing before him who had so completely taken over his will. He looked at the lean face, the lank hair, the black singlet marked with fire and lightning which stared luminously back at him as if saying *This is what I am* and thought: *You were a silent little thickhead and now you're not only dangerous but highly articulate, far more than I am, and with talents of sleight of hand and quickness of eye far above anything I could ever dream of, and who knows what other talents beside? How come the metamorphosis, Gary?*

Gary spoke.

"Let's get all this straight," he said.

Julian still said nothing.

"You were the young master," said Gary. "I was the cleaner's son. I was nothing to you. I was scum, I was an oik."

"I never said so," Julian replied uncomfortably.

"Oh, but you did," said Gary. "You did. An oik who came out of the gutter. Born on the shitheap."

The old Julian suddenly flared up inside. *And that's just what you were*, he wanted to say. *Nothing more.* But he stayed quiet.

"You don't know where I came from. You don't know whose son I am," said Gary. "Neither do I. And now I never will."

Some drunk who lurched off into the night again, Julian thought but did not say.

"But that's not why you're here now," said Gary quietly. He held the wicked knife in his hands and for the first time Julian was nearly sick with the fear he should have felt all along – a paralysing, mind-numbing, helpless dread of what had to follow.

"You're here because you're the cause of everything bad that happened to me. When I was a little boy and miserable and quiet and *shat* on by everybody, and when all the things I could do were squashed out of me because I was too *thick* instead of cleverer than the lot of you put together, it was *you* who put me there. Just *you*, Master Julian."

Julian managed to find words.

"That's ridiculous, Gary. We were only toddlers."

"It was *you*. You were my enemy. From the very first day, I knew it in here." He put his hand on his heart, right over the flames on his singlet. "I grew up in complete silence and I knew all the time that you were the cause of it all. Every little bit."

Rubbish! Julian wanted to say. But words had deserted him in the face of this – he could only call it *passionate* eloquence.

"That's why I wanted to kill you when I was only eight. That's why I wished you'd been in this summerhouse that night. That's why I went on burning. One day I would have burnt *that*" – he extended his knife towards Mockbeggar House – "and you would have been in it. But I was taken away and locked up. So that was all due to you as well."

This is twisted, crazed logic, thought Julian. *And it will be the end of me.*

"And I know now that it was all really true," Gary went on. "Wanda Gates told me."

Now Julian could speak, derisively.

"Wanda Gates? Where did you find that devious old trout?"

"Wanda Gates was at my mother's funeral. Your mother was not. Wanda Gates told me what in my heart I knew. You got the credit for all I did. It led you to Oxford and me to cardboard boxes by the Thames."

Julian was silent again. There was nothing to say.

"Go on," said Gary. "Say something. I want to know if you've got any defence."

There was none. None that would work.

"I didn't know. I didn't mean..." Julian started.

"Oh, come on!" said Gary. "Do better than that."

"What's going to happen?" Julian managed fearfully.

"Neither of us will ever leave the summerhouse," said Gary calmly. He held up his knife. "This is for both of us."

Julian stood and swayed. Gary seemed to move, near and far, in front of him, one instant so close that he could see the stubble on his chin; the next, far away as if standing on the head of a pin. And then he knew: he saw the truth standing in front of him like a grinning ghoul. *"You got the credit for all I did." It was true. Everything that had made him, Julian, what he was; everything that had caused his father to set the wheels in motion of his unfolding career; everything that had justified that fatuous opinion "he really is most extra-*

ordinarily able" – *every one of those things had been done by Gary. They were his achievements and nobody else's. Gary in the nursery, Gary with the Lego bus, Gary with the paper and crayons, Gary, Gary, Gary... And so his own life had been built on somebody else's foundations. His life was a lie. His life was a fraud. He was where he was solely through his father's delusion and the self-perpetuating myth it had led to.*

He stared at his tormentor.

"Don't bother to run away," said Gary. "I'll catch you."

Julian knew he could never run, never move either foot again.

"As soon as you're gone it's my turn," said Gary.

So that was it. Everything had narrowed itself down to this final meeting. Julian looked helplessly at his foe.

And a new urge came to him: a sort of desperate strength. *Sod it!* he thought. *I won't die without a murmur on my own ground.*

"OK," he said. "If that's how you want it."

"I do," Gary replied.

Julian's new-found strength was suddenly augmented with something that made him dizzy with its force. *Whatever was I thinking just then? My life a lie? Nonsense! My father deluded? Rubbish! My life justifies itself. All means justify the final end of my temporal success. If a worm like Gary Brady is expended in that process, then so be it.*

He spoke. His voice shook with his new-found right-eousness. "But just listen to this, Gary Brady. If you really want to know, I *do* think you're dirt. You're not fit to bother with. I was right from the first. It's no use trying to reason with your sort."

"What's reason when it was you who put me here?" said Gary.

They stood before each other, breathing hard, and Julian waited for Gary's move.

The grounds of Mockbeggar House seemed vast, like some mid-Western prairie dropped into England. No part-time superannuated gardeners could be seen – perhaps they were absorbed in the greenhouses, Grizelda thought. The journey seemed more and more pointless to her. Her feet were useless as in a dream. Three times she nearly turned back to the car and drove off but each time she thought, *Sir William is wrong. If I leave here, it's my own decision, not his. And if I leave here I have left Julian. Even if he is miles away now.*

But then she saw he was not miles away. Here was the tract of fine grass where Georgina had recalled the past. And there, in the present, was a sudden flash of sunlight on bright metal. Grizelda focused her eyes and saw the two figures standing motionless, like garden statues, unaware of her. She stopped on the path which edged the clearing and heard half of what they said.

One figure: "This is for both of us ... as soon as you've gone it's my turn."

The other: "If that's how you want it... It's no use trying to reason with your sort..."

For a moment, Grizelda was a statue as well. Then she acted.

She screamed, "No! This won't happen!"

She convulsively plunged forward the last few metres and faced Gary, shielding Julian.

"*No!*" she screamed, a long, wailing howl.

The grounds were not so deserted now.

After Grizelda had left, Sir William and Georgina had

stared silently at each other, Sir William bristling with indignation. They listened.

"I hear no car," said Sir William. "Did she bring one?"

Georgina said nothing.

Sir William rose, opened the door, shouted. "Melanie!"

"Sir?"

"Did Miss Grissom come in a car?"

"Yes, sir. It's still there. I think she's in the garden."

"We'll see about that," said Sir William and strode through the hall towards the back door. After a moment's hesitation, Georgina followed.

They heard a woman's voice shrieking a long way off.

The rules had changed. The game had gone wrong. Gary looked at Grizelda uncomprehendingly. Then a dull film crossed his eyes. The new face in front of him was the sort he yearned for, the sort that was beyond him...

"Then we'll go, all three," he said. But there was no conviction in his voice.

Grizelda found words. "Gary, you must stop this. You have everything: you're brilliant. You've talents no one's seen yet. I *know* what it was like for you. I've been there. You can win. You *can*, Gary."

"I've got a nice little career," he said.

Grizelda heard the bitter sarcasm and understood what he meant. Then: *Oh God! I never said that, did I?*

"Gary, you've got far more. You could have the lot."

"Not while he's here and not while you're part of him."

His mouth clamped shut: Grizelda wondered what next she could do.

* * *

Melanie followed her employers into the garden. She too

heard the scream from far off. Without hesitating, she ran back into the house to the nearest phone and dialled the police.

Out of the corner of her eye, Grizelda saw Georgina there, watching. And Sir William, helpless, out of his depth. *Ignore them. Try again.*

"It will be all right, Gary. You'll have a lovely life. I can help you."

"No, you can't. I won't let you."

Gary stepped back as if surveying the two of them. There was a sort of frozen immobility for a short time which yet seemed without measure. Grizelda kept her eyes on him. His face showed expression like a book: acceptance, defeat, envy untinged with jealousy, a sort of love. Grizelda wondered if he were seeing a procession of the events which had led to this moment. Finally his eyes left them and surveyed the whole expanse of grass round them, as if he were taking it all in – and perhaps seeing again the summerhouse which once stood there, flaming, crackling, with him a little boy watching in the dark. Then: "No," he said. "I can't let you."

What happened next would stay in Grizelda's dreams for the rest of her life. With deliberation, Gary moved. He raised his knife in an oddly graceful movement and leant, blade foremost, towards her. She flinched as, with consummate care and gentleness, he nicked the flesh of her neck just above the collarbone. Her hand flew to the sudden sharp pain and she felt the trickle of blood. Then she watched him put both hands round the knife's handle and turn the blade towards his own body. He lunged forward hard, unhesitatingly, leaning on it. The blade drove deep into him, just under the divide in his rib-cage. With a sort of grunt, he fell. On the ground, his open eyes seemed looking at her, as if he was still saying, "No, I can't let you..."

There was a scream from close by. Georgina. She crumpled into Sir William standing next to her and he awkwardly placed his arms round her.

Grizelda stooped to Gary, touched him. He was dead. Blood soaked the flames on his singlet. She stood, tears blinding her eyes.

She turned to Julian. She held out her arms to him. He was standing as if in a trance. They looked at each other. Julian made no move towards her. She tried to understand the expression in his eyes.

Then Julian moved. Only now did Grizelda know what his eyes had been saying. He turned away from her, went to his parents and enfolded both their shocked bodies in his arms.

Grizelda watched for a moment. Then she made up her mind. She walked quickly, resolutely, without looking back, to the Calibra. She was just about to open the door when the first police car turned through the gates.